ROBOTECH

ART I

ROBOTECH
ART I

by Kay Reynolds
and
Ardith Carlton

STARBLAZE GRAPHICS

From the animated series
ROBOTECH
A Harmony Gold, U.S.A., Inc.
Production in association with
Tatsunoko Productions
Company, Ltd.
Story Editor—Carl Macek
Executive Producer—Ahmed
Agrama

The Donning
Company/Publishers
Norfolk/Virginia Beach

Robotech Art I is one of many art books published by The Donning
Company/Publishers. For a complete listing of our titles, please write to the
address below.

Copyright © 1986 by Kay Reynolds and Ardith Carlton

The Donning Company/Publishers
5659 Virginia Beach Boulevard
Norfolk, Virginia 23502

10 9 8 7 6 5 4 3 2

First Printing April 1986

Library of Congress Cataloging-in-Publication Data:
Robotech art.
    1. Robotech (Television program).   2. Animation (Cinematography)
I. Keynolds, Kay, 1951- . II. Carlton, Ardith.
PN1992.77.R543R6   1986   791.45'72   85-16291
ISBN 0-89865-412-2 (pbk.)
ISBN 0-89865-462-9 (lim. ed.)

Printed in the United States of America

CONTENTS

Carl Macek (facing far right) and team
set up the Harmony Gold/
ROBOTECH booth at the 1985 San
Diego Comic Convention.

INTRODUCTION

If there is one word which accurately describes the initial inspiration behind **ROBO-TECH,** it would most certainly be coincidence. A chance meeting with Jim Rocknowsky, a product director from Harmony Gold, led to a "roller coaster ride" of intense brainstorming and creative development in regard to the possibility of transposing some of the most imaginative animation to have been produced in Japan in the past few years into a unique and revolutionary television series destined to be syndicated throughout the United States and the rest of the world.

Once the dreams of **ROBOTECH** became a reality, the idea of coincidence blossomed into a full-time obsession for everyone involved in the project. From Harmony Gold's early meetings with people from the various toy manufacturers and potential licensees to the actual syndication of **ROBOTECH** to well over 90 markets in less than a year, this 85-episode science fiction serial adventure has been blessed with a sense of good fortune which is almost uncanny. The assembly of a team of professionals by Frank Agrama, President of Harmony Gold, with roots in various branches of the entertainment conglomerate was a feat in itself. Pulling diverse talents together to work as a cohesive team in a time frame and production schedule that resembled live television was just another example of the concept of good timing which seemed to follow **ROBOTECH.** For many reasons, everyone involved with the project seemed to feel that the time was right for American audiences to experience the true dramatic range that animation can obtain—even when produced under the constraints of daily television syndication. The idea of creating a "soap opera" for the after-school prime time slot was totally unheard of before **ROBOTECH.** Likewise, the concept of bringing legitimate and realistic portrayals of human drama into animated productions was something that was completely against all that animated programming had stood for during the three decades of its existence. The fact that a company like Harmony Gold was willing to put characters from their series into life-and-death situations with the outcome often less than ideal, again, was totally revolutionary.

But beside all the innovation and technical expertise which remains the core of **ROBO-TECH,** there is a universality which is totally unmistakable. It was something that could only be experienced by observation. For years it was practically an underground phenomenon that thousands of average Americans were meeting in libraries and conventions to watch Japanese animation in its original language. Most of these viewers were not able to speak or even remotely understand the actual dialogue spoken by the characters in these films. And yet this audience would sit in spellbound amazement of the striking visuals and imaginative storytelling—caught up in the momentum of the action and in some mysterious way, follow the complexity of the convoluted plots and storylines. Cults formed around certain groups of animators and studios. Members of the Cartoon Fantasy Organization would dream of the time when someone would be able to interpret these films in an honest and sophisticated manner. Fans knew full well that the creative teams behind these films were not gearing their message to a mindless audience. Rather the goal was to present serious science fiction through the medium of animation.

After Harmony Gold had produced a number of episodes of **ROBOTECH,** Kenji Yoshida, the head of Tatsunoko Studios (the original producers of the animation shown in the series shown in Japan) came to the United States to visit his friends and business associates at Harmony Gold. Naturally Mr. Yoshida came to visit Intersound Studios, the high-tech workshop which did all the re-production of **ROBOTECH** for Harmony Gold. What he saw was a group of actors led by Robert Barron taking pride in creating personalities to match images produced half a world away. He also saw talented artists such as Joel Valentine working to tie the music, sound effects and re-recorded dialogue of **ROBO-TECH** into a cohesive whole which improved on the original material from Tatsunoko Studios. Mr. Yoshida also heard music produced under the supervision of Thomas A. White which had an orchestral presence usually reserved for feature film productions. What he saw was a studio, headed by Ahmed Agrama, committed to excellence. His fascination led him to a screening room in which he sat down and watched episodes of **ROBOTECH** in their entirety. He laughed, he felt apprehension, he became totally involved in the storyline of his original work now re-interpreted as **ROBOTECH.** The funny thing was that Mr. Yoshida does not speak a word of English.

The point is that through **ROBOTECH** everyone at Harmony Gold learned a valuable lesson. We learned that the audience for animation is not bracketed by age or nationality. The audience for animation is, by and large, intelligent and inquisitive. And given programming which recognizes these factors, the audience for animation is quite large and very faithful.

The book that you hold in your hand tells the story of the making of **ROBOTECH.** It also tells the story of a company, Harmony Gold, which is trying to introduce a philosophy of quality storytelling and superior animation into the world of American television. Throughout the world, animation is looked on as a legitimate entertainment medium. In America, animation is looked on as a vehicle to sell cereal and toys to young children. And although **ROBOTECH** will eventually do that as well under the supervision of John Rocknowski and his marketing

and licensing department, it is, first and foremost, an important step in the ongoing process of redefining the scope and direction of television programming for the future.

With all this out of the way, I invite you to enter the world of **ROBOTECH.** It was designed as a multilevel series which can be enjoyed again and again. This book will capture the art and politics which went into the making of this milestone of American animation.

Carl Macek
Los Angeles, California
August, 1985

Later, Svea Macek (art director), Susan Christison (Director of Licensing) and Carl Macek talk with one of the many fans who attended the convention.

CHAPTER 1

Part One— The Macross Saga

I n the year 1999, Earth has been ravaged by a global civil war. Brother battled brother as the conflict raged across the planet, but the devastation paled in comparison to a new threat which appeared to alter the course of human history forever. Astronomers discovered an alien spaceship that had broken through hyperspace on a collision course with Earth. Alarm increased as reports of the giant spaceship were confirmed by scientists around the planet. Eventually, they determined that the landing site would be Macross Island in the South Pacific.

The uncontrolled descent produced shock waves of incredible force; however, there was little damage to the island or, surprisingly, to the spaceship itself. The armored hull had taken the brunt of the fall, leaving most of the sophisticated technosystems intact. The gigantic craft was explored with a mixture of awe and anxiety. There was no sign of the alien crew, but the remains of the battlefortress gave evidence of a civilization that was light-years ahead of Earth's most advanced thinking. That alone was the most sobering discovery. Neither the look of the spaceship nor the material found inside indicated its creators were a peaceful race. Annihilation by invaders from another planet had become a terrible possibility.

The Global Civil War ground to a halt. A cease-fire was ordered, and world leaders banded together to form the United Earth Government. Under this new administration, a research team consisting of the most brilliant minds on the planet was formed to investigate

A global civil war ravages the planet Earth.

and restore the battlefortress. The team labored to decipher parts of documents from an incredibly complex technology called Robotech.

For the next ten years, the resources of the entire planet were focused on the restoration of the spacecraft on Macross Island. A great city grew up around the Robotech Project. On the eve of the ship's maiden flight, every citizen—man, woman, and child—gathered to celebrate the achievement and to witness the launching of Earth's new defender under the name of the Super Dimension Fortress One.

As the SDF-1 prepares for takeoff under the command of Captain Henry J. Gloval, inhabitants of Macross City enjoy opening festivities hosted by war hero Lieutenant Commander Roy Fokker. The ceremonies are interrupted when Fokker's young friend, Rick Hunter, crashes the air display with a fantastic demonstration of his own aeronautical abilities. To the public's delight and Fokker's distress, the young man all but steals the show. However, when the two meet after Hunter landed his plane, all friction is

forgotten as the two renew their friendship.

Their enjoyment is short-lived as another warp-fold splits the fabric of space. Yet another huge alien ship enters Earth's solar system. These are the Zentraedi, a race of giant warriors bred for thousands of generations for the sole purpose of military conquest. They are in pursuit of the Robotech battlefortress. The alien finder-beam locks in on the SDF-1's position, and the rest of the armada follow its flagship to an orbit circling Earth. Under the command of Breetai and his assistant, Exedore, the Zentraedi prepare to reclaim their lost property.

When the spacefortress senses the presence of the Zentraedi armada, it automatically begins to prepare defense mechanisms. The bridge of the SDF-1 dissolves in chaos. Captain Gloval leaves the opening ceremonies to join his crew. Lieutenant Commander Lisa Hayes and Bridge Officer Claudia Grant advise him of the ship's unusual behavior. As the SDF-1 bridge crew become aware of the invaders and regain control of their ship, a combat alert is ordered and all personnel are called back to the ship.

Breetai and Exedore don't know what to make of the Micronians' (the Zentraedi term for humans) initial attack. Their defense seems erratic. It does not put the Robotech spacefortress to its most effective use. The Zentraedi can hardly guess that their foes lack sufficient knowledge to control the massive Robotech defense mechanisms.

Rick Hunter is literally caught napping in one of the Veritech Fighters as the combat begins. Lisa Hayes orders him into battle. She assumes he's one of their combat veterans. Rick obliges her, taking off with youthful nonchalance only to find himself in the midst of a situation he's not prepared to deal with. Fortunately, Roy Fokker comes to his aid.

The alien craft crash-lands on Macross Island.

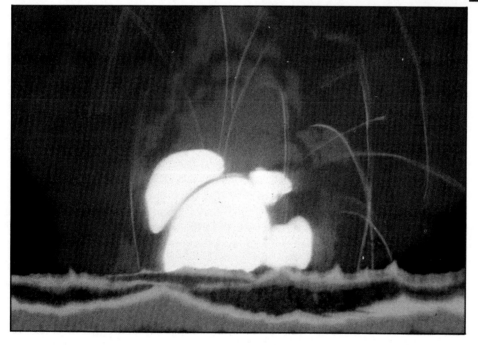

A great city grows up around the Robotech project.

Inhabitants of Macross City gather to watch launch-day festivities.

Lieutenant Commander Roy Fokker

The air show is crashed by Rick Hunter.

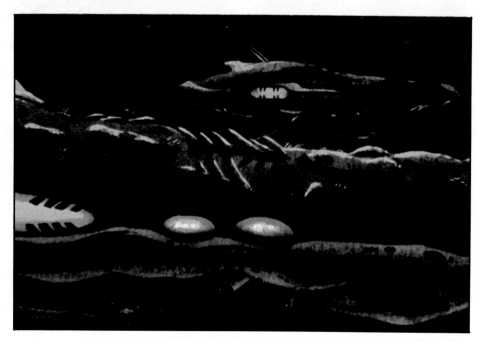

The Zentraedi Armada, led by Breetai and Exedore, breaches the fabric of space in search of the lost Robotechnology.

The Zentraedi attack.

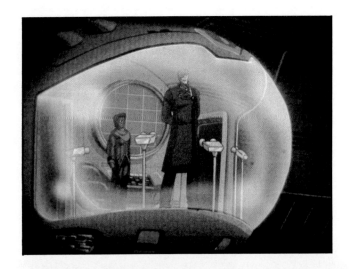

Chaos ensues as the SDF-1 prepares
its own defense!

Lisa Hayes rallies the flight crews.

Captain Gloval is recalled to
the SDF-1.

Rick Hunter, unwilling fighter pilot

Captain Gloval argues against using an inexperienced crew in a major military confrontation.

Rick Hunter meets the beautiful Lynn Minmei again.

As Rick Hunter desperately tries to make heads or tails of the VF-102 and survive, Captain Gloval comes to an uncomfortable realization. In order to protect Earth and her people, he will have to take an inexperienced crew and an untested alien ship into space to do battle with the invaders. While Gloval himself is a battle-hardened veterans, none of his immediate crew has either flown in space or served in combat. It's an impossible situation. Still, the Captain knows he has no choice if they are to have any chance of defeating the aliens. His only alternative is surrender, and this is something he is not willing to do.

On the all-but-deserted streets of Macross City, Rick Hunter meets Lynn Minmei, a charming Chinese girl. He would like to impress her with his flying expertise—if he can only figure out how the VF-102 works! The mecha transformations are as puzzling as they are amazing. Once again, "big brother" Fokker comes to his rescue.

The Zentraedi begin to level the city with a bombardment of firepower that Gloval and his crew are powerless to stop. They can only be grateful that the civilians of Macross City have been safely evacuated to shelters on the island. Little do they know that one little civilian remains behind. The irrepressible Lynn Minmei has returned home to get her diary. Once again, she runs into Rick Hunter. They are attacked by one of the alien aircraft. At the last moment, the alien mecha is destroyed and Hunter gets his first look at a Zentraedi warrior. While human in appearance, the Zentraedi is enormous, standing well over sixty feet in height. The events of the day coupled with this revelation are too much for Rick. In a deep state of shock, he freezes at the controls and is unable to do anything more for himself or his new-found friend.

Rick impresses Minmei with his aeronautic abilities.

Scull Leader Roy Fokker comes to the rescue.

Zentraedi troops level the city.

Rick Hunter in action

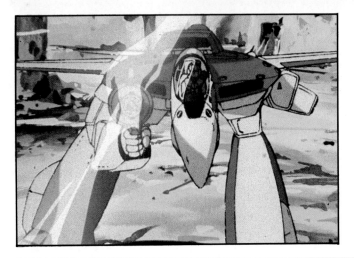

Rick encounters the Zentraedi giants
for the first time.

In shock, Rick freezes at the controls.

SPACE FOLD
Episode 3

Fokker returns to transport Rick and Minmei to the SDF-1.

Rick's plane is safe!

Lieutenant Commander Fokker returns to bring Hunter and Minmei to the safety of the SDF-1. Captain Gloval tries to determine the Zentraedi strategy while Breetai puzzles over how to capture the SDF-1 with the least amount of damage. Exedore warns his commander that, once free of the planet's gravity, the ship can execute a hyperspace fold that will carry them beyond the reach of Zentraedi weapons. Breetai reluctantly increases the laser bombardment.

On board the SDF-1, Fokker shows Rick that they have managed to salvage the young man's flying circus aircraft. Rick is happy to give up the Veritech Flyer in exchange for his old familiar racer—a vehicle that doesn't change shape or fire lasers. His first taste of battle was more than enough; Rick has no

desire to become a fighter pilot. Fokker returns to duty, leaving Rick and Minmei with the little plane. Minmei wants to return to her aunt and uncle in the evacuation shelter on Macross Island. Rick still wants to impress the girl and, although he has promised Fokker he won't wander off, he decides to fly back to the island so that the girl can rejoin her family.

In the interim, Captain Gloval has decided to make an emergency jump into hyperspace at an altitude of 2,000 feet above Macross Island. To the Zentraedi's amazement, the SDF-1 executes a space fold maneuver that places them beyond reach of battle. In minutes, the besieged SDF-1 and her crew find themselves in the icy expanse of deep space, but they also discover that their proximity to Earth during the fold has caused Macross Island to be transported with them. Disaster piles on disaster as they find themselves orbiting the planet Pluto instead of the

The space fold maneuver

moon. Then, when they prepare to re-fold to get back to Earth, they discover that the fold system has vanished into thin air.

Gloval observes that it's going to be a long trip back home.

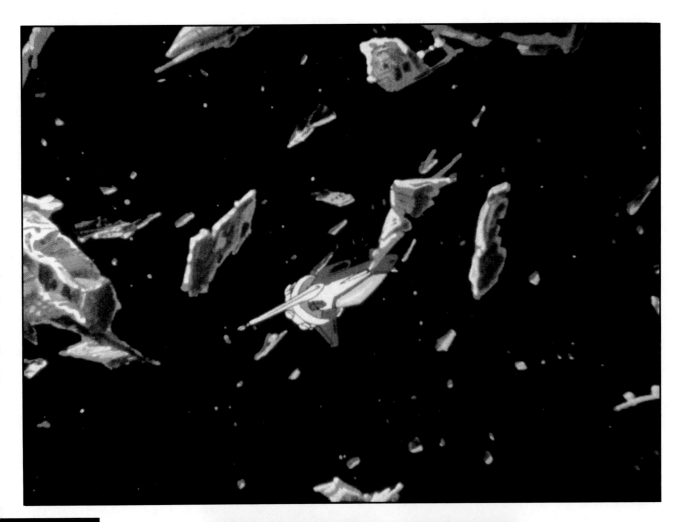

Rick and Minmei lost in the debris of space

"It's going to be a long trip back to Earth."

THE LONG WAIT

Episode 4

While the bridge crew of the SDF-1 plans its next course of action, Rick Hunter tries a maneuver of his own. Initially trapped in the vacuum of space outside the battlefortress when the SDF-1 executed the fold, Rick and Minmei enter an unexplored area of the ship. With the radio broken, they have no way to call for help. Although Roy Fokker quickly determines that his friends are missing, he is ordered to assist in retrieving the surviving 70,000 civilians of Macross Island. The two young people are left to their own resources.

While Fokker and his pilots salvage what they can, Rick and Minmei explore their surroundings and try to find their way to the center of the ship. However, the size of the

Rick re-enters the SDF-1.

Rick and Minmei look for a way out.

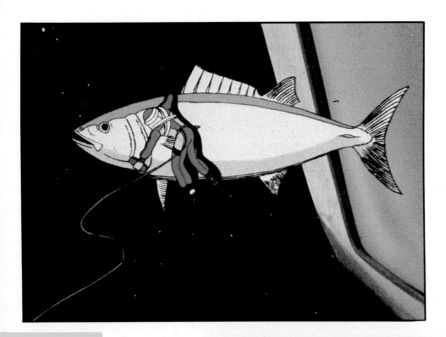

battlefortress is more than they can handle, and eventually they are reduced to simply finding the means to stay alive. They pass the time in conversation, becoming good friends. Rick Hunter finds his companion charming as well as beautiful. His sense of responsibility for Lynn Minmei evolves into genuine affection.

They spend many days trapped in the confines of the ship, but just as they lose hope of ever seeing friends and family again, a freak accident caused by a construction crew assembling Macross City within the SDF-1 results in the rescue of the two young people.

Bringing home the bacon. . .
uh, tuna!

Becoming friends

A freak accident...

...and rescue!

TRANSFORMATION
Episode 5

The first Chinese restaurant in space

Rick is unhappy.

Despite the incredible disruption in their lives, the citizens of Macross City make the best of their situation. Reunited with her aunt and uncle at their restaurant, Lynn Minmei persuades them to reopen. The first Chinese restaurant in space—and Minmei—prove to be very popular with the inhabitants of the SDF-1.

Meanwhile, still in orbit around Earth, Breetai and Exedore discuss the origins of the Micronians found in their most ancient records. The legends are vague but express a strict warning advising Zentraedi to keep away from all planets inhabited by Micronians. Breetai is puzzled. How could such tiny creatures pose a threat to the magnificent Zentraedi warriors? Intrigued, the commander orders a space fold of the flagship and armada in an attempt to follow the SDF-1.

Rick Hunter is unhappy with his new life on board the battlefortress. His conversations with Roy Fokker and Lynn Minmei are strained and strangely dissatisfying. Roy encourages him to join the Robotech forces and put his talents to good use, but Rick is unwilling to go into battle again. He does not want to become a soldier, a professional killer. Minmei cannot understand his point of view. Their argument is interrupted when Captain Gloval and crew discover the means to transform the SDF-1 into a robotic configuration—just in time to do battle with the approaching Zentraedi armada.

The SDF-1—transformed!

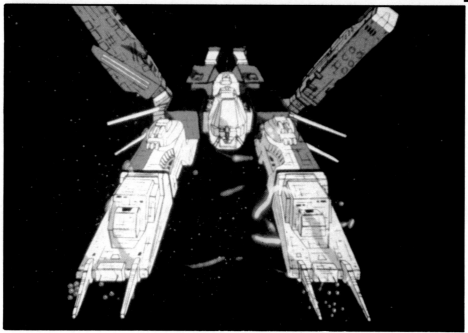

In its new configuration, the SDF-1 is able to repel the attacking Zentraedi forces, although at great cost to Macross City. The modular transformation destroys much of the city, due to the radical effects on the fortress's basic structure. In the months that follow, the citizens pull together and repair the damage. Once again, they try to lead normal lives.

Rick Hunter decides to join the Robotech Defense Force after all and becomes a Veritech fighter pilot. As Rick gets the unsettling information that his new commanding officer is Lisa Hayes, someone he still refers to as "that old sourpuss," Captain Gloval receives his own bad news. In trying to trace the missing fold system generator, his crew has discovered that its disappearance

Gloval and crew face a new attack from the Zentraedi forces.

Lisa Hayes presents her plan.

may have distorted the actual fabric of the space/time continuum. Gloval can only guess at how this will affect their attempt to return to Earth.

The Zentraedi track the SDF-1 to its hiding place in the rings of Saturn. Captain Gloval attempts a blitzkrieg maneuver to take them past the alien armada. As the SDF-1 battles its way through, Rick Hunter takes part in his first official combat duty. On the bridge, Lisa Hayes comes up with an offensive strategy of her own—the Daedalus maneuver—which allows the SDF-1 to defeat the main Zentraedi destroyer.

Blitzkrieg!

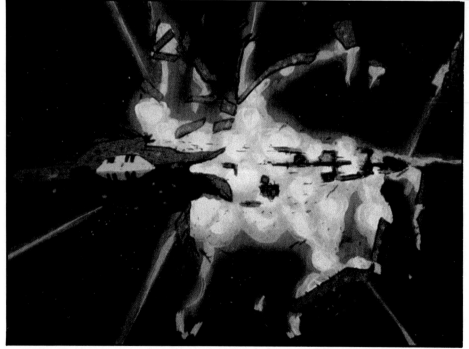

Exedore and Breetai are amazed at
the Micronians' success.

BYE-BYE MARS
Episode 7

Warlord Khyron, the "Backstabber"

Emerging from hyperspace above Mars, Breetai sets an ambush for the SDF-1. He also calls up reinforcements—the 7th Mechanized Division of the Botoru Fleet. Exedore is alarmed at this turn of events. The Botoru division is commanded by Khyron, a ruthless Zentraedi warlord who has earned himself the nickname "Backstabber." Khyron's motto is victory at all costs—even at the unnecessary risk of his own men. Breetai agrees that Khyron's measures are extreme at best, but so far, the warlord's division has remained undefeated. Breetai cannot afford to lose the SDF-1.

In Macross City, Rick Hunter receives a personal invitation from Lynn Minmei to the girl's sixteenth birthday party. Minmei is excited about the event and pleased with the announced news of the recent Zentraedi defeat. Rick regretfully advises her that the announcement is only so much morale-building propaganda. The Veritech squads have suffered heavy casualties and didn't hit half the reported targets. Minmei brushes the sobering news aside. She can't imagine why anyone would want to stay depressed on her birthday.

As the SDF-1 attains orbit around Mars, they try to establish contact with Sara base. Lisa Hayes is particularly interested in reaching Sara since her fiance, Karl Riber, is stationed at the observation post. A gentle young man, Riber had optioned for space duty in order to avoid the Global Civil War. Lisa had joined the armed forces in order to apply for duty on Mars so that she could be with him. It's been a long time since they've seen each other. Lisa is devastated when she learns Sara base has been destroyed and that there are no survivors.

Captain Gloval lands the battlefortress close to the base itself. He deploys a company of destroids to secure available supplies. Veritech fighters are launched to observe the area and cover the transport vehicles. Lisa requests

A Zentraedi ship

Rick receives an invitation to Minmei's birthday party.

permission to leave the ship and check out the base personally. Gloval cautions her to be careful and allows her to go.

As Lisa explores the base and the last of the supplies are being loaded on the SDF-1, Khyron's forces attack. Gravity mines prevent the battlefortress from taking off. The SDF-1 is unable to escape.

Gloval orders Claudia Grant to contact Lisa at Sara base. He tells Lisa to find the reflex furnace controls and place them in overdrive. Lisa follows through, knowing that it will destroy the base as well as the gravity mines. She hopes the explosion will destroy her, too. Without Riber, Lisa has no desire to live. At the last minute, Rick Hunter arrives to take Lisa back to the ship. Rick actually has to carry her out. They escape with no time to spare.

Khyron endures his first defeat at Micronian hands. He finds the sensation annoying—and intriguing.

Lisa remembers her fiance,
Karl Riber.

Lisa explores Mars Base Sara.

Involuntarily rescued

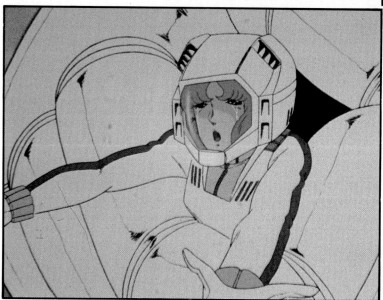

SWEET SIXTEEN

Episode 8

Minmei prepares for her party.

Ben Dixon, Rick Hunter, and Max Sterling

As Minmei prepares for her sixteenth birthday, the SDF-1 continues to orbit Mars. Operating on auxiliary power, the battle-fortress is under a constant barrage of fire from alien ships and battle pods. With its main engines damaged and the fold system inoperative, the SDF-1 is unable to escape. Khyron and his Zentraedi troops press their advantage at every turn, despite Breetai's orders to the contrary. The commander wants to capture the ship intact.

To his chagrin, Rick Hunter finds that he's not the only man invited to Lynn Minmei's party. The popular girl has requested the presence of almost every fighter pilot on the ship. While he finds her natural enthusiasm and innocence pleasing, Rick can't help but wish Minmei would focus her attentions on one specific individual—like himself! Before he can press his case, Rick is called back to headquarters, where he is presented with the titanium Medal of Valor for distinguished service for his rescue of Lieutenant Commander Lisa Hayes. He is also promoted to the rank of lieutenant and introduced to the members of his new squad, Corporals Maximillian (Max) Sterling and Ben Dixon. The three young men go to Minmei's party only to be called back to duty when Khyron begins another accelerated assault. Yet because Khyron has attacked against Breetai's orders, the Zentraedi commander orders a manual override that pulls the battle pods away from the space fortress—just as Khyron is about to defeat the SDF-1.

Max distinguishes himself as an excellent fighter pilot. Unfortunately, Ben Dixon is a more enthusiastic than effective combatant. Rick is more concerned with the fact that he's all but missed Minmei's party, not to mention the fact that he's been too busy to get her a present. When he returns, he gives her his Medal of Valor. Minmei is delighted.

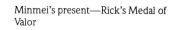

The Vermilion Squad in action

Minmei's present—Rick's Medal of Valor

MISS MACROSS
Episode 9

Minmei—one of 28 contestants

The swimsuit competition

The citizens of Macross City hold a beauty contest to boost morale among soldiers and civilians alike. Lynn Minmei is one of twenty-eight eager and attractive contestants chosen from nearly four hundred applicants. Minmei's charismatic charm has already made her the darling of the SDF-1. She wins the title of Miss Macross hands down and becomes the official Queen of the City.

The Zentraedi pick up the beauty pageant broadcast and are mystified by what they witness. Their culture does not permit close association between males and females. The aliens are aghast to see Micronians of opposite sexes mingling with each other, actually touching each other. The concepts of music, dance, and fashion are totally foreign to them as well. Breetai dispatches a reconnaissance squad to investigate. In pursuit of their mission, the three spies—Rico, Bron, and Konda—are nearly destroyed by Rick Hunter. They return to the Zentraedi flagship more confused than before.

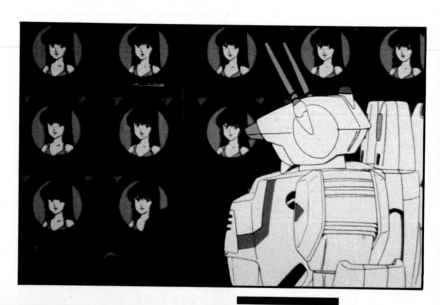

The contest is broadcast across the ship . . . and into space.

Zentraedi spies, Konda, Rico, and Bron, are dispatched to investigate Micronian eccentricities.

BLIND GAME

Episode 10

Khyron at the helm

Lisa volunteers.

Captured!

Ordered to fire a warning shot across the bow of the SDF-1, Khyron takes matters into his own hands again. The blast knocks out the radar tower of the giant spacefortress. The stress of constant battle has already taken its toll on the SDF-1, and much of the sophisticated electronic equipment no longer functions properly. The aliens make contact with Captain Gloval, demanding the ship's surrender. Gloval retaliates by planning a new defense.

Lisa Hayes volunteers to pilot a radar vessel into Zentraedi-controlled space under the protection of Rick Hunter's Vermilion Squad. The defense of the ship is more important than ever. The bridge crew has received a disturbing first transmission from Earth. The United Earth Defense Headquarters has forbidden the SDF-1 to return. Earth defense has calculated that the Zentraedi are more interested in the battlefortress than they are in the planet itself. As long as the SDF-1 remains in space, they are certain that the aliens will stay there, too, It's superficial reasoning at best; however, the spacefortress is now the only home the troops and the 70,000 residents of Macross City have. Lisa knows it must be protected!

FIRST CONTACT
Episode 11

While performing their mission, Lisa, Rick, and Ben are captured by the Zentraedi. Max Sterling manages to escape. They are interrogated by Breetai, Exedore, and Dolza, the supreme commander of the Zentraedi armada. In the course of the questioning, the Zentraedi officials demand that the Micronians tell them what they know about protoculture—something the humans protest they have never heard of. The Zentraedi want to learn about Micronian customs and are shocked to learn that human children are born from a female parent. Rick and Lisa provide an example of the affection humans demonstrate for each other by kissing. The Zentraedi are so shocked that they have the prisoners removed to other quarters.

After they are gone, Dolza tells Breetai and Exedore that the Zentraedi were once the same size as the Micronians and that both sexes lived together before they abandoned the custom and evolved through the use of protoculture. Dolza describes protoculture as "the essence of Robotechnology developed by our ancestors" and, although those secrets have been lost, he suspects that they are somehow stored within the SDF-1. That is why the battlefortress must be regained!

Lisa, Ben, and Rick are brought before Supreme Commander Dolza.

Lisa brings out the worst in Dolza.

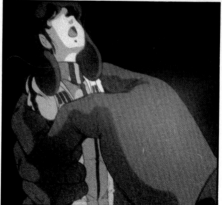

Rick and Breetai confront.

A demonstration of Micronian customs

THE BIG ESCAPE
Episode 12

The Zentraedi commanders are eager to learn more about the Micronian culture and investigate their knowledge of protoculture. Rico, Bron, and Konda volunteer to be reduced to Micronian size so that they may infiltrate the SDF-1 and report their findings to Breetai and Dolza.

Meanwhile, realizing the effect they had on their interrogators, Lisa and Rick try kissing in front of the next guard who appears, as part of an escape plan. The next guard turns out to be Max Sterling in disguise. He has come to rescue his friends.

Humiliated by his failure to recapture the Micronian prisoners, Breetai also finds himself relieved of active duty. Dolza places another Zentraedi warlord, Azonia, in charge. Observing their conversation, Rick and Lisa realize that the aliens' tremendous size comes about through the use of protoculture.

They complete their escape and make their way back to the SDF-1.

Max Sterling to the rescue!

Lisa takes pictures of the Zentraedi ship, but the camera is lost in the escape.

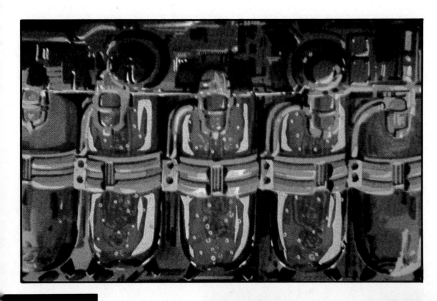

The secret of the Zentraedi—
protoculture-induced growth

Azonia, now in command of the
Zentraedi armada, talks with one of
her pilots, Miriya.

BLUE WIND
Episode 13

On board the battlefortress, Lisa, Rick, Max, and Ben relate their experiences and observations as prisoners of the alien invaders to their superior officers. There are promotions all around, and their exploits are cause for celebration among the civilians and soldiers of Macross City. Rick is briefly reunited with Lynn Minmei, who has become quite a star, a virtual singing sensation. He can't help but feel that they are growing apart. The three Zentraedi spies observe the festivities with all the enthusiasm of children in a huge toy store. They are beginning to enjoy the Micronian culture.

Following a course of his own design. Captain Gloval executes a daring plan to take the SDF-1 back to Earth. Khyron prepares to destroy the battlefortress rather than allow it to reach the planet. He is stopped by Azonia, who threatens to destroy the warlord herself if he harms the spacefortress. Seething with rage, Khyron allows the ship to pass. The bridge crew of the SDF-1 observes this incredible drama between the two Zentraedi forces and is amazed—except for Captain Gloval. He has calculated this move all along.

The battlefortress lands in the Pacific Ocean with minimum reentry damage. The inhabitants of the giant spaceship are glad to be home.

Zentraedi spies try to assimilate themselves into Micronian society.

Azonia berates Khyron for disobeying orders.

The SDF-1—home at last!

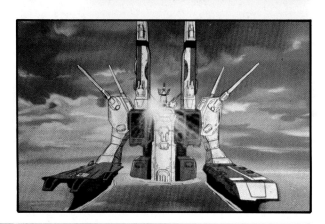

GLOVAL'S REPORT
Episode 14

Captain Gloval prepares a report that describes all that has happened to the SDF-1 and her inhabitants, from the fateful maiden launch festivities up to and including their return to Earth.

HOMECOMING
Episode 15

Gloval and Hayes are met with a cool reception.

After two years of fighting its way back to Earth, the SDF-1 is home. Captain Gloval and First Officer Lisa Hayes prepare to meet with the United Earth Defense Government at its secret headquarters in the Alaskan wilderness. Their mission is crucial. They want to convince the governing council to work toward a truce between the Zentraedi and the people of Earth.

Lisa and Gloval are met with a cool reception. The council hears them out, then dismisses them with a vague promise to consider their proposals. Gloval is convinced that something is very wrong.

While the two officers puzzle over the council's seeming indifference, Rick Hunter and Lynn Minmei encounter a mystery of their own. Rick flies Minmei back to Japan so that she can visit her parents in the Chinatown section of Yokohama. Minmei's parents are shocked—but delighted—to find their daughter alive. Minmei's cousin, Lynn Kyle, hears the commotion and comes in to find out what is going on. Rick and Minmei learn that the Earth government has circulated the story that everyone living on Macross Island had been killed. Kyle is pleased to learn that his parents, Minmei's aunt and uncle, are

alive. Although Minmei's parents would prefer that the girl remain with them, she persuades them to let her return to her career on board the SDF-1. Reluctantly, they agree to let her go, but they send Lynn Kyle to accompany his young cousin. Kyle is a cynical opportunist. War has made him a bitter young man. He can see only the negative sides of situations. Kyle and Rick are not destined to be friends.

Captain Gloval and Commander Hayes are called back into the council meeting, where they are advised that their request for a peace negotiation has been rejected. Gloval demands to know how the council thinks it can win against the Zentraedi forces. The council wants to know why Gloval thinks they can't. Their decision is based on insufficient knowledge regarding the alien culture. They cannot be sure the Zentraedi would participate in a peace settlement in good faith.

To Gloval's additional dismay, the Earth council refuses to allow the 70,000 inhabitants of Macross City to return to the planet. Press censorship had been exercised from the day the Robotech battlefortress disappeared. The government did not want anyone to know that the world was at war with invading aliens. In an effort to circumvent global panic, they released a story that a guerrilla force had attacked and destroyed Macross Island after the ship had left on its test flight. They do not want their propaganda invalidated by the return of 70,000 supposedly dead friends and relatives. The council concludes that it is more crucial that the SDF-1 draw the enemy forces away from the planet—at any cost.

Rick takes Minmei home to her parents' restaurant.

Lynn Kyle, Minmei's cousin

The council reaches a decision.

Returning to the SDF-1—the only home they have

BATTLE CRY

Episode 16

The announcement of the governing council's decision not to allow the residents of Macross City to return to Earth is met with a rage-induced riot on board the SDF-1. The civilians resent their subordinate position. A strong anti-military feeling prevails—with Lynn Kyle as an able spokesman. He had been a member of the peace movement on Earth. Charisma seems to run in the family; Kyle creates as much of a stir as his cousin, Minmei.

Acting against Azonia's orders, Khyron leads an attack on the battlefortress. It is only with the greatest effort and good fortune that the SDF-1 manages to escape the onslaught. During the battle, Lisa Hayes finds herself distracted. She is unhappy over her father's part in the Earth council's decision. Lynn Kyle reminds her too much of her fiance, Karl Riber. Kyle's anti-war statements echo her lost one's sentiments perfectly, yet she senses a kind of insincerity that was never present in Riber. At the conclusion of the battle, Rick Hunter is critically injured; suddenly, Lisa begins to realize that the affection she feels for the fighter pilot is something more than friendship.

Rick Hunter is injured during Khyron's attack on the SDF-1.

PHANTASM

Episode 17

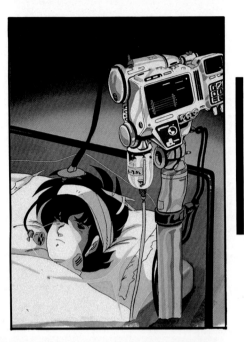

Rick Hunter lies in delirium in a base hospital.

The young pilot's dreams center on rescuing Minmei from an enemy that seems to be a cross between Breetai and Kyle.

The fantasies conclude with a growing awareness of his interest in Lisa Hayes.

Rick Hunter has survived a direct hit during an incredible aerial dogfight—but just barely. He has bailed out of the plane and now lies wounded in a base hospital. While his body fights for its life, his mind races through an emotional journey. It is a delirious dreamscape filled with distorted memories of the past two years that particularly concern his relationship with Lynn Minmei and his new feelings for First Officer Hayes.

FAREWELL, BIG BROTHER
Episode 18

Rick Hunter comes out of his delirium and spends a long time recovering from his wounds. He is quickly bored with having so much time on his hands and so little to do. Lisa Hayes arrives to visit Rick in the hospital. She is awkwardly apologetic and only stays for a short time. Claudia Grant is the first to guess the reason for Lisa's unusual shyness and confronts her with the fact. Claudia knows Lisa's in love with Rick. Her advice? "Stop moping around and act like a woman."

Zentraedi forces still under Azonia's command prepare a new attack. One of her best fighter pilots, a strikingly beautiful woman named Miriya, takes Khyron to task because of his inability to defeat the Micronians. Khyron advises caution: "Your ego is going to become the cause of your ultimate destruction. Because you have never faced a worthy opponent, you believe that you are something special, but take care, Miriya—for there is one aboard the alien ship whom even you cannot best." Miriya is intrigued by the thought that there might be a fighter pilot better than herself.

Roy Fokker visits with Lynn Minmei on the set of her first movie before he takes off for battle. He is concerned about Rick Hunter's depression and tries to persuade Minmei to visit her friends. Minmei is as charming as usual. She knows that if it weren't for Rick, she wouldn't be around to fulfill her dream of becoming a motion picture actress. She goes to visit Rick but is so exhausted that she falls asleep across his bed.

Miriya leads the assault against the Veritech fighters. She searches for the flying ace Khyron warned her about. Geared for conquest, she is especially ruthless in her actions. She discovers her primary foe in— Max Sterling!

Her pursuit of this one pilot becomes obvious to the bridge crew of the SDF-1 and Sterling is recalled from the fight, but Miriya follows Max into the ship itself. They do battle

Lisa visits Rick in the hospital.

on the streets of Macross City until an overhead hatch is opened, forcing her away from her prey.

That evening, after the end of the battle, Roy Fokker visits with his fiancee, Claudia Grant. As she prepares dinner, she tells him: "I don't think you realize how terrified I get every time you fly off on a combat mission. It's almost as if you pilots think that it's all some kind of wonderful game that you're playing when you go up in those Veritechs."

Roy responds, as if to himself: "It isn't a game, Claudia . . . it has *never* been a game."

Claudia is amazed when Roy seems to pass out. She thinks he's simply exhausted from the fight, but when she cannot wake him, she suspects the worst. A doctor explains later that when he was wounded in combat Fokker suffered internal injuries and lost too much blood. It is a terrible tragedy. Fokker will be sorely missed by his crew and his friends.

Lisa Hayes visits Rick Hunter to personally tell him of his "big brother's" death.

Roy Fokker defends the SDF-1.

The Scull Squad leader is hit!

Widespread destruction in Macross City as Sterling and Miriya battle

The Zentraedi spies are fascinated by Lynn Minmei dolls.

Fokker collapses at Claudia Grant's apartment.

The catastrophes of war have reduced the civilian population of Macross City to 56,000. Captain Gloval is desperate to have the survivors relocated on Earth before anyone else is killed. He broadcasts his request over open airspace, realizing that he will be refused again but hoping that someone in the government will hear and do something about the impossible situation. Gloval will not rest until his orders are changed. His persistence pays off. The North American Ontario quadrant agrees to accept as residents any civilians from the SDF-1 who wish to return to the planet.

Azonia and Khyron are quarreling again when Miriya requests permission to be reduced to Micronian size so she can become a spy for the Zentraedi. Azonia is puzzled but grants the pilot's wish. Miriya has an ulterior motive. She wants to find and eliminate the Micronian who defeated her in battle.

The Zentraedi proceed with a new attack plan which quickly goes awry. Khyron takes matters into his hands, and Azonia ends up having to fight a two-front battle trying to keep the warlord from destroying the Micronians while she attempts to capture the vessel herself.

Captain Gloval decides to test a new barrier-shield system. It protects the ship but renders the weapons system inoperable. Khyron blasts the shield with all he's got and eventually, the system overloads. Rick Hunter, now the leader of Fokker's famed Skull Squadron, is ordered to evacuate the surrounding area as the barrier control begins an explosive chain reaction. Not all of the squad is able to pull out in time. Ben Dixon is killed. By the end of the debacle, they learn that the attacking Zentraedi fleet has been wiped out and, because of their proximity to the planet, the Earth's surface has been leveled over a radius of twenty-five miles.

On board the SDF-1, Lynn Kyle holds a press conference for his cousin. Lynn Minmei

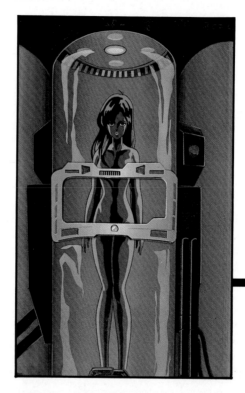

Miriya has herself "micronized" to infiltrate the SDF-1 and confront **Max Sterling**.

Captain Henry J. Gloval executes new defense strategies.

Khyron blasts the SDF-1 until his ship's system begins to overload.

has collapsed from stress, and her public is anxious to hear how she's doing. Kyle chides the newsmen on their priorities: "I don't understand how, with all that's been going on, you people can be chasing after a star who passed out from a little overwork! Now forget that and let's find a way to make these military leaders stop this war. This fighting is totally non-productive. . . . There are no winners, only losers. We must get out of this destructive, inhumane, no-win situation at once."

While the crew of the SDF-1 is alarmed at Kyle's underlying suggestion of total surrender to the Zentraedi, the three spies—Bron, Rico, and Konda—are astonished at their gut reaction to these new ideas. An end to fighting would negate the Zentraedi reason for existence, yet the thought of life without constant warfare is somehow appealing.

PARADISE LOST
Episode 20

Captain Gloval's dream of evacuating the civilians aboard his ship has come to a disastrous end. He learns that the barrier overload has wiped out an entire city as well as its surrounding countryside. The people of Earth know nothing of the circumstances that led to the explosion, only that the battle-fortress is a threat to life and property. The Ontario quadrant withdraws its offer to take the civilian refugees. The SDF-1 finds itself homeless again. Gloval receives his orders: *The United Earth Council hereby orders you to remove your vessel from any proximity to the Earth. You are also ordered to keep the civilian refugees on board your ship. If these orders are not followed to the letter, we will be forced to take steps to see that they are.*

At Zentraedi Command Headquarters, Dolza, Breetai, and Exedore review a video record of the battle and are shocked. From all appearances, it would seem that the Micronian are utterly ruthless, that they would sacrifice an entire population center to defeat four small divisions of attacking battlepods. Dolza decides to place Breetai in charge of the Zentraedi forces again. Breetai accepts the position and requests that the Imperial Class Fleet—a war force of over one million ships—be deployed under his command.

Bron, Rico, and Konda regretfully return to Zentraedi Command to make their report. Breetai and Exedore don't know what to make of Micronian culture—movies, music, dolls, candy, and other artifacts—but Exedore, for one, decides that he would like to examine it firsthand! While the two commanders ponder the new information, the spies enthusiastically relate their experiences on the SDF-1 to their fellow soldiers.

Meanwhile, Captain Gloval makes an announcement to the residents of Macross City. He tells them about the council's decision but breaks down at the end and cannot continue. Lynn Minmei interrupts. She talks to the crowd as only she can, saying:

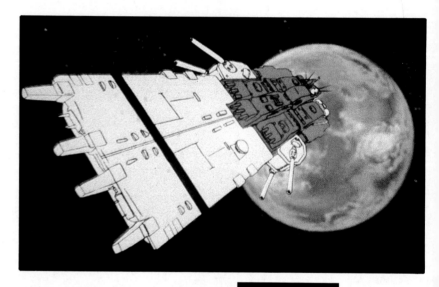

After the overload disaster, the SDF-1 is ordered to leave Earth's orbit.

"I don't understand anything that has to do with politics, but I do know that the only way we'll survive this is to pull together....I think of the SDF-1 as my home now. We've all been through quite a bit, but look at how strong we've become because of it. I have more friends here than I ever did on Earth. You've been like a big family to me. Someday we'll return to Earth—we'll **never** give up hope. But for now, I'm proud to be a citizen of Macross City and this ship."

Minmei's speech bridges the gap between military and civilian residents. Her words find a place in everyone's heart.

A NEW DAWN

Episode 21

Minmei and Kyle arrive for the premiere of their film in Macross City.

Observing Zentraedi are impressed with Lynn Kyle's on-screen fighting.

Taking advantage of a lull in the war, the citizens of Macross City look forward to the premiere of Lynn Minmei's first film. It's a martial arts epic featuring the young singing star and her cousin. Kyle's Kung Fu expertise has made him a natural for the hero of the picture. The crowd finds the film delightful as they watch the romantic story evolve around the two stars. They enjoy the action sequences when Kyle vanquishes Zentraedi villains with all the panache of a new Bruce Lee.

Observing the film from their ship, Breetai and Exedore are concerned. They do not understand that what they're watching is a work of fantasy. As Lynn Kyle decimates the huge alien invaders, the Zentraedi commanders wonder if the Micronians have developed a new weapon. They are further disturbed by their own feelings as they observe the love scenes.

Breetai and Exedore are not the only ones upset by the film. Neither Rick Hunter nor Lisa Hayes can enjoy the picture. They leave the theater and run into each other outside. Kyle is still a painful reminder of the man Lisa once loved. Rick can't bear to witness the close friendship that seems to have evolved between Minmei and her cousin. Coupled with the love scenes from the film, it's more than he can bear. Lisa and Rick find themselves becoming unwilling allies. Their feelings of friendship for each other increase.

The aliens have no concept of "special effects."

Unwilling allies

BATTLE HYMN

Episode 22

Dolza, Breetai, and Exedore plan their next battle strategy, unaware that the seeds of defeat are being sown from within. Bron, Rico, and Konda have decided that they prefer the Micronian way of life, and they have convinced several of their fellow soldiers to defect with them. Meanwhile, Khyron is up to his old tricks. With the commanders in conference, he can strike without having to advise his superiors of his plans.

Khyron begins his new assault while most of Macross City is gathered to hear Lynn Minmei in concert. Despite the destruction around her, the young girl continues to sing, hoping to distract the crowd from impending disaster.

On the night of Lynn Minmei's biggest concert . . .

Warlord Khyron launches his greatest attack ever!

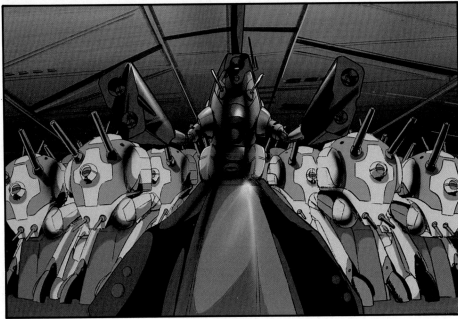

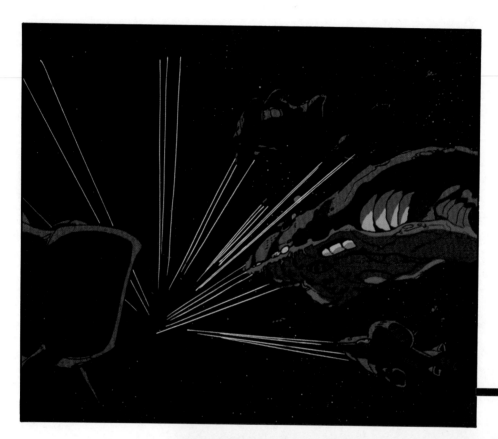

Warlord Khyron launches his greatest attack ever!

RECKLESS

Episode 23

The Zentraedi rebels are interviewed by SDF-1 command and granted political asylum.

The crew of the battlefortress has responded to the Zentraedi's latest attack with a great show of force, but the fighting works its way inside to the streets of Macross City. Khyron's troops overrun the civil defense patrol's resistance. The warlord is positive that this time, victory will be his. However, his gloating is interrupted when he notices odd behavior among some of his men. When he questions them, they explain that they're looking for Minmei. Khyron forbids them to pursue their quest. They ignore his orders and run away.

At Zentraedi Command Headquarters, Breetai and Exedore receive news that Khyron's troops are deserting. Exedore tells Breetai that this must be the secret weapon that the Zentraedi legends warned of.

The officers of the SDF-1 are as stunned as the Zentraedi when confronted with the alien deserters. They hardly know what to make of the situation, but a subsequent examination shows that the Zentraedi blood types and genetic structures are identical to those of humans. The aliens aren't as alien as they appear to be. Gloval decides to grant them political asylum.

SHOW DOWN
Episode 24

Lisa plans to return to Earth.

The alien defectors have provided Captain Gloval and First Officer Hayes with new hope that peaceful co-existence is possible between the people of Earth and the Zentraedi. In light of this development, Lisa volunteers to return secretly to Earth and try once again to persuade her father, Admiral Hayes, and the other military commanders to begin peace negotiations with the alien leaders.

As Lisa prepares to do verbal battle with the military, Miriya zeroes in on Max Sterling at the video arcade. She feels certain that she'll win at any game he chooses to play. She is defeated time after time. Meanwhile, Max finds himself enchanted with this unusual girl and makes a date to meet her at the park in a few hours.

Lynn Minmei is greeted by the press corps as she leaves the hospital with the now-recovered Lynn Kyle. The press makes much of the fact that she spent so much time with her cousin, who was wounded at the concert on the day the aliens attacked within the city. Kyle astounds her by proposing marriage on the hospital steps in front of the crowd.

Miriya and Max meet face-to-face in the video arcade.

Lynn Kyle proposes to Minmei.

WEDDING BELLS
Episode 25

Miriya faces defeat at the hands of a mere Micronian—Max Sterling.

Max and Miriya prepare for their wedding.

Max Sterling anxiously waits for Miriya in Macross City park. Until now, he has spent most of his time in pursuit of battle. Now he finds himself involved in a totally different crisis, but it's not the one he expected. Miriya attacks on sight. Max demands an explanation as he frantically tries to protect himself. Miriya snarls: "Time and again you have made me look like a fool. I am the Zentraedi's greatest pilot and will not be humiliated by a Micronian. The first time you were lucky; the second was your final victory. Nothing can save you now. This time, I will win. I will defeat you!"

Miriya boasts too soon. Max overcomes her. Thoroughly vanquished, the alien girl begs him to end her life since she cannot live with defeat. It's the last thing Sterling can bring himself to do. Miriya is the only girl he's ever been attracted to. He proposes on the spot, and Miriya finds that the feelings she's harbored all along for the young man are not warlike at all.

Preparations for the wedding begin immediately. The full squadron of fighting mecha aboard the SDF-1 shows its colors. Not only is this the first wedding in space, it is the first joining of a human and a Zentraedi. Observing Zentraedi find the broadcast ceremony extremely interesting. At first they wonder if Miriya is taking her job as a spy a bit too seriously, but finally conclude she obviously cannot resist the charm of the Micronian pilot. The danger of direct contact with the Micronians is plainly evident.

Prior to the ceremony, Captain Gloval addresses the crowd: "This wedding carries with it a great historical significance. As you all know, Miriya was a Zentraedi warrior who destroyed many of our own ships. She comes from a culture that we have grown to fear and hate. It is the Zentraedi who have caused our present situation. They alone prevent our return to Earth, our homes and our beloved families. It is they who have caused destruction and endless suffering. Now, I know what you are thinking—'Why is he choosing this time to remind us of all these terrible things?' I remind you of these brutal acts, ladies and gentlemen, because we must learn to forgive . . . not blindly, not out of ignorance, but because we are a strong and willing nation. We cannot blame the Zentraedi for this inexplicable lust for war. They have never known any other way of life, and it is their only means of survival. Nor can we condemn the individuals of that society for the mass insanity of a war machine. Instead, we must look to their good nature. Some have made a request to stop the fighting, and I believe it is a genuine request. We must respond with equal integrity. The blood of both these young people was tested before the ceremony. Zentraedi blood was found to be the same as human blood. There is no reason why we cannot coexist in peace. Let this occasion represent a future where all people live in harmony. . . . Each and every citizen must develop a responsible attitude toward the prospect of peace. We must learn from our mistakes. To live with different people, different nations—think of the challenge! I am not proposing laying down our arms but extending them so that if there is a chance of a peaceful solution, we may find it together."

While Gloval's words make an impact on the inhabitants of the SDF-1, not all listeners are as impressed. Admiral Hayes does not agree with the Captain's sentiments. Commander Dolza orders Breetai to lead Zentraedi forces into battle immediately. Breetai follows his orders, but some of his soldiers are having second thoughts about their mission.

Miriya joins Max in his Veritech fighter. Once in space, she shows him how attacking Zentraedi flyers can be put out of commission without killing the pilots. Rick Hunter and other SDF-1 pilots follow their example. Meanwhile, on board the Zentraedi flagship, the alien warriors are refusing to engage the Micronians in battle. Breetai soon has a full-scale mutiny on his hands.

Captain Gloval addresses the citizens and crew of the SDF-1.

Even with the best intentions, some things need to be worked out.

THE MESSENGER

Episode 26

Exedore is greeted by an officer of the SDF-1.

The Zentraedi ambassador demonstrates the Micronian "psychological advantage."

Despite Kyle's protests, Minmei volunteers to assist the military in their efforts to bring the war to an end.

An uneasy truce is called between the two combatants. Following orders from high command, Breetai contacts the SDF-1 and requests permission to negotiate a settlement between the civilizations. Exedore is escorted to the battlefortress as a representative for the Zentraedi people.

In the first official meeting between alien and human, Captain Gloval tries to explain some of the so-called Micronian secret powers. He describes the special effects used in the film that made Lynn Kyle seem so powerful as well as some of the processes they have used in fighting off the Zentraedi war machines. Exedore is amazed at their ingenuity. The one thing Gloval cannot explain away is the "psychological assault." Eventually he comes to realize that Exedore is talking about Lynn Minmei's singing. The Zentraedi minister explains that it is the girl's singing that has caused so many of their warriors to desert in droves. He explains the ancient warning that forbids Zentraedi contact with Micronians.

After their discussion, Exedore speculates that once he reads the report, Supreme Commander Dolza will most certainly order the main fleet to launch an all-out attack on Earth. He suggests that the SDF-1 prepare to escape the star system. Dolza will arrive with the main fleet consisting of more than 4,800,000 battle-ready warships. Not only will they take Earth, they will destroy the Micronian-contaminated Zentraedi as well. Exedore and Gloval now have a common enemy.

FORCE OF ARMS

Episode 27

The entire Zentraedi force, commanded by Dolza, emerges from hyperspace and surrounds Earth. Once again, the crew of the SDF-1 prepares to do battle, but now the humans have allies in Breetai and Azonia. Khyron, true to his self-serving nature, deserts, planning to return and conquer the weakened victor.

Dolza's attack is brutal. He begins by firing on Earth. Whole cities are obliterated across the face of the planet. In an attempt to disorient the new Zentraedi forces, Breetai comes up with a plan to broadcast Minmei's singing. Meanwhile, the United Earth Defense Council plans to put its most valuable weapon, the Grand Cannon, to use.

As Minmei's song is broadcast from a planet base, Gloval launches the SDF-1 into its ultimate strategy. He rams the battlefortress into Dolza's flagship. The ensuing explosion destroys the hostile alien armada. The incredible spacefortress, terribly damaged, crash lands on Earth.

RECONSTRUCTION BLUES
Episode 28

Rick Hunter notices flowers growing near the ruins of the SDF-1.

Only a handful of survivors remains scattered across the planet two years after the final confrontation. The destruction has been overwhelming, leaving only vast, pock-marked desolation where great cities and beautiful forests once stood. The remaining Veritech fighter pilots routinely patrol the deserts to investigate anything out of the ordinary. As Rick Hunter flies over the remains of old warships, he notices that life begins again. Flowers are growing in the ruins.

In spite of the horror that follows such devastation, the spirit of man prevails. A new city has risen over the remains of the SDF-1. Where there had been only chaos, survivors have somehow managed to rebuild. The battered hulk looks silently over peaceful homes, schools, libraries, and parks. There is even a new overhead rapid transit system linking the city with the suburbs.

During this period, Rick Hunter and Lisa Hayes become close friends while cousins Minmei and Kyle drift further apart.

Zentraedi and humans enjoy a concert together.

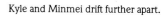

New life on Earth...Max and Miriya's baby, Dana Sterling

Kyle and Minmei drift further apart.

ROBOTECH MASTERS
Episode 29

Dissatisfied Zentraedi warriors leave to rejoin Khyron's troops.

At their distant home, the Robotech Masters receive a telepathic message that Zor's lost battlefortress has been located. A routine scan indicates that it is surrounded by a large discharge of protoculture mass. While it seems impossible that any single force could have been responsible for the destruction of more than four million battleships, the Robotech Masters receive information that that was exactly what happened. They prepare for a hyperspace fold to investigate the truth behind their data.

On Earth, the surviving Zentraedi are unhappy. They are not used to a life without the excitement of war. Peace grates on their nerves. Thousands of dissatisfied warriors are leaving town after town, heading out into the desert wastelands. It is just the kind of information Warlord Khyron likes to hear from his spies. Now, with Azonia fighting at his side, he is certain nothing will stand in the way of his desire for total conquest.

VIVA MIRIYA
Episode 30

Somewhere within the recesses of another galaxy, the Robotech Masters attempt to resurrect a being in the likeness of Zor, the genius who developed the secrets of proto-culture and Robotechnology, the being who took those secrets to his grave.

On Breetai's flagship, the Zentraedi commander meets with his old associate, Exedore, and representatives of Earth. Admiral Gloval, Commanders Hunter, Hayes, and Grant, as well as Max and Miriya Sterling, are part of the expedition. The Sterlings have even brought their baby daughter, Dana, along.

The Zentraedi commander organizes a raid on the last remaining Robotech factory in an effort to hold the upper hand in case the wandering Robotech Masters find their way to Earth. He wants them to believe that the remaining Zentraedi are the new masters of Robotechnology. His human friends are willing allies in his scheme.

Breetai greets his former comrades.

Breetai executes a raid on the last Robotech factory.

KHYRON'S REVENGE
Episode 31

Lynn Kyle leads a group of angry citizens against Rick Hunter.

Kim, Sammie, and Vanessa are dismayed over recent events.

Lines of Zentraedi are converted back into giant warriors.

Commander Hunter attempts to deploy a small squadron to guard the last protoculture chamber used for altering the size of the Zentraedi. He encounters unexpected resistance from civilians led by Lynn Kyle. To prevent a riot, Hunter leaves.

The protoculture chamber is placed by its civilian owners inside New Detroit City. Khyron quickly discovers the new location. On the eve of a major concert by Lynn Minmei, the warlord attacks, hoping to regain this vital piece of Robotechnology.

In the SDF-1 Conference Center, Admiral Gloval and crew compare notes with Exedore over the history of the Zentraedi race. Their studies indicate that the Robotech Masters discovered and developed protoculture over 500,000 years ago. Proud of its advanced and powerful civilization, the Robotech Masters decided to develop an intergalactic police force that would protect them from hostile alien life forms. A race of giants was created by proto-genetic engineering. Intended as peace-keepers, the giants developed ideas of their own. Their warlike natures caused them to begin fighting among themselves and, eventually, they discovered that their superior physiques could make them the masters of anything smaller than themselves. Gloval theorizes that if the giants had been programmed with emotions such as love, trust, and empathy, the fighting and destruction might not have taken place. The Robotech Empire collapsed, caught in the crossfire of the fighting giants—giants who evolved into Zentraedi.

In New Detroit, the civilians are not able to withstand Khyron's attack. The warlord takes the protoculture chamber to his ship. Lines of Zentraedi wishing to be converted back into the giant warriors they once were grow longer and longer. Khyron rejoices at the sight of his increasing army.

BROKEN HEART
Episode 32

Earth's Veritech forces are deployed to combat Khyron and his Zentraedi troops, but it is an impossible situation. In the course of the battle, Minmei and Kyle are captured by the giant warlord. The two are held hostage against the return of the spacefortress.

Rick Hunter and Lisa Hayes execute operation "Star Saver" and rescue Minmei and Kyle before any harm can come to them. Minmei begins to realize how much Rick means to her. They exchange vows of affection as Rick races off in pursuit of fleeing Zentraedi hostiles.

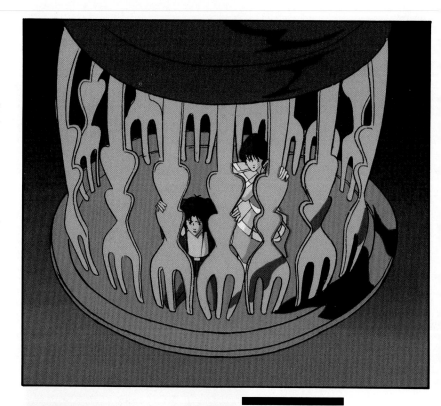

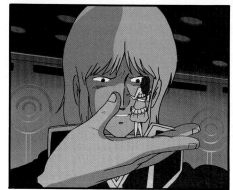

Kyle and Minmei are captured by renegade Zentraedi.

Khyron gloats.

A RAINY NIGHT
Episode 33

Lisa Hayes is miserable. Her potential relationship with Rick Hunter has just come crashing down around her. She knows Rick is still in love with Minmei and now, Minmei seems to be returning his sentiments. Lisa feels that she's lost him—this time for good.

Claudia Grant tries to console and counsel her friend. She shares memories of her relationship with Roy Fokker. It was a stormy courtship filled with as many difficulties as Lisa has experienced with Rick. She advises that the worst problems come from non-communication. "Don't keep him waiting, Lisa," Claudia advises. "Don't let too much time go by before telling him how you feel."

Lisa promises to try.

Claudia counsels—and consoles—Lisa regarding her unhappy romance with Rick Hunter.

PRIVATE TIME
Episode 34

Rick Hunter asks Lisa Hayes to join him on a picnic, but at the last moment he receives a call from Minmei, who asks him to meet her. It's a rare opportunity he can't afford to miss.

Afterwards, Commander Hunter rushes to meet Lisa, who has patiently waited for him throughout the day. All seems well until Lisa recognizes the scent of Lynn Minmei's perfume on Rick's new scarf. Hunter finds himself alone again.

As Claudia explains, her romance with Roy Fokker got off to a very shaky start.

Young Roy Fokker

SEASON'S GREETINGS
Episode 35

The "missing" Lynn Minmei shows up on Rick Hunter's doorstep.

Rick hears a disturbing news bulletin announcing that Lynn Minmei, originally reported as ill, is now missing. He is surprised to open his door and find his friend waiting for him outside.

Minmei is unhappy and tells him that she wants to stop singing and spend her life with him. In the midst of this confession, Lisa Hayes stops by to try to explain her feelings. Of course she sees Minmei and Rick through the open door and decides against it. How can she hope to compete with a star like Lynn Minmei?

Khyron chooses the holiday season for a new attack.

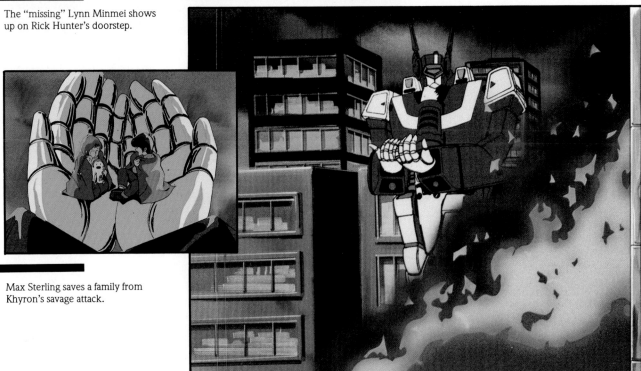

Max Sterling saves a family from Khyron's savage attack.

TO THE STARS
Episode 36

Lisa and Rick try to escape the devastation.

As they prepare a counterattack against the Zentraedi warlord, Admiral Gloval promotes Lisa Hayes to the rank of captain of the new SDF-2. Before she takes command, Lisa finally gathers the courage to tell Rick how she feels about him. In the midst of battle, Rick confronts his own feelings for both Lisa and Minmei. He discovers that it's Lisa he loves after all. He leaves Minmei behind as he and Lisa race to their battle stations.

On board the repaired SDF-1, Gloval makes a final desperate stand against Khyron the Destroyer. A crowd gathers and cheers as the battlefortress soars into the sky. The SDF-1 only has enough power for one shot. The blast cripples Khyron's ship and the SDF-1, its power depleted, crashes on the planet's surface, its fall cushioned by water. Khyron knows the fallen vessel can't erect a defense barrier without power. In their lust for total annihilation, Khyron and Azonia lock their ship's guidance system into a head-on collision with the helpless battlefortress. The impact destroys the SDF-1, the SDF-2, and Khyron as well.

Rick finds Lisa after the crash. At the last minute, Gloval had managed to shove her into one of the ejection modules. She is the holocaust's only survivor. Saddened by the loss of their friends and shipmates, they decide to build a new life for themselves and the people of Earth. Rick and Lisa plan to oversee construction of a new SDF-3 so that future generations can join them in their journey to the stars.

The ruins of the majestic SDF-1 rise out of the water to do battle one more time.

Khyron fires on the SDF-1 as . . .

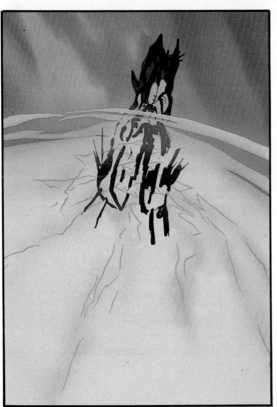

...the SDF-1 fires on the warlord's
flagship.

Khyron and Azonia are destroyed
with their ship.

The two ships are destroyed. The
First Robotech War is over.

Rick Hunter and Lisa Hayes...
to the stars

Part Two— The Robotech Masters

DANA'S STORY
Episode 37

Fifteen years later, the first graduating class of the United Earth Forces Military Academy prepares to carry on in the tradition of the officers and crew of the SDF-1. The descendants of the Zentraedi Holocaust are a tough breed. Earth is not the pleasant planet it used to be. Although several cities have been rebuilt, including New Macross City, many of them have had to be sealed off to avoid radiation contamination. The current feudal society is unstable, made up of human beings who have survived all but insurmountable odds in the face of the alien invasion. For the most part, they are an aggressive and suspicious lot.

However, everyone is cheerful at the close of graduation ceremonies. Everyone except Bowie Grant, Claudia Grant's younger brother. Bowie is a musician. He doesn't feel that the military way of life is his true vocation. Fellow graduate Lieutenant Dana Sterling senses his depression. In an effort to buoy his spirits, she tells him the story of how her parents, Max and Miriya Sterling, met and fell in love. "There's a lot more to the military life than just maneuvers," she concludes. Although heartened by her story, Bowie remains unconvinced.

Their discussion is interrupted by an emergency alert. It is not a drill. The Robotech Masters have arrived in force. They have traced the lost protoculture factory to Earth.

Lieutenant Dana Sterling— graduation day!

FALSE START
Episode 38

The 15th Squadron on practice drill

In the brig

The irrepressible and ingenious Dana Sterling leads her squad in a practice drill while the Southern Cross goes from red to yellow alert. The green troop runs afoul of seasoned combat veterans led by Lieutenant Marie Crystal. The verbal battle dissolves into physical conflict and, after leading the military police on a wild chase through Monument City, Dana finds herself thrown in the brig to reconsider her behavior in solitary confinement. Later, Dana is berated by Colonel Alan Fredericks. She has not exercised conduct becoming either an officer or the daughter of war heroes. The young women begs for another chance.

Fredericks agrees to give her one more opportunity to prove herself. Dana is released in time to lead her squad into their first official combat.

The initial confrontation between Earth Defense and the Robotech Masters results in a draw. The aliens are stunned. They had been certain they would recover their lost protoculture factory with little effort. They did not reckon on the strong fighting spirit demonstrated by the Southern Cross Defense Corps.

Because of her splendid efforts against enemy forces, Dana is directed to take command of the 15th Squadron. Their previous commander, Captain Sean Philips, is demoted to private second class for yet another of many indiscretions—this particular one involving a colonel's daughter. Sean takes the setback in good-natured stride. Meanwhile, Dana is troubled by visions of an alien being she has never seen before but is somehow strangely familiar.

SOUTHERN CROSS

Episode 39

Citizens of Earth are advised that war has been declared with the Robotech Masters. Military discipline becomes the order of the day. Sterling's 15th Squad is ordered to take position as rear guard defense. Civil Defense is too tame a position compared to what the young lieutenant has in mind for an active military career but she carries out her orders—until she sees the main base going up in flames. Mobilizing existing troops, Sterling returns to the base and attacks the invading bioroids.

When the battle is reconstructed later, Earth Command Headquarters discovers that the turning point which saved the day came about when the 15th Squad forced the bioroids to return to their mother ship. Dana is promoted again—to first lieutenant. She appears astride her hover tank at the awards ceremony and jokingly tells the audience: "It was a hare-raising experience, folks, but through the miracle of 'rabbit-technology,' we were able to pull a victory out of our hats."

VOLUNTEERS
Episode 40

To cover their impending invasion, the Robotech Masters have interrupted the communications link between United Earth Command Headquarters and its strategic orbital observation outpost, Space Station Liberty. The United Earth Government's High Command decides that a team of Robotech defenders will have to be deployed to reestablish communications and to test the strength of the invaders. Lieutenant Marie Crystal of the tactical armored space corps and Lieutenant Sterling volunteer to carry out the mission.

In the course of the battle to regain the post, Dana sees the red bioroid that has been the focus of her disturbing visions. It is an unusual mecha, but Marie and Dana manage to defeat it and rout the invaders from the space station.

Communications between United Earth Command Headquarters and Space Station Liberty are reestablished.

The red bioroid attacks

HALF MOON
Episode 41

On a routine night patrol, Dana and Bowie discover a trespasser in a forbidden sector outside what was once New Macross City. They investigate despite receiving negative orders from their command post.

The "intruder" turns out to be enemy aliens led by the pilot of the red bioroid. In the skirmish that follows, Bowie is captured.

Dana reports her findings but is denied permission to rescue her aide. Once again, she circumvents orders. Dana gathers the 15th Squadron. A midnight drill seems suddenly in order—with live ammunition and full combat gear.

At Headquarters, Military Intelligence confirms that the aliens are digging at the crash site of the old SDF-1. They are mystified as to what the Robotech Masters could possibly want or salvage from the old wreck. Their meeting is interrupted by a large-scale bioroid attack.

Convinced the Robotech Masters mean to kill him, Bowie wastes no time discovering a means to escape confinement. He breaks out of his cell and finds a way outside as the 15th Squadron engages the enemy. Once again, Dana finds herself face to face with the red bioroid pilot. This time, both experience an unsettling moment of recognition.

Reinforcements arrive to help the 15th rescue Bowie. The Robotech Masters' huge advance command ship retreats, rising slowly into the air carrying not only the compliment of bioroids but their strange commander as well.

Bowie Grant

DANGER ZONE

Episode 42

The confrontation accelerates.

The 15th volunteers.

Since neither side is willing to make even the smallest concession, the war between Earth and the Robotech Masters escalates into another serious military confrontation. Supreme Commander Leonard deploys the bulk of their tactical armored space corps to engage the enemy in space in an attempt to avoid turning the planet surface into a battleground, but his strategy is based on insufficient data. Most of the troops are wiped out while the survivors are left to drift helplessly in space. On the hasty decision of one stubborn man, hundreds of lives have been lost in a single hopeless gesture. The Robotech Fortress continues to orbit Earth, untouched, unscathed, and apparently unbeatable.

Professor Miles Cochran and his colleague, Dr. Samson Beckett, examine trace remains of a downed bioroid pilot and make a disturbing discovery. Their analysis. of the alien's genetic code determines that the invaders are human—not micronized Zentraedi as they had originally suspected. They are horrified at the thought of brother fighting brother.

Dana Sterling volunteers the 15th Squad to rescue the space corps. Louie Nichols has determined that the alien ship twists opposing forces in a series of hyper folds to move from place to place. Dana devised a plan to upset the hyper-balance of the alien craft. While everyone agrees that the plan could work, they run into difficulty with Chief of Staff Rolf Emerson, Bowie Grant's guardian. After the recent disaster, Emerson does not want to risk his ward's life in another futile military maneuver. Bowie, Dana, and Louie convince Emerson to see their point of view.

The 15th Squad not only rescue their fellow defenders, they destroy the alien ship. What was once an invincible source of terror crashes to the planet's surface, a fiery symbol of mankind's first victory.

PRELUDE TO BATTLE

Episode 43

After their recent success shooting down the enemy ship, the 15th Squad find themselves "volunteered" for another dangerous mission. Supreme Commander Leonard has begun to consider them his lucky ace in the hole. General Emerson's protests in the matter are disregarded.

In preparing for their next encounter, the members of the 15th psych themselves up, each in his or her own way. Unfortunately, Bowie Grant gets into more trouble than he can cope with alone. The young musician is arrested twice by the Global Military Police, once for frequenting a restricted bar, the second time for brawling in the same off-limits area. Although his excuses seem valid, Bowie's recent lack of concentration has caused him to make small, but potentially serious, mistakes on the battlefield. Dana can't afford to take a chance on the possibility that Bowie will become distracted on their new mission. She orders him confined to the guardhouse. The young man is forced to acknowledge his childish behavior. At the last minute, Emerson procures a release allowing Bowie to join his comrades on the mission. Bowie determines to become the best soldier he can.

THE TRAP

Episode 44

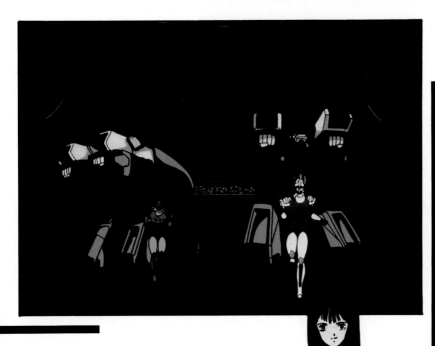

Dana Sterling in armor

Musica

Dana Sterling leads the 15th Alpha Tactical Armored Corps into the alien ship. Helmet monitors transmit their findings to Central Command. However, as they scout the ship's interior, the Robotech Masters are making their own observations in return.

The team discovers a bio-mechanical operation that indicates the aliens are able to create perfect androids. Separated from the group, Bowie meets a beautiful alien woman, Musica, the mistress of the Cosmic Harp. Musica manipulates the electronic beams of the fantastic instrument. However, the two are attracted to each other by more than their love of music. Bowie is enchanted, but Musica finds her own reactions too disturbing; they go against all her conditioning. After she helps Bowie to defeat attacking sentries, she runs away.

Meanwhile, the Robotech Masters trap Dana and her crew. Sterling blasts her way out through the floor. Guessing their welcome is over, the squad heads for an exit—any exit! On their way out, Sterling captures an enemy bioroid.

METAL FIRE

Episode 45

An analysis of the 15th Squad's observations supports Command Central's theory that the Robotech Masters have come to Earth in search of the last known protoculture matrix. A preliminary report on the captured bioroid indicates the bio-mechanical weapons are controlled by programmed androids. The bioroids cannot be stopped unless the cockpit controls are destroyed. Dana objects. Blasting the cockpit will kill the pilots. Supreme Commander Leonard seems to find this information especially satisfying and announces: "Gentlemen—it seems to me our course is clear. We must commit ourselves to the destruction of these androids whenever they appear. You don't believe we could ever come to terms with a group of barbarians like them? Their advanced technology leaves us no choice. Even if we could negotiate, we'd be doing it from a position of weakness, not strength, and that would be fatal. It's out of the question."

Although Dana suspects Leonard's orders evolve from fear and prejudice, there is no way she can successfully contradict him. She is concerned that not all the bioroid pilots are mechanical androids but actual living aliens— aliens like her mother. The lieutenant leaves the conference feeling very disturbed.

The Robotech Masters are in a perplexing situation. The secrets of protoculture production have been lost with the passing of their creator, Zor. All attempts to rediscover those secrets through the cloning of Zor have ended in failure. Confrontation is their final alternative. The true threat to Earth and the protoculture matrix derives from the approach of another alien race, the parasitic Invid. The Elders are desperate to recapture the matrix before their civilization collapses around them, but too many of their bioroid pilots have been injured in battle to mount an effective attack. The Robotech Masters decide to capture human beings to determine if they can be reprogrammed to pilot the bioroids.

STARDUST

Episode 46

Alien troops capture more than 200 civilian hostages. Leonard has them listed as casualties of war despite the protests of Rolf Emerson.

At Command Central, Dana Sterling tries to stop Leonard from killing a captured alien pilot. Although she knows her actions place her career in extreme jeopardy, she cannot stop herself from protesting an action she instinctively feels is wrong. Dana can't believe the enemy troops are unthinking androids. Her continued attraction to the red bioroid pilot makes this theory particularly upsetting.

Dana is reduced to seeking solace at a bar. Bowie Grant accompanies his commander. Sterling meets an interesting entertainer, Jordan Sullivan. Hoping she's found the answer to her romantic dilemma, Dana slips backstage for further conversation only to discover that the man is an agent for the Global Military Police. He convinces her to help him and she agrees. However, the mission goes awry and Sullivan is killed.

OUTSIDERS

Episode 47

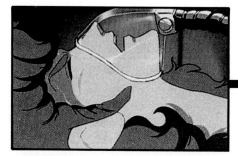

Zor, captured by the humans

The red bioroid pilot is captured, and Dana Sterling finds her problems are just beginning. The more she tries to dismiss the mysterious warrior, the more compelling he becomes. She has no way of knowing he is Zor Prime, first clone of Zor, the genius who created the science of Robotechnology—and, inadvertently, Earth's continuing conflicts with invading alien forces. Long ago, the first Zor escaped with the secrets of Robotechnology on the SDF-1 to prevent their abuse by the Robotech Masters. Now, the Robotech Masters seek to manipulate Zor Prime in ways they could never control the original. With a neuro-sensor implanted in his body, the clone will serve as an unknowing spy for the alien invaders.

Dana is not the only person on the 15th Squad suffering from romantic difficulties. Bowie Grant, obsessed with the beautiful alien musician, finds himself the object of ridicule among his fellow soldiers because of his affections. Bowie has never considered himself a real member of the military establishment. Now he becomes more alienated than ever.

A reconnaissance vessel from the SDF-1 lands near the outskirts of Monument City. Dana Sterling and Sean Philips arrive to pick up Major John Carpenter and his aide from the Robotech Relief Expedition. They are taken to United Earth Command for debriefing. Leonard is staggered to hear there will be no reinforcement arriving from the SDF-3. It would seem Earth's survival rests on strategic information gathered from the mysterious alien prisoner.

Sean Phillips

DEJA VU

Episode 48

Lieutenant Nova Satori of the Global Military Police begins a complex psychological profile on the alien pilot identified only as "Zor." Zor suffers from amnesia and is haunted by agonizing nightmares. The clone doesn't know his dreams are based on memories he shares with his cell donor. Zor's interrogators do not suspect their prisoner is anything other than human. They believe they have captured a brainwashed civilian who has been forced to serve the Robotech Masters.

Sean Philips, the Casanova of the 15th Squad, visits Marie Crystal, who is recuperating from wounds suffered in battle. Lieutenant Crystal attempts a little reverse psychology to ensure the private's attention and wonders later if she's overplayed her hand.

The indomitable Nova Satori

Marie Crystal wonders if she's got Sean's attention—or not.

A NEW RECRUIT
Episode 49

It is decided to induct Zor into the army of the Southern Cross in the hopes association with a military environment will spur his lost memory and provide important clues to the origin and tactical strengths of the Robotech Masters. He is assigned to the 15th Squad.

Although Dana revels in her special kinship with the new recruit, there are other members of the squad who resent Zor's assignment. These are soldiers who have lost friends and family in the alien attacks. Despite the fact that Zor exhibits all the abilities of a truly exceptional soldier, he cannot find acceptance in the squad.

Inside the mother ship, the Robotech Masters observe their spy with concern. Zor Prime's association with Dana Sterling has aroused emotions that are bringing back the original Zor's memories. Still, they remain confident of their control and their ability to annihilate their human adversaries.

Dana Sterling dreams of the alien, Zor Prime.

TRIUMVIRATE

Episode 50

Robotech Masters—the three who act as one

The United Earth Defense mount a full-scale attack on the armada of the Robotech Masters. Dana Sterling and the 15th Tactical Armored Division are left behind to continue deprogramming Zor. The clone encounters more resentment. The fighting 15th does not enjoy babysitting assignments.

Meanwhile, transmissions from Zor Prime continue to be received by the invaders. Commander Leonard's attack is doomed from the start.

Zor, Dana, and Bowie investigate the wreck of the SDF-1 and find the ruins filled with unusual flowers. The plants seem to throb with power, more like sentient beings trying to make contact with something far away. Zor notices the blossoms grow in clusters of three and remembers a connection between the plants and a mysterious Triumvirate that is the essence of the alien lifestyle—the three who act as one.

CLONE CHAMBER
Episode 51

Leonard's desperate frontal assault proves to be a disaster. The shattered Earth fleet withdraws toward the dark side of the moon, but the Robotech Masters aren't celebrating yet. Transmissions from Zor Prime alert them that the "Invid Flowers of Life" growing within the ruins of the SDF-1 are in full bloom. It marks the first signal of the approaching Invid invasion force. The Robotech Masters' biosynergetic reservoirs of protoculture are running dry. Weapons and defense systems are a constant drain, consuming more energy than they create. If the Robotech Masters cannot secure an infusion of fresh protoculture, their civilization will come to an end.

Musica and her sisters, Allegra and Octavia, are approached by the mates chosen for them by the Robotech Masters. Musica still remembers Bowie Grant. Tormented by feelings she cannot understand, Musica refuses to obey the Robotech Masters. Her behavior does not go unnoticed. Like the Zentraedi, Micronian culture has had an unsettling effect on the clones. The mistress of the Cosmic Harp has become as unpredictable as Zor Prime.

Air Cavalry One relief forces led by Lieutenant Marie Crystal succeed in rescuing Leonard's decimated Earth fleet. On her return to the planet, she finds Sean Philips waiting for her. It would seem that her military and romantic strategies have paid off.

Zor Prime puzzles over memories that are not his own.

LOVE SONG

Episode 52

General Rolf Emerson

Supreme Commander Leonard places his arch-rival, General Rolf Emerson, in command of a second offensive against the enemy. Despite conjecture to the contrary, Emerson rejects speculation that he is piloting a suicide squad. Yet all the officers appointed to the mission are those who consistently oppose Leonard's decisions, and the odds for success are very much against them this time. Still, Emerson is determined to return victorious.

Marie and Sean's important date becomes a disaster. The lieutenant finds Sean apparently involved with a girl from his past. Marie runs away. Sean tries to explain, but she departs with Emerson's fleet before he gets the chance.

THE HUNTERS

Episode 53

The members of the 15th Squad relax in the video arcade. Trying to improve his game, Louie Nichols invents a device activated by organic impulses produced when the player's eyes intercept reflected light from the game target—a vision trace firing system or "Pupil Pistol."

Two senior officers observe the excitement and suggest that Louie and Dana develop the machine for use in simulation training for new recruits. Louie is more than willing to help until he learns his device has been integrated into real combat weapons. Dana and Louie try to destroy the prototype. Zor stops them, saying: "I understand how you feel, and believe me, I know the pain bioroids go through when they revive. I'll be aboard this hovertank...some of my frinds might die. I don't want any more deaths, but this new machine is our best hope."

Angelo Dante finds himself agreeing with Zor for the first time. "It's because we must succeed in our mission invading the battleship. You know that's our only sure means of achieving peace."

Louie is not convinced and while the squad argues, General Emerson engages the alien enemy in deep space.

Louie Nichols

MIND GAME
Episode 54

Angelo Dante and members of the
15th Squad

A savage battle rages around the armada of the Robotech Masters. Utilizing Louie's new Robotechnology, the Earth Defense Fleet puts up a valiant struggle until an orbital warp-blast paves the way for another alien offensive. The 15th Tactical Armored Squad is sent to reinforce Emerson's fleet.

For the first time in her fighting career, Dana Sterling is uncertain about a military engagement. She's not the unquestioning, gung-ho academy graduate she once was. Recent experiences create doubts regarding her training. Zor tries to help her regain confidence, saying: "Understand that the better we perform our mission, the better this planet's hope for survival. I wish I could remember more than I do, but one thing I do remember—I was much less than a human being while under the control of the Robotech Masters. I want to destroy them now to make sure I'll never have to be like that again. I'm sure everyone in this room would prefer death in combat to slavery."

Zor's speech seems to help everyone focus positively on the upcoming crisis, particularly Dana. They proceed with their attack, eventually blasting their way into the alien flagship. Victory seems close until the Robotech Masters reestablish direct control over Zor Prime and the 15th Squad find themselves attacked by a man they believed to be their friend.

DANA IN WONDERLAND
Episode 55

Another mystery

Dana's decision

Trying to escape Zor, the 15th Squad makes a scattered retreat into the depth of the giant ship. The Robotech Masters mobilize their sentries in an attempt to capture the Micronians before they spread more emotional contamination.

As they race through the ship, Dana discovers many disturbing facts about the true nature of the civilization living on board the ship. Independent thought and emotional response are strictly forbidden. Transgressors are destroyed. All clones live to serve the Robotech Masters. What they believed to be androids are actually clones, biogenetically evolved from the organic cells of living beings. They are not mechanical creatures devoid of feeling.

In spite of their abilities as a fighting team, the cards are stacked against the 15th this time out. They are captured and brought before the Robotech Masters.

CRISIS POINT

Episode 56

With the Micronians safely in hand, the Robotech Masters try to locate their missing clone, Zor Prime. His prolonged association with human emotions has turned him into an unstable unit. In another part of the ship, Musica tries to describe her feelings for Bowie Grant to her sisters. She longs for the time before the Triumvirate when each of them was able to act independently, when each was "capable of feeling pleasure, pain, happiness, or even loneliness." However, in the turmoil surrounding the Micronian prisoners, Musica learns the missing Zor Prime is to be deprogrammed, possibly damaged, when he is found. She goes in search of him herself.

The Mistress of the Cosmic Harp finds Zor Prime in a deserted part of the ship. Once again, he suffers from memories that aren't his. Musica explains the truth about his origins just as clone sentries arrive to take them away.

Zor and Musica rejoin the 15th Squad. The crew manages to overcome the guards and escape. As they search for an exit, Musica tells Zor the reason behind his mission on Earth—he was an unwitting spy for the Robotech Masters. Zor Prime is upset: "I betrayed my friends and now, the only way to redeem myself is to betray my people. Everything I touch turns to ashes."

In a daring one-man stand against a legion of bioroids, Zor clears the way for Dana and the 15th to escape and rendezvous with Emerson's fleet. At first given up for dead, Zor also manages to escape to the fleet.

DAY DREAMER
Episode 57

A new crisis

The remnants of Emerson's force withdraws toward Moon Base Aluce-1 as a shuttle bearing the 15th Squad, Zor and Musica return to Earth.

Musica and Bowie are happy to be together again, and the alien beauty tries to assimilate herself to her new environment. Their plans are cut short when Nova Satori and the military police seek Musica out as a spy.

FINAL NIGHTMARE
Episode 58

Musica

Bowie

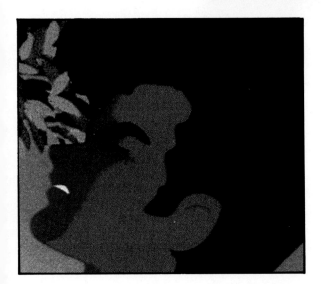

The Robotech Masters call a full-scale assault on Earth. Nearly 70 percent of their remaining protoculture pods have been invaded by the Invid Flower of Life. The infected mass has degenerated to the point where it is no longer of any use to them. They are concerned that the Earth factory has been similarly contaminated. They must retrieve what they can before the Invid arrive.

At Command Central, Leonard decides to join Emerson and launch a final offensive: "We will knock them out of the skies or die in the attempt." His fellow officers agree.

Bowie and Musica hide within the wreck of the SDF-1. The flowers have changed since Bowie's last visit. Musica recognizes the blossoms at once and realizes that the Invid Flowers of Life have completed their mutation. Even now, the drifting spores are drawing the Invid to Earth across the cosmos. Bowie demands an explanation. Musica tells him: "The Invid are the enemies of both our people...The Flower of Life survives by feeding off the protoculture matrix." The young fugitives have found the factory everyone has been searching for, but it is too late to be of any use to Earth or the Robotech Masters.

Dana and crew track the couple to the ruins. They are followed in turn by Nova Satori and Zor. When confronted by the spores, Zor Prime remembers his past. He knows all of Zor's plans and dreams. He becomes the original Zor once again.

THE INVID CONNECTION
Episode 59

Marie Crystal

The final offensive is underway. Alien warships move silently toward Earth. Their plan is simple—attack without retreat or surrender until they reclaim the fallen protoculture factory. General Emerson engages the enemy once again. Leonard launches his fleet.

As the battle escalates, the Robotech Masters cast their infirm and aged citizens adrift in space. They drug their clone soldiers with anti-pain serum to enable them to fight longer. Merciless maneuvers give them the advantage. They issue an ultimatum to Supreme Commander Leonard: "Evacuate the planet within thirty-eight hours or we will be forced to destroy your homeworld."

Leonard orders all remaining squadrons to assemble at Monument City and prepare for an attack. Emerson returns the battered remains of the Southern Cross Defense Force to protect the planet and its people as his ship explodes. Marie Crystal manages to get the general into an escape pod, but they are picked up by the Robotech Masters before they can reach their own troops.

The aliens contact Zor Prime for a trade—Zor, Musica, and the dismissal of remaining Earth forces for the general and his crew. Zor accepts.

CATASTROPHE

Episode 60

The Robotech Master gloats.

As the prisoner exchange is in progress, a trap set by the Rotobech Masters on their ship claims the life of Rolf Emerson. Chaos reigns as the 15th Squad desperately attempts to pull out of the area. Dana tries to relocate Zor while Sean, Marie, Bowie, and the rest of the crew look for Musica's sisters.

Dana Sterling finds Zor determined to personally destroy the Robotech Masters. After a frantic search through the depths of the gigantic ship, Dana and Zor discover the Robotech Masters preparing a new two-front assault against the fleet and the planet.

The aliens do not believe Zor wants to destroy them: "You are the embodiment of Zor, creator of the first protoculture and the Master responsible for our development. It was Zor who developed the Zentraedi people. Zor who became the prime force behind all the advancements of our society. Your most important achievement was the protoculture which brings the promise of eternal life . . . . Surely you are not prepared to destroy your most precious creation, the embodiment of your hopes and dreams? Without it, your native civilization will wither and die."

Zor replies: "My civilization is already dead."

He eliminates one of the three masters. Dana upsets the terminals that control a container of protoculture matrix. She accidentally causes the seeds inside to blossom, releasing their energy. Its usefulness to the remaining Robotech Masters has been destroyed, but for Dana the energy has unleashed racial memories buried within her Zentraedi cell structure. Somehow, Dana finds the strength to reject instincts that urge her to become a part of the Robotech Masters' culture. Hallucinations brought on by the spores leave her half-stunned.

In another section of the ship, Musica leads a battle of her own while the 15th Squad rescues civilian clones—including Musica's sisters—marked for destruction.

"I have freely chosen a new way of life!" Musica tells the sentries. "The truth is, we are all individual beings with free will—and you know it!"

In the ensuing struggle, Octavia is killed. The 15th Squad, with Marie Crystal and Musica, load the surviving aliens into troop carriers and evacuate to Earth.

For the Robotech Masters, the moment of retribution is at hand in the form of their rebel clone. Zor kills them. He sets Dana adrift in one of the escape modules, then prepares to destroy the ship. As he locks the controls into a crash-land position over the ruins of the SDF-1, Zor thinks to himself: "There is no other way. The destruction of this ship over the site of the battlefortress is the only guarantee that the protoculture will be obliterated before it brings the Invid to this planet!"

Zor is tragically wrong. His sacrifice only compounds disaster. Instead of rendering the protoculture matrix useless, the explosion frees the mutated spores. They scatter over the planet's surface, turning Earth into a vast, fertile garden awaiting cultivation by the rapidly approaching Invid.

The survivors of the second Robotech War enjoy a bittersweet victory. With morale, supplies, and population depleted, Earth must rebuild once again—this time in the face of another massive invasion they know they cannot win.

Zor's tragic decision

Part Three—
The New Generation
THE INVID INVASION

Robotech warriors prepare to defend Earth.

Scott Bernard proposes to his girlfriend, Marlene.

Marlene hopes the mission will be successful.

Weary from the war with the Robotech Masters, the armies of the Southern Cross are no match for the battle-hungry Invid invaders. Led by the Invid Regis, the supreme ruler of the protoplasmic parasites, the aliens turn the planet into a wasteland. Earth becomes a slave colony whose sole purpose is to harvest and process protoculture.

A contingent of interstellar ships responds to the crisis. They have been deployed from Admiral Rick Hunter's expeditionary mission which is in search of the Robotech Masters' home planet. This latest generation of Robotech warriors is equipped with new and powerful weapons. There are members of the fleet who have not visited Earth in twenty years. Most of the space-born crew have never seen their homeworld. However, Rick Hunter has commissioned them to reclaim their ancestral planet and has every faith in their ability to do so.

As the fleet prepares to defold near Earth, Lieutenant Scott Bernard proposes to his girlfriend, Marlene. Marlene teases him, saying: "It's a bit sudden...You'll have to speak to my father first. Or perhaps even my mother." Scott plays along with the game as the fleet enters the fourth quadrant and locks its target on Reflex Point, headquarters of the Invid Regis.

Unfortunately, the Invid are aware of Hunter's force and are waiting for them. The fleet commander deploys Veritech fighter squads while the fleet establishes orbit. As Scott boards his craft, Marlene gives him a holo-medallion to bring him luck.

There are more Invid fighters than anyone anticipated. The Veritechs are overwhelmed on their first assault. As the aliens fire on the command ship, shields drain rapidly. The gravitational pull of the planet becomes more than the depleted power source can take. Despite their best efforts, the fleet is sucked into the atmosphere. It meets a fiery death on the planet surface while the Invid eliminate the remaining Veritech fighters.

Scott Bernard's incredible skill and ability enable him to land in a remote area far away from Reflex Point. In a state of shock and despair, he stands on Earth's soil for the first time. It's not the homecoming he anticipated. As he opens the holo-medallion, he sees a three-dimensional image of Marlene. Her recorded message says: "Scott my darling, I know it isn't much but I thought you'd get a kick out of this trinket....I'm looking forward to living the rest of my life with you. I can't wait till this conflict is all behind us. Till we meet again, my love."

Scott sees the holographic message of Marlene.

It begins to rain, a phenomenon the young lieutenant has never encountered. As he tries to adjust to his current situation, Scott takes what comfort he can from military instilled discipline. He recalls orders: "Even if only one of you survives, you must find Reflex Point and destroy it along with the Invid Queen, the Regis."

As Scott considers how to accomplish this, a young man arrives on the scene and discovers an undamaged cyclone. His name is Rand. He draws the attention of Invid scouts as he examines the vehicle. Scott Bernard comes to his rescue.

After they defeat the aliens, Scott asks Rand for information regarding the location of Reflex Point while the youth enthuses over his newfound mecha. While Scott persists, Rand snaps: "Hey...do I look like some kind of travel agent? I don't know anything about their headquarters. I hate those creeps."

Scott explains: "The Invid wiped out an entire combat wing of the reconnaisance forces sent by Admiral Hunter. That's the reason I'm looking for them...I'm the only survivor, too."

Rand notices Scott looking at Marlene's hologram message and compliments the lieutenant on his luck in girlfriends. Scott becomes very distant.

Something about the forlorn but determined soldier appeals to Rand's sense of fair play and responsibility. He agrees to help. Although he's too emotionally drained to understand the significance of Rand's commitment, Scott Bernard nevertheless gains his first friend on Earth.

Off to a good start—Scott Bernard
meets Rand.

THE LOST CITY
Episode 62

Searching for information regarding the Invid stronghold, Scott and Rand question the inhabitants of a peculiar town. It's a desolate place. Downed spacecruisers, bioroids, and scorched Zentraedi battle pods litter an otherwise peaceful lake. The streets are still covered with debris from the last Robotech war, and people regard the newcomers with suspicion. Visitors are rare. The Invid shadow hangs over everything.

Rand and Scott meet a spunky young girl named Annie. The orphan is an outrageous flirt, by turns delightful and obnoxious. For some unknown reason, Annie is being forced to leave town. The child follows the two young men, more relieved to see friendly faces than she cares to admit.

They are taken to an island to look for more survivors of the expedition that might have been forced down in battle. As they wander through the rubble, Scott finds functional hovertanks, cyclones, and other mecha. It's more graveyard than junkpile. Suddenly they find themselves alone in the eerie place—but not for long. Invid scouts appear on the horizon. The townfolk have betrayed them to the enemy.

These Invid aren't used to humans that fight back. Scott and Rand put them out of commission posthaste. In the midst of the battle, a mysterious cyclone rider arrives to help them and then disappears. After the fight, the trio returns to town and demands an explanation. They are received with hostility.

"Nobody here wanted your Robotech expeditionary force," a townsman says. "If it weren't for you soldiers, we'd still be living in peace! Now why don't you just pack it up?"

Scott is confused. "Don't you realize that without any kind of resistance, you've got no hope? You're going to sit back and let the Invid keep control of the Earth?"

"Fighting the Invid only aggravates the situation. All we want is to live in peace, even

Rand and Scott can't leave Annie behind.

Scott Bernard is haunted by memories of Marlene.

if it means doing without freedom." The townsfolk are adamant. "Anybody who doesn't see it our way has already left. Please get out."

Disheartened and angry, Scott takes off with Annie and Rand following. The lieutenant can't believe what he has just encountered but remains determined to reach Reflex Point. Rand loses his temper.

"That again! Ever since we got together you've been talking about this reflex thing as though it were the most important thing in the whole universe. You know what your problem is? You don't know how to communicate with people. Wouldn't you be a lot happier back in space with your girlfriend?"

The lieutenant's reaction indicates that Rand has said the wrong thing. He apologizes. Scott finally tells his friend that his girlfriend is dead and rides away. Rand and Annie ride after him.

LONELY SOLDIER BOY
Episode 63

The unstoppable Rook Bartley

Yellow Dancer, a.k.a. Lancer; the "she" is a "he."

The trio make their way to another half-dead town. There seem to be more people, but they're not much friendlier. Still, they are attempting to recapture some of the pleasures they knew before the invasion by hosting a rock concert in one of the less run-down bars. The performer is a popular singing star named Yellow Dancer who has modeled her career after the legendary Lynn Minmei.

Scott, Rand, and Annie enjoy the music. They appreciate any sign of real civilization, especially after their long trek through the war-torn countryside. The fun is over too soon when the ugly side of humanity rears its head in the form of a drunken thug who attacks the beautiful singer in the middle of her performance.

Playing along with the brute, Yellow tries to regain order. Obviously, she can hold her own on stage and in a fight. Still, she's just one person and things get out of hand when the drunk is joined by his friends. Before Rand and Scott can intervene, a quick-tempered blonde woman appears to put Yellow's assailants in their place. Scott recognizes her as the cyclone rider who helped them when the Invid attacked at the island.

Rand can't just stand by. He has to lend the newcomer a hand. She does not appreciate it, but to Rand's delight, Yellow Dancer seems grateful. He is thrilled to meet his favorite singing star. Yellow seems as charming in person as Rand had always imagined she'd be.

While Rand admires Yellow, Scott has a word with the singer's manager. It seems there's no way to combat the thugs who broke up the concert. They are in charge of the town by force of numbers and mean-hearted brutality. The alien victory has brought out the worst in a lot of people. Humans suffer at the hands of their own kind as well as by the Invid slavers. Surrounded by the results of defeat, Scott suspects it's no wonder that people have lost the heart to fight back.

After another demonstration of cruelty, Scott, Rand, and Annie improvise a posse to counteract the gang's hold on the town. They are joined by the young woman they met at the bar, who introduces herself as Rook Bartley, and a muscle-bound combat veteran named Lunk.

In this lawless time, the old adage "might makes right" is the unwritten law of the land. There are no police, no courts of law. Justice is obtained by a clenched fist or at the end of a gun. As Scott Bernard leads his new comrades into battle, he is aware that it's not a simple skirmish against a band of well-armed toughs, but the first blow against the wall of anarchy that threatens to engulf Earth.

Although they've never fought as a team before, the five work together and defeat the gang as if they'd known each other for years. The town is heartened by this turn of events. Lunk and Rook decide to join the search for Reflex Point—at least for the time being. Yellow Dancer wants to come along, too.

Scott is against it. "Don't be ridiculous. This is no job for a cocktail lounge chorus girl."

Yellow is amused. "There's a whole lot more to me than meets the eye."

True enough. Beneath the slinky clothes and lavish makeup, the "she" is a "he." Yellow Dancer turns out to be the alternate identity of a male resistance fighter named Lancer.

Rand breaks down in tears. The girl of his dreams is no more. Scott accepts the revelation with more enthusiasm. He has three new recruits in the war against the Invid.

The end of a fantasy—Rand is devastated.

Episode 64

The ranks are growing—Annie, Scott, Lunk, Rook, and Rand.

Survival techniques in the big woods

Scott Bernard's luck has changed—from bad to good. Not only has he gathered a band of experienced resistance fighters, Lunk has contributed a fully armed and operational Veritech alpha fighter. The former soldier had hidden the vessel from the Invid and human spies who would have destroyed it.

However, while the alpha fighter is a strategic plus in combat, it consumes more protoculture energy cells then the team can easily get their hands on. Whenever they try to replenish their supplies, the Invid always show up to interfere.

Finally Rand discovers the problem: "We've been giving ourselves away every time we switch on our cyclones or laser blasters. I think they can detect the bioenergy given off by our Robotech mecha when it's activated."

Lunk agrees: "Remember how they found us at the river? Well, Scott left the panel gauges of his cyclone on. They might have been homing in on that."

"It makes sense," Rand concludes. "After all, the Invid thrive on protoculture, right? It's like they can smell the stuff the same way a shark is able to smell blood in the water."

The conversation dissolves in a squabble between Rook and Rand. The two seem to antagonize each other at every turn. Scott advises them to save their energies for the aliens. They quiet down—for a full minute—before they're at it again.

Later, country born and bred Rand tries to show the others how to survive in the forest and make the most of their surroundings. A fishing demonstration is interrupted by attacking Invid. Trapped in open fire, Rand gains firsthand insight into how fish feel caught on a line.

They escape using the alpha fighter, but there is little rest. Too many aliens patrol the area for them to remain in one place long. As Scott leads the group to safety, he tries to come up with a way to acquire more of the badly needed protoculture energy cells.

CURTAIN CALL
Episode 65

Lancer's transformation into singer Yellow Dancer is effective—but startling, too.

Resistance fighters must be sneaky. It is the backbone of the "freedom fighter" code. An unhappy truck driver makes this discovery when he stops to assist Rook and Annie. The two girls hijack the truck and head back to their friends. It's the first step in a plan to replenish their fuel supplies and strike the Invid at the same time.

In his guise as Yellow Dancer, Lancer stages a rock concert to serve as a diversion while the others break into one of the largest protoculture storage units in the area. Rand is sure their strategy will go off without a problem. "When folks find out Yellow's coming to town, people go berserk."

Rand is right. As Yellow, Lancer is greeted by a town official who assures the singer: "To make sure your performance runs smoothly, I'm obtaining the cooperation of the president's personal police department."

Those words are music to Lancer's ears. They want to tie up the entire security department—a department created to guard the immense protoculture storage area—while the group completes the raid.

As the concert begins, Scott, Rand, and Rook breach the unit using a map provided by Lancer. The system is complicated. They encounter a few heart-stopping difficulties getting the material they need. Once security discovers the raid, the freedom fighters create a double-diversion using the hijacked truck. While police chase the vehicle, the stolen protoculture is carried away by helium-filled balloons released at the end of the concert.

When the team regroups, they waste no time in celebrating even though their first mission has been a fantastic success. They take off immediately, seeking cover with the Invid and their allies in pursuit.

HARD TIMES
Episode 66

Rook Bartley has never been considered the "life of the party" at any time, but as the combat troop approaches her hometown, she grows more introspective by the minute. Her teammates notice her quiet mood and try to bring her out of it, but Rook remains lost in bitter memories.

She remembers when she worked with another team, a gang of motorcycle riders called the Blue Angels. They were dedicated to helping others and spent most of their time fighting a rival group, the Red Snakes. Then the Angels were disbanded by a man Rook had believed to be her friend. Romy...the same man who refused to show at a designated rumble where Rook was mercilessly beaten by Red Snake warriors. Rook has not been home since that black time.

There's no putting off a return now. Rook rides into town to visit her family. Talking to her sister, Lily, she receives bad news. Since Rook's departure, the Snakes have had the run of the town. The gang wars are worse than ever. Romy and the Blue Angels have lost the desire to fight.

Bartley is not surprised. It's just what she expected from the coward who left her to be savaged by their enemy. Lily protests; it wasn't like that at all. She tells Rook that Romy and the Angels were ambushed the day of the rumble. It wasn't that they wouldn't help Rook—they *couldn't* help her. Romy was never a fighter like Rook anyway. He did what he could for as long as possible, but he was not cut from the same cloth as Rook Bartley.

While the truth does not set Rook free, it puts a scab on a few open wounds and gives her the courage to make a new stand against the Red Snakes. She challenges their leader to a race—on a thin wooden beam more than fifteen stories high. Although he'd never admit it out loud, Rand has been concerned about Rook. He shows up in time to keep the race a fair one-on-one competition. Rook wins easily.

Afterward, Rook and Rand stop to say goodbye to Lily. Rook is surprised to hear Rand met and spoke with her mother. "She said for you to stay well...that's all she wants," Rand explains. "She told me to tell you to just take care."

Rook is even more surprised when the woman appears, smiling from a distance. "And I always thought she was so ashamed of me for the way I behaved. I'm sorry for leaving, Mom. I love you so much...." Rook is unable to say what she feels out loud. As she rides away, the girl is lost in thought again, but they're the best thoughts she's known in a long time.

Rook suffers at the hands of the Red Snakes.

Rook and Rand put on a show for Rook's friends as she prepares to leave town.

PAPER HERO
Episode 67

Invid shock trooper

Scott Bernard and crew blast their way through Invid scout troops again. It's the kind of engagement they've become very familiar with. After the battle, Lunk is pleased to find they are near a village he's been trying to visit for a long time.

"I want to make good on a promise I made to a friend to deliver this book for him," Lunk tells his friends. "I really don't know what the book's about, but it was important to my buddy and he gave it to me to bring to his father, Alfred Nader, here. I only wish he could have delivered it himself. . . . It was during the Invid invasion. . .my friend was on recon patrol and I was detailed to drive out and pick him up. When I found him, he was trying to get away from a couple of Invid, and I could see he had already been wounded. As I watched, they blasted him again. How he could get up and run after that I'll never know—but he did and started for the truck. I thought I might still be able to pick him up, but the Invid caught up with him before I did. He didn't have a chance. He cried out to me, calling me to come get him, but there was nothing I could do. The Invid spotted the truck and started after me. I had no choice but to run for it. I don't know how I got out of there, but I made it. And do you know, I can still hear my buddy's voice coming over the intercom as loud and clear today as I heard it then. . .calling me to help him. There's no way I'll ever forget that day. Well. . .the book had some sort of special meaning for him, I suppose. The one thing he wanted most was for his father to have it."

Rand is touched. "Lunk, you and I have a book to deliver. Let's go."

Lancer, Rook, and Annie join Lunk and Rand on their trip into the village. Scott stays behind with the mecha.

The village is a spooky place. As they walk along deserted streets, it seems as if everyone has decided to pack up and run at once. The restaurant won't serve them. The shops are closed. Lunk finally corners a villager and asks

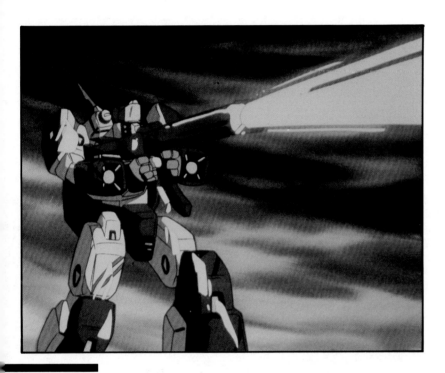

Rand in action

about Alfred Nader. The man says that no one has ever heard of him. Lunk is sure the villager is lying. His friends agree.

Lunk and Rand search the area on their own until confronted by a gang of angry villagers. Outnumbered, they run for the truck, but when they reach the rendezvous area, they find their friends and vehicles missing.

Game time is over. Rand and Lunk force information from the mayor. Lancer, the girls, and the mecha are returned. After another quick but deadly Invid encounter, they are told the story behind Nader's disappearance.

In a town committed to violent aggression, Alfred Nader maintained a philosophy of passive resistance. Although he was repeatedly beaten by the town radicals, the old man refused to change his beliefs. In the end, he was killed. Guilt has made the villagers suspicious of every stranger. They feared the day that someone would come to punish them for their crime.

Retribution of this nature is not the freedom fighters' responsibility. Besides, conscience has provided its own punishment. No one is sorry to leave the village behind. On the way back to camp, Lunk remembers his buddy and Alfred Nader: "We never met, but I feel as though I know you, and I'll always think of you as my friend. I'm going to keep this book with me wherever I go and look at it from time to time. It'll remind me that there are people in this world who will stand up for what they believe in. Goodbye to you, Alfred Nader. You were a fine man."

EULOGY

Episode 68

Deep inside Reflex Point, the Invid have performed a strange, primordial ritual. As the Regis surveys the new empire, she is aware of the human renegades still at large. Although their numbers are growing, they pose no immediate threat to Invid domination. Still, the Regis thinks it best to terminate them before they do. It would be especially distressing if they were to stumble on the Genesis Pits before the larvae evolve into their ultimate form.

The Invid Mother increases her search for the remaining hostiles.

Scott Bernard gets good news. Colonel Jonathan Wolff, a volunteer from Admiral Hunter's Reclamation Force sent against the Robotech Masters, is alive. Wolff's legendary exploits have made him one of the best-known heroes of the Robotech Wars and an inspiration for all young Defenders. Scott is thrilled to meet the colonel face to face, holding his ground against the Invid in a small town. "I can still remember the day Colonel Wolff left after joining the Earth Reclamation Forces," Scott tells his friends. "He turned up missing, and we thought he was dead. Amazing. He's been here fighting the Invid all this time."

Rand agrees. "With a guy like that blasting away at your side, it's no wonder the soldiers here aren't worried."

"Yeah...but there's something going on here. This town's too lax." Scott is puzzled as he watches the carefree troopers. "Do they think Jonathan Wolff's going to keep beating back the Invid all by himself?"

Lancer is skeptical, too. "This town really has a party mentality. I don't know what they're thinking, but it sure seems weird."

Scott keeps the rest of his observations to himself. He's disturbed by the careless atmosphere so close to Invid strongholds, but forgets his misgivings when Colonel Wolff asks him to be a member of the new Wolff Pack. Wolff wants Scott's help in an assault against an Invid hive.

The mission is a disaster. Invid are waiting for them. Jonathan Wolff is the only member of the team to return. Rand and Rook insist on going back for Scott immediately. Wolff reluctantly agrees to help.

Rand and Rook split off from the colonel to cover more ground and are almost killed by Invid. Then Rand doubles back, only to find Wolff accepting protoculture energy cells from an Invid scout.

Rand is furious when he confronts the colonel: "So the hero's a traitor! No wonder the town's full of laughing soldiers. It's so safe and secure while you're around. The great Robotech hero's made a deal with the Invid. The great Jonathan Wolff leads his own soldiers to the Invid's doorstep for protoculture. Isn't that right? That's why you always come back to town alive and unhurt after every mission, isn't it?"

"You don't understand, kid," Wolff begins. "My efforts keep this whole town alive."

"All but your own soldiers—they're being annihilated!" Rand continues. "You were a god to us, the reason we became soldiers in the first place. We all worshipped you, wanted to be just like you...until now."

"Welcome to the real world," Jonathan tells him. "Now you know the dark side of being a hero, don't you?"

Rook calls Rand and Wolff. She has found the wounded Scott Bernard. Rand blurts out what he has just discovered. Scott is livid with rage and pain. Before Wolff can attempt to justify his actions, they are attacked by more Invid. As they battle their way out, Colonel Wolff is severely injured.

Afterward, when Scott tries to take Wolff back to town, the colonel remains behind. He wants to die: "A traitor should die on the open plain like this so the buzzards can pick at his body. When I think of the lives I traded to the Invid so I'd be spared....My wife... my boy...."

Although upset by Jonathan Wolff's betrayal, Scott Bernard continues to fight.

The Invid Regis receives a report advising that the human informer has been killed. She is unconcerned. Other agents—Invid bred— will keep her informed of the freedom fighters' progress.

THE GENESIS PIT

Episode 69

The greatest concern of the Zentraedi and the Robotech Masters was the survival of their race. The Invid are no different. They have not traveled across the universe on a whim. Desperate need spurs them to conquer. In order to survive, the Invid use any means at their disposal to become as strong as possible. Now, the Regis observes a crucial experiment, the Genesis Pit, from the great Hive and considers: "The living creatures of this world have evolved through their long history into many different levels and forms. A large number of these forms are highly specialized and adapted to specific environments. In order to carry out our plan to find the ultimate life form suitable for life on this planet, we have utilized Genesis Pits to carry out experiments in biogenetic engineering. We have cloned creatures from all significant eras of the planet's history . . . designed them to recreate all native forms exactly as they evolved. We shall use this knowledge to transform our race into the ultimate power it is destined to be."

But, the best-laid plans of mice, men, and even Invid are often doomed to go astray. Human intruders, in the form of Scott Bernard, Rand, and Annie, stumble into the deep pit as they scout for a safe camp. When they regain consciousness, they can't believe their eyes. They are trapped within a dense jungle, surrounded by creatures that have been extinct for years. As they look for a way out, Rand and Scott see animals from different periods of Earth's history and, surprisingly, Invid. Even more surprising, the Invid are not attacking but disappear as soon as the humans spot them.

"None of this makes any sense to me," Rand tells the others. "First of all, there are prehistoric monsters running around who should be extinct. Second, there are Invid running around and they don't attack us. Why? How can these exist in the same space and time? It's got to be artificial. . . . On the other hand, these plants and animals are here.

They're definitely real—dangerously real in some cases, that's clear enough."

Scott speaks for himself and Annie: "What's clear? I'm completely lost."

"Everything's been thrown into a prehistoric pot . . . primeval plants from the Paleozoic era, reptiles from the Mesozoic era—it's like viewing the biological evolution of the Earth in a living museum," Rand continues. "But who would have the interest or power to create such a thing except the Invid? It must be a test base! They're playing with the history of life on Earth—the evolution of biology from ancient times to today. That's it! They're doing evolution experiments!"

The youth has touched on the truth. Observing the revelation from the Hive, the Regis Mother possesses and speaks through Annie: "Earthlings, your time on this planet runs short. The age of humans is coming to an end. Now a new era begins on Earth. Humans are transients on the long road of evolution. The Earth is entering an era of domination by another form of life which has traveled a different evolutionary path. Be warned!"

When Annie comes back to herself, they try again to find a way out of the Pit. The animals begin to behave strangely, stampeding toward a single area. Following a hunch, they chase after the herd.

The cause of the panic is an earthquake, and the trio manages to climb to safety as the Genesis Pit collapses around them. They are the only ones to escape. Annie is upset: "What about the poor dinosaurs?"

"The Invid created them, and it's probably better that they left them down there to be destroyed," Rand says. "Those dinosaurs would never have been able to survive. The conditions on Earth aren't right for them any more. Time simply passed them by."

"You mean like when the Invid say the time for human beings has passed?" Annie wants to know.

Trapped

"They're wrong," Scott tells them. "Humans have plenty of time. It's the Invid who'll soon be extinct!"

As they walk away to look for the rest of the group, Rand and Annie hope Scott is right.

ENTER MARLENE
Episode 70

The destruction of the Genesis Pit has proved to be a major setback for the Invid. The Regis Mother finds it necessary to introduce a simulagent among the freedom fighters. She will learn what she can from the rebels and then eliminate them. The creature is taken from the dark recesses of the biogenetic laboratories. When hatched, the larva will take on the characteristics of a human female. It is transported inside a crystal cocoon and carried to the site of a recent Invid victory. But the scouts are careless. They handle the fragile egg roughly. A beautiful woman emerges from the cocoon, as planned—but without memory or cultural loyalties. Still, her alien cells form a psychic link with the Regis at the Great Hive. The Invid Mother receives the simulagent's transmissions perfectly.

Scott and crew arrive at the scene of the terrible battle. As the young lieutenant surveys the ruin, his hopes are dashed. They had received information concerning another Expeditionary Force from Admiral Hunter consisting of 6,000 fighting men and women. The freedom fighters have arrived too late. The Invid had not only Massacred the troops, they have destroyed all of the innocent townsfolk as well.

Scott falls into a deep depression. The others decide to leave him alone while they check among the wreckage for supplies and usable weapons.

Lancer, Lunk, and Annie find a beta fighter plane and more alphas. Lunk tries to get Scott to share in the excitement: "With five fighters and three cyclones we'll probably be able to knock the Invid right off the planet!"

Annie agrees. "This is so terrific, Scott! We're gonna have enough firepower to turn us into a miniature army."

"Five lousy fighters won't make any difference against the Invid," Scott snarls. "We'll all end up like this."

Lancer cautions the others away while he has a word with their unhappy friend. "Scott, listen to me, okay? We're all together with you—ready to follow you, the leader. And we want to keep traveling with you, to help you in your fight against the Invid. They're awesome . . . as aliens come, they're probably the worst. But if you give up now, there is nobody here who can lead us. Don't you remember what you said? 'We're all soldiers and we have to follow orders—whatever the cost, no matter what happens.'"

Scott Bernard is unconvinced. As Lancer walks away, he can't help thinking: "What do you think you're trying to prove, you idiot? There's no way to defeat the Invid. Not now or ever!"

He settles back into sad, angry thoughts. His head is filled with painful memories of Marlene.

Rand and Rook happen upon the female simulagent. They believe her to be a shell-shocked war victim. The newly hatched Invid larva has no idea who or what she is, but she is grateful for the duo's friendly overtures.

Back at camp, the pitiful girl causes quite a stir. She touches everyone's heart. Even Scott takes notice. Her fragile beauty reminds him

Rook's cyclone . . .

. . . converts to her unique battle armor.

of Marlene, but when they try to question the newcomer, she collapses, whimpering. Suddenly, they are surrounded by hordes of Invid fighters.

Scott leads the crew into battle. Lancer takes the new beta into combat. The others man their weapons with deadly accuracy. Rage gives Scott the edge to rout the aliens. Victory brings fresh determination for them all. Still, the savage battle depletes their fuel supplies. They take to the skies in a search for more protoculture.

The Invid girl goes with them.

THE SECRET ROUTE

Episode 71

After beating back the Invid, Scott and crew attempt to cross a treacherous mountain range but find their path blocked by an avalanche. Since the planes are too small to carry all the equipment and passengers, they drive to a nearby village in the hope they can get information about an alternate route.

The news isn't good. They are warned of an Invid fortress in the mountains. Alien scouts patrol the area to keep humans from crossing over to the desert. A map to a secret passage is available, but it costs more than the freedom fighters can afford. Lancer is not concerned with money. He assures the group they can quickly increase their fortunes.

Later, disguised as Yellow Dancer, Lancer meets with the village mayor, Donald Maxwell, to set up a rock concert. The mayor's home is opulent and unusual. The cavernous living quarters host a small fleet of antique planes, Maxwell's most prized possessions—except, perhaps, for the lovely girl at the piano. Lancer's arrival interrupts the conversation between the mayor and his fiancee—an old friend of Lancer's named Carla. The two recognize each other immediately, and Lancer recalls a time three years ago when he was trapped in the middle of an Invid raid. Even the townspeople were helping the aliens to hunt down freedom fighters. Lancer's rebellious ways were too well known for the youth to avoid capture. It was Carla who had the inspiration to disguise Lancer as a woman in order to escape. Thus the identity of Yellow Dancer was created. The years have not diminished Lancer's feelings for Carla—or hers for him—but he knows there is no point in renewing their relationship while the Invid are still at large. Life on the run has proved to be tougher than he could have imagined. Carla is too frail to endure that kind of hardship for long. She is the same gentle, lovely woman he remembered although somewhat sadder. Unfortunately, melancholy has become the curse of the times they live in.

Carla and Lancer share pleasant memories.

Carla disguises Lancer so that he can escape the Invid.

When Lancer rejoins his friends, it's to bid farewell to the departing Annie. The fickle youngster has found herself another family. The are heading across the secret route to a new home. She provides her old friends with a copy of the map they have just purchased, but Lancer senses something amiss and visits Carla again.

Carla is pleased to see him until Lancer insists she provide information about Donald's business. She becomes evasive. There are some things that she will not admit knowing—even to herself.

Lancer senses a problem: "This town is no good for you, Carla. . . . You weren't like this before. Listen to me—there's something terribly wrong about this map business. Tell me what it is before anyone gets hurt. Then we can leave together."

Carla is enthusiastic. "Let's try to go someplace to the south—you and I—where

Lancer confronts Carla over Maxwell's secret.

there's sunlight. Please. We could be happy there."

"But the threat still exists unless we go over those mountains."

"The Invid control everything up there! You'll never be able to stay alive. The map is a fake," Carla says miserably. "That's Donald's business. He sells fake maps that lead people to their doom."

"And no one else knows because no one comes back." By now, Lancer has seen enough of human nature to know truth—no matter how gruesome—when he hears it. There seems to be no end to what some men will do for profit. "So that's how Donald acquired all his wealth. That crook! Those innocent people have come to this town believing there was some hope...some chance. But—Annie!"

Remembering the girl, Lancer runs off to tell the others what he has found out. They take off to find Annie and her new family under attack from Invid scouts. They defeat

the aliens only to face another danger—Donald Maxwell.

Maxwell aims artillery at them. "Congratulations on being the first to come back from these mountains. However, I can't allow anyone who knows my secret to return. Line up over there."

Rand gets the drop on Maxwell before the man can destroy his friends. In order to save himself, Maxwell gives them his copy of the map with the correct route. It is something he has had in his possession all along and had been saving for his own fast getaway. Carla turns from him, more in disappointment than in anger. As Maxwell watches her leave with the freedom fighters, he realizes he's lost the one thing that meant the most to him.

As the caravan makes its way over the frigid pass, they notice Maxwell has created a diversion for the Invid using his collection of antique mecha. "You are special to him," Lancer tells Carla. "He sacrificed his most important machines for you. He saved your life even if it meant giving up everything he owned."

Only Carla can know how much the sacrifice meant to Maxwell. At the last moment, she heads back to town. Briefly, Lancer watches her go, then continues on his way over the pass.

THE FORTRESS

Episode 72

Having successfully crossed the mountains into Invid territory, Scott prepares an offensive against the invaders. He holds a council meeting to share gathered information and strategy.

"There's an old mountain offense outpost that the Invid have converted into a fortress," Scott explains. "Unfortunately, it lies between us and Reflex Point, so we're going to have to take it out. I don't need to tell you it's not going to be easy. Our alien friends have the place pretty well defended. Now...don't everyone volunteer at once, okay? Lancer, what did you find out?"

"At 6:30 every morning, most of the scoutships and shock troopers go out on patrol," Lancer tells them. "That would seem to me to be the best time to make our move. Whatever our move is!"

Annie is not happy. "Rats! So what are we gonna have time to make for breakfast if we have to leave so early, huh?"

"How 'bout ham and eggs and pancakes with lots of butter on 'em?" Lunk teases. "And plenty of syrup—and tea and toast and—"

"Why don't we just waltz in and raid the Invid's refrigerator while we're at it?" Rook breaks in.

"Yuck!" Lunk makes a face. "You know what protoculture tastes like? I may be hungry, but I ain't that hungry!"

Lancer becomes serious. "I really hate to interrupt all this, but if we're not careful we may not be around to have breakfast. Get it?"

"Lancer's right," Scott agrees. "This opera-tion's not going to be any picnic."

They continue with their plans. Rand shapes several pairs of skis to take them across the snow-laden woods to the fortress. As they divide into patrols, the Invid simulagent collapses in pain again. They have named her "Marlene" at Scott's suggestion. "After all," the lieutenant had said, "we can't keep calling her 'hey, you.'" They comfort the girl the best they can and go about their business.

Rand and Annie make their way into the fortress. Inside, the building has taken on an eerie, organic appearance. It looks like a giant beehive. They spy on the Regis, watching as she transforms protoplasmic material into scout troopers, but are discovered when they attempt to leave. They are cornered by the living, jelly-like substance. It swirls over them, suffocating them beneath its bulk.

Outside, Scott, Rook, and the others have picked up their friends' signal. Although Rand has successfully managed to sabotage the hive's interior, neither he nor Annie has made an appearance. They follow the emergency tracking beam to their friends' location and find them beneath the unformed Invid creatures.

During their escape, the resistance fighters manage to blow the reflex-furnace. The mechanism overloads and reaches critical mass—just as the group battles its way past the fortress. Scott feels special satisfaction at this victory—an entire Invid hive destroyed and all the freedom fighters and mecha left intact. He allows himself to feel a little hope.

SANDSTORMS

Episode 73

Rand surveys their surroundings.

The group leaves winter behind when they make their way onto the desert. A scalding wind roars across the dunes as they hide from a posse of Invid shock troopers. The Regis does not take defeat well. She suspects the simulagent of having provided the information that caused the destruction of the cortex center. Scott and crew decide to lie low for a while—at least until the search lets up. The extreme temperatures make it difficult to travel anyway. Not only that, Marlene has become ill. Nothing they do seems to help.

They cannot know that the simulagent was psychically tied to the great hive that has just gone up in flames. She has experienced the deaths of her alien brothers and sisters, although she suffers without actually knowing the cause herself.

Rand feels sorry for Marlene. He hopes water will help her condition and goes in search of fluid-bearing cactus that will provide it. After he leaves the cave, he is caught by a sudden sandstorm and falls into a pit. The impact leaves him unconscious. While he lies there, he inhales hallucinogenic spores from the Invid Flower of Life—the same kind of spores that once infected Dana Sterling. They

work on his subconscious mind in the form of incredible dreams.

The Regis appears in the vision, intoning an awful prophecy: "All things change. . . all things die. So it is that we have come from the farthest reaches of the cosmos to regenerate ourselves, to take the Earth from the dying hands of humanity. From the ashes of your people, we shall arise—reborn!"

After the sandstorm, Rook goes in search of his missing friend. When she finds him, she brings the still-delirious Rand back to the cave. As he come to, Rand tries to explain what he learned in his dreams: "The Invid—they're trying to survive by plugging themselves into the Earth's evolutionary process. . . . You can hardly blame them. It's the same sort of thing any of us would try to do if we faced certain extinction."

"So we're supposed to surrender, is that what you're proposing?" Scott demands. "This may come as a surprise to you, but I couldn't care less whether the Invid survive or go the way of the Zentraedi. I'm not just going to roll over and play dead!"

Heat, stress, and illness have left everyone short-tempered. Rand wisely keeps his peace as he sits beside Marlene and watches her wake up. The girl seems to be better, although still quite weak. He continues to sit beside her as he contemplates the message in his dreams.

While traveling through a forest of trees which were once active Invid Flowers of Life, the Robotech rebels run afoul of a group of primitive outcasts. The tribe has canonized the aliens as their sacred protectors. They pray and make offerings to the Invid as if they were gods. Somehow Scott manages to convince them that the Invid are enemies. He helps them to regain their humanity. Their encounter is not without cost. Young Annie, ever on the lookout for a husband of property, believes she has found one in a young warrior named Macgruder. It's love at first sight for the mercenary-minded girl. "Hold your horses, Annie," she says to herself. "If you play your cards right, this guy could make you a jungle princess...or a queen....Who knows? They might even make you a goddess!"

She almost loses her catch when he decides to take on the Invid all by himself in order to prove his manhood. Annie determines to help him. It's obvious Macgruder is unable to handle even the simplest situation without her assistance. They hijack Rand's cyclone and, luckily, manage to create a diversion that allows the others to destroy the attacking aliens.

Afterward, with the help of the grateful tribe, Scott and the others build a flotilla of rafts to move themselves and their mecha downriver. Annie elects to stay behind with her newfound security. The group is unhappy to see her go but don't try to stop her. They're sure Annie will be safer with the tribe anyway.

As they travel down the river, Rand breaks the melancholy silence that has enveloped them since their departure. "Oh, come on. Why the long faces, everybody? You all look like your puppy just died. Pull yourselves together. It's really a blessing Annie's gone. I mean, now we don't have to worry about that little bundle of energy getting herself into trouble. With her gone, us big kids are free to get on with some serious freedom fighting."

"You're as transparent as glass," Rook jeers. "You put on a brave front, but you miss her as much as the rest of us. Admit it."

Further comment is put aside as the rafts land and the group comes face to face with a strange Invid hive. It is surrounded by mecha they've never seen before. Knowing the ingenious aliens as they do, they can't help but feel that they're about to do battle with some of the most powerful weapons they've ever faced.

Annie...scheming, uh—*dreaming* again

Macgruder...at the mercy of feminine wiles

Lancer's cyclone...and transformed armor

Macgruder and Annie—to the rescue!

SEPARATE WAYS
Episode 75

Searching a deserted city for more supplies during a night reconnaissance results in disaster. The group is attacked by an Invid patrol. They retreat to a subway tunnel only to be trapped when the aliens create a cave-in behind them. The front of the tunnel is blocked by rubble as well.

Tension, self-doubt and hidden anger erupt violently among the close-knit crew. The underground confinement causes Lunk to lose control. He jumps Scott. When Lancer and Rand pull him off, the big man diverts his rage to Rand until he is beaten down to sit, sobbing, on the floor of the tunnel. Ashamed of being frightened, Lunk considers himself a coward and doesn't feel worthy to be a part of the group anymore.

The scene leaves everyone shaken. Rand and Rook walk away to look for another exit, but they find nothing useful.

"I'm beginning to wonder if we're going to get out of here," Rand tells her. "It looks like that business about whether Lunk should stay with the group might have been discussed a little prematurely. . . . Even if we do get out, the group won't be the same."

"I guess I should tell you something," Rook says quietly. "I've been thinking of dropping out of the group myself. It's been on my mind for some time."

"How could you be thinking that? You know this is an important mission. Annie's gone, and Lunk's in trouble. We're counting on you more than ever."

"Well, maybe I'm tired of people counting on me, you know? Or maybe I'm just tired of running for my life all the time."

Rand is incredulous. "You expect me to believe that? You're just like me. You thrive on danger."

"Up to a point."

"Well. . . maybe you're right," the young man speaks thoughtfully. "I'm only kidding myself when I say fighting is fun. Maybe I keep saying that to keep from admitting I'm scared sick most of the time."

It is Rook Bartley's turn to show disbelief. Still, there's no doubting Rand's sincerity. She stumbles onto a new thought. "Maybe if we both pulled out, we'd be saving everyone's life. Scott would have to postpone his mission while we went looking for more people."

It seems like a workable idea, but Scott is more stunned than impressed with her logic. Still, Rand has come up with a plan to use their remaining protoculture to blast their way through the rubble and out of the tunnel. Working together to rig the explosion, the five rebels renew their friendship. Rand's idea works, and they soon find themselves on the streets again. They are surprised to find Annie waiting for them.

The girl is thrilled to see them. "Can you picture me as a jungle princess? They expected me to gather nuts and fruit! I told them 'so long—gotta go!' Dumb, huh?"

Her pleasure at finding her friends turns to tears when she discovers Rand and Rook have decided to break off from the team. She pleads with them to stay, but they ride away. They seem to form a team of their own. By now, Rand has admitted that he's willing to follow Rook anywhere.

He races after her, concerned. "What's the hurry? Take it easy before you get us both killed. I'm sure you're upset about the group deciding to push ahead to Reflex Point, but wiping yourself out at ninety miles an hour on a wet road isn't going to help."

"What makes you so sure everybody's going to be all right? We just left some people who didn't have the sense to come in out of the rain!"

"Missing them already, aren't you?"

Although she tries, Rook has no real comeback to that. It isn't long before they see Scott and Lancer soaring overhead in the alpha fighters. It's too much. Rook turns her cyclone around and heads back to the team. Rand follows.

Rook and Rand discuss parting with the freedom fighters.

METAMORPHOSIS

Episode 76

Rook saves the day, but is wounded in battle.

Disturbed and suspicious because of the simulagent's inability or refusal to maintain contact with the hive, the Regis creates two new agents from the protoplasmic culture. She addresses them personally. "You have both been summoned to the protoculture chamber to assume your rightful place in the new order of our society. However, you must first undergo transformation into the ultimate life form of this planet....My children, you are truly the inheritors of my lineage within the society of the Invid. You are a prince and princess of our race and shall be known hereafter as Corg and Sera. We must begin the mass transformation of our people to the humanoid life form. This form which you have now assumed has been determined to be the most advanced and flexible configuration for survival on this planet. However, there may be hidden dangers in this physical form. An earlier experiment with humanoid reconstruction appears to be malfunctioning. Our spy, Ariel, who has joined the human resistance force, has failed to establish a communications link with our headquarters. You must contact Ariel and determine the cause of her dysfunction before we commit ourselves to a complete metamorphosis. You must prepare the way for the final phase of our domination of this planet. Now go—and prove yourselves worthy of your heritage.

As the Invid royalty speed away from Reflex Point, across the ocean, on the coast of a nearby tropical landmass, the members of Scott Bernard's resistance unit are trying to combine work with pleasure. Having located a derelict naval base, they have combed the area searching for protoculture fuel and supplies. Scott determines that they could slip quietly past the Invid in boats and save fuel as well. However, while the men and Annie check out their new transportation, Rook Bartley encounters Invid scouts.

Rook is wounded in the brief battle, so

they decide to stop for a bit of R & R at a deserted resort hotel. The group has spent so much time on their guard that they find it difficult to relax and have fun. Lancer takes off on his own and discovers a beautiful tree-lined grotto complete with waterfall. He quickly discards his clothes and treats himself to the delights of the sparkling water.

But his solitary swimming is interrupted by the arrival of the Invid princess, Sera. She appears to be no less human than Marlene. When Lancer chases the spy, he is startled to see her jump into Invid battle armor reserved for alien commanders. The implications are horrible. Lancer can only assume the aliens have brainwashed human beings into fighting for the Invid as the Robotech Masters had done during the Second Robotech War. Lancer runs to advise Scott and the others of this terrible discovery.

Confused and shaken by her encounter with Lancer, Sera flies off to join Corg and the reassembled Invid attack squadron. They prepare to seek out and destroy the resistance fighters. Led by the Invid royalty, the aliens attack. Scott and crew scatter for their mecha under a barrage of fire. In the midst of the fighting, Lunk is hit. Lancer tries to help. As Sera dives for the kill, she notices the handsome young man she met at the lake and hesitates. Lancer gets off the first shot and knocks her out of the sky. Sera remains in her body armor, shaken by her failure to destroy the ship. She has never experienced the power of human emotion, and as she picks up a variety of sensations from her departing sister, Ariel, she becomes more confused and fearful. Sera can only watch helplessly as the human convoy makes its way to dry land, out of range of Invid attack.

Sera, the Invid princess, in battle armor.

THE MIDNIGHT SUN

Episode 77

The enigmatic Yellow Dancer

The Robotech rebels leave the warm serenity of the tropics to tackle a snow-covered mountain pass. Cataclysmic changes have altered the planet's surface during the three Robotech Wars. Rand can hardly believe the abrupt change in climates: "It seems impossible that when we crossed into these mountains two days ago it was summer."

As the group sets up camp, Marlene undergoes another painful attack. During the past few months, the young woman has developed the ability to think for herself. She has also developed a vocabulary to relay her thoughts, but Marlene, known to the Invid as Ariel, still remains puzzled. She loves the freedom fighters as much as she fears the Invid. Her origins are a mystery. She cannot understand her confusing dreams and pain-filled reactions.

Marlene is not the only one suffering from the complexity of unfamiliar emotions. As the Invid Princess Sera deploys her squad against freedom fighters, she thinks of Lancer. "What is wrong with me?" she wonders. "Why do I keep seeing his face over and over again in my mind? What is it about this human that haunts me so? Part of me is repelled by the very thought of him and yet, somehow, part of me wants to see that human's face again. This is wrong—it's not the Invid way."

During the attack, Sera leads her troops against every member of the group except Lancer. To her dismay, she finds she simply cannot harm him. At the last, Sera confronts both Lancer and Marlene. In a face-to-face showdown, the unarmed human male stands up to her: "I know you . . . but why are you fighting for the Invid? Listen, I don't know what kind of game you're trying to play, but I want some answers. Can't you hear me? I said—look, forget it. In fact, go ahead and shoot me if you want but spare this girl. Please."

Sera can only stare at him. "That face . . . it's like time has stopped and I can look into my past and future—at the same time. . . . What is wrong with me? I'm so confused!"

Marlene experiences her own reaction to Sera: "It's as though I know her . . . like sisters somehow."

Sera's perplexity saves the day for Lancer and Marlene when Lunk and the others arrive to drive her away. Later, the rebels speculate over the alien's failure to shoot. "That's easy," Scott says. "We distracted it with our cover fire. It was just enough to confuse it so it didn't hurt them. Like Lunk said—we were lucky. We were *real* lucky!"

Marlene tries to understand her attraction to the Invid with Lancer's help. She is upset. "I can't do it. I don't belong with you. Please, Lancer, I'll just bring trouble."

Lancer soothes the frightened woman. "You'll be safe with me, Marlene. Trust your emotions."

"All right," Marlene agrees. "But I'm afraid for us all."

As they return to camp, the singer can't help thinking: "Strange, that Invid pilot acted like she knew Marlene, and now Marlene is scared to death. I wonder. . . ."

Lancer and Marlene are not the only ones wondering. In the hive, Sera is lost in her own thoughts. "I have failed the Regis, but still, I feel no shame over my defeat. I could have destroyed them . . . I know that. Now I must find out why I spared them."

GHOST TOWN

Episode 78

The freedom fighters journey through another deserted town.

The search for Reflex Point brings the rebels to another vast desert. They find a bandit outpost inhabited by elderly veterans of the war against the Robotech Masters. The old men have been living off their ancient mecha. Their most valued possession is a transceiver. Scott is elated until he is told the machine does not transmit messages. Still, they are able to hear orders directly from the fleet for the first time since Scott's patrol was destroyed.

A message comes across the screen: "This is Expeditionary Force calling Earth. If anyone is reading this message, here are your orders. All Invid military outposts must be destroyed. Admiral Hunter is planning a major offensive, and he calls upon all surviving forces to help destroy any military objectives."

The message confirms Scott's working objectives. He is excited to hear even this one-sided broadcast from central command. Inspired by the freedom fighters' enthusiasm, the oldtimers respond with their own call to glory. They plot an offensive against nearby Invid scout towers. Before Scott and his crew can stop them, they execute their strategy. However, the fight is more than old soldiers with equally old battle armor can withstand. They are killed while completing their mission.

The freedom fighters find themselves high in the Rocky Mountains with Invid in close pursuit. They can't use their Robotech mecha for fear of detection by squads too numerous to withstand. As they make their way across the ice-covered pass, Rand's scanners pick up a heat source beneath the snow.

Further investigation reveals a subterranean city enclosed within the Earth. The rebels locate an entrance and make their way to the street level. While Lunk and Lancer overhaul the mecha, the rest of the team go in search of food and supplies. They are quickly carried away with the fun of exploring the abandoned city. The stores are well stocked with food and clothing. Annie introduces Marlene to her favorite food—peppermint chocolate. Rand discovers Vienna sausages, but spoilsport Scott interrupts the festivities: "I want to load these supplies and get out of here. You may have forgotten, but there's a war going on."

"Give it a rest, Scott," Rand urges. "I mean, I know you were born in space and this place might not be very important to you—"

"But we were born right here on Earth," Annie breaks in. "Leaving this place now would be like turning our backs on our historical heritage."

Looking down at Annie's chocolate-smeared face, Scott knows the last thing on the girl's mind is the desire to study old Earth civilization. However, Scott relents and decides to relax himself as he strolls away with Marlene.

The lieutenant has come to enjoy Marlene's company. She reminds him of his fiancee in many ways. They enjoy shopping in the deserted mall and each other's company. It is the first time Scott has felt at ease since he landed on the planet. Meanwhile, at the arcade, the magnitude and the loneliness of the place begins to wear on Rook Bartley. The deserted city reminds her of all Earth has lost. The gigantic city calls out for people who

Rook remembers better times.

will never return so, when the Invid attack again, Rook is more than willing to leave. Marlene is almost overcome by the psychic trauma she experiences whenever the aliens are nearby. Scott helps her to safety.

The assault is led by Prince Corg. He has not been affected by any human emotion save lust for victory. The joy of battle stimulates him into taking unnecessary chances, and Rand is able to shoot him down. The rebels have no choice but to use their mecha to escape. Behind them, the city bursts into a tower of flame. Lunk has rigged the main generator to feed back on itself. The mile-high city blows a mile high.

Lancer stares at the flames. "If it wasn't a ghost town before, it certainly is now."

"But those were some fireworks, huh?"

"Golly gee, Miss Rook, I'm sure glad we were able to provide you with some excite-

ment today," Rand teases.

Scott ignores the friendly bickering. "How did Marlene know the Invid were coming?" he wonders. "And why didn't that one warrior fire at us when he had us both in his sights? It was almost as if he recognized her somehow...as if...Marlene was one of them!"

Scott and Marlene find something in common.

Lancer gives Annie a hand.

BIRTHDAY BLUES
Episode 80

Rand lines up an enemy target.

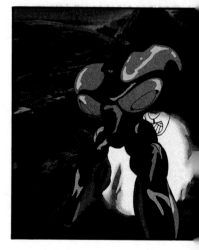

Prince Corg attacks.

The hit of the party—Annie!

Soaring in one of the alpha fighters high above Earth with Rand and Marlene, Annie is more excited than usual: "Yahoo! What a bee-yoo-ti-ful day! Do you know what day it is? Do you? I bet you don't! It's my birthday!"

"If you don't stop screaming in my ear, it'll be the last birthday you ever celebrate," Rand promises.

Rook buzzes across their flight path to advise that they're about to fly into an Invid hive. The freedom fighters investigate the acitvity from the air. It looks as if the aliens are expecting them. The small band makes its way cautiously around the outskirts of the hive with their mecha cruising at the lowest possible speed in the hope alien sensors won't pick up the vibrations.

"Count your blessings, Mint," Rand advises. "We're lucky to still be alive."

Rand tries to console his young friend as they land. The group takes cover in an abandoned village. As night falls, Annie and Marlene sit together, waiting for the others to return. "I guess birthdays are very special days," Marlene says. "I wish I could remember if I ever had one."

"You've had one," Annie tells her. "I don't think there's a way around that."

"Do they make you unhappy?"

"It's hard to be happy when every single one of your birthdays was a disaster. I remember my mother and father going away and leaving me to celebrate alone. I don't know how many times I prayed that just once I could have a real birthday party with friends and family just like everybody else. I don't think there's anything worse than being alone on your birthday. Thank goodness the day will be over soon."

Lancer, Rand, Rook, Lunk, and Scott complete a protoculture-baited trap. Rand is sent to retrieve Marlene and Annie. He takes them into the darkened village to a house where the rest of the crew waits for them.

Annie's special dream comes true. Her friends have prepared a surprise birthday

party. She is delighted, but soon uninvited guests invade the party. A patrol of Invid troopers led by Corg converge on the house—only to fall into the freedom fighters' trap. The shock troopers don't know what to make of Lunk's Roman candle-enhanced explosives. They retreat into the night. In the village safe-house, the resistance fighters enjoy the fireworks.

Although the evening provided just a brief moment of fun in the never-ending Robotech War, it is a time that will be remembered by all of the young people who lived through it. By fulfilling the dreams of one little girl, they have unconsciously answered a need felt by all. On this night, they are more than a band of freedom fighters. They have become a real family.

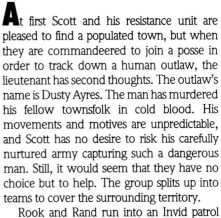

Episode 81

Rook thinks about the odd stranger she's just met.

At first Scott and his resistance unit are pleased to find a populated town, but when they are commandeered to join a posse in order to track down a human outlaw, the lieutenant has second thoughts. The outlaw's name is Dusty Ayres. The man has murdered his fellow townsfolk in cold blood. His movements and motives are unpredictable, and Scott has no desire to risk his carefully nurtured army capturing such a dangerous man. Still, it would seem that they have no choice but to help. The group splits up into teams to cover the surrounding territory.

Rook and Rand run into an Invid patrol and are helped by a mysterious man. After the fight, Rook bandages their deliverer's wounds and notices an unusual prosthesis on his right arm. The stranger offers a bitter explanation of his metal arm: "This is a perfect example of the Invid's evil—of how men can be evil to one another. The Invid used the right side of my body to experiment on, but what was worse was that my friends stood by and did nothing to stop them. They made no attempt to save me from the horrible pain. They could have rescued me. It would have been easy—but they didn't."

The two rebels begin to understand why the newcomer seems so unfriendly, why he places so little trust in his fellow man. They take their leave and head back to town. Rook is sympathetic toward the stranger, but Rand feels suspicious. The Invid ran as soon as they saw him. It's the first time the aliens have shown that kind of fear toward any human being.

Rand and Rook meet the rest of their friends. A member of the posse has found a picture of Dusty Ayres. Somehow the two are not surprised to see a photograph of the man they just met. Rook Bartley is more disturbed by this news than she thought possible and sets off on her own to find the killer. There are answers she must have.

Rook finds Dusty. As soon as he sees her face, he guesses that she knows who he is.

He promises to tell her the truth behind the killings as long as she swears to keep the story to herself.

"Look closely," Dusty begins. "I'm only half human—my whole right side has been replaced. Remember when you saw my arm? That was only where the Invid began their experiments. Apparently, the aliens were studying the functions of my body... trying to get data on the process of human evolution. Piece by piece they replaced my entire right side with protoculture-generated prostheses and organs. The experiment was done without anesthesia....It was more painful than you could ever imagine."

Rook is shaken. "What about your friends?"

"Ahhh...now you bring me to the part about my friends. My very closest friends," Dusty continues. "They stood there and watched when I was captured and never made an attempt to rescue me. They left me to die! But now, they're the ones who are dying. Each mark on this metal arm is a name I'd just as soon forget, but I can't until I've finished every one of them."

Rook understands his need for revenge. She knows what it is like to feel betrayed by friends. Dusty's experiences are more terrible than any she has known. As Dusty begins to leave, they receive a frantic call from Rand. The unit is surrounded by Invid. They need help. Rook and Dusty hurry to their rescue.

During the ensuing battle with the aliens, Dusty Ayres sees his two remaining targets, the men who left him with the Invid, and fires on them. The freedom fighters mistake his intentions and fire back. In return, Ayres lines them up in his sights with practiced ease. Killing has become easy for him. But this time, Rook intervenes.

"Dusty—they're my best friends! They didn't know you didn't mean them any harm," she explains. "They mean more to me than life itself. If you have to kill someone else, take me. But spare them."

Ayres is amazed. "I couldn't do that to you, Rook. I just couldn't. But...if I'd had friends like you when I was captured, my life would have been completely different."

As Dusty achieves this final realization, a battered Invid trooper makes a desperate effort to destroy them. Ayres fires on the alien, throwing himself in the way of the

Rand is suspicious.

Lancer rides for help.

trooper's final blast when he does. Both alien and human are destroyed.

Later, as the morning sun stretches across the valley floor, the Robotech rebels gather around the ashes and rubble which serve as a monument to an unlikely hero.

"I don't know if I coulda done what he did, Rook," Lunk says.

Rand shakes his head. "He saved all our lives. No matter what he did in the past, he redeemed himself in the end."

"Rand is right," Lancer agrees. "Besides— Dusty Ayres is lucky. He died with great courage...and he died for friends."

THE BIG APPLE
Episode 82

While Invid Shock Troopers invade the city...

...Lancer gives a concert to keep the civilians from panicking.

Rook Bartley holds invaders at bay.

After several defeats, the Invid have resumed their search for the freedom fighters. Guessing that the rebels must be nearly out of protoculture energy cells, the aliens deploy an elaborate surveillance network designed to capture the elusive humans.

In the once-proud city of New York, Lancer leads Rand and Annie in a search for fuel. He is obviously in familiar territory. His expertise leads them to a building where the Invid store protoculture.

Rand can't believe their good fortune. "There's enough here to carry a whole army to Reflex Point!"

"Provided, of course, that we can get it without being spotted," Lancer warns.

"Hah! Don't worry about a thing. Protoculture Express at your service. We deliver overnight or your money back, right?"

"Right!" Annie chimes in. "In fact, if we don't make good, we pay you!"

Lancer sighs, unhappy. "Gee... I remember what a beautiful place this building was. This is Carnegie Hall, the greatest concert hall in the world. It was everybody's dream to play here. It was my dream, too, even though I never got the chance. I suppose those days are gone forever, now that the Invid have turned everything upside down. But what a thrill it would have been to appear here. I can almost imagine it.... I won't let the Invid destroy my dreams! Somehow, someday I am going to play this hall!"

"Awww, come on," Rand urges. "Let's get out of here. Let's grab as much stuff as we can and take off before we get caught, okay?"

The singer agrees. For the moment, he has no choice. Dreams are put away as the trio scoop up as much of the precious fuel cells they can carry. In her enthusiasm, Annie takes too much and drops one of the canisters—loudly—on the cement floor. A guard peers about anxiously. Lancer, Rand, and Annie stay low, but finally the sound of a mewing cat distracts the guard at last.

He blames the noise on the animal and walks away.

The cat turns out to be a young boy. He leads the others to the safety of another building. Inside, an old friend of Lancer's, Simon, is holding a rehearsal for a stage production. The two men are pleased to see each other. Lancer is surprised to learn the Invid are allowing musical performances in the city. "Well, they haven't tried to stop us yet," Simon tells him. "I guess they figure this keeps the slaves happy and out of their hair. Anyway—you know what they say. The show must go on!"

In an Invid hive atop the tallest building in the city, two very different people are involved in conversation. Sera and Corg are arguing.

"You must stop this indiscriminate destruction," Sera commands. "We have not completed our observation of these life forms. You seem to forget our instructions—to study their behavior patterns and learn from them."

"Sera, I must protest your lenience in dealing with the humans. Our experiments have been completed. It's time to exterminate them."

"Do not challenge my authority. The Regis has placed me in charge."

"For the moment." Corg is smug. "You've known all along that we planned to save only a small percentage of the humans to use as workers on our protoculture farms. The rest have been scheduled for extermination. It's obvious you have no stomach for destruction, and, orders or not, I intend to begin that process immediately."

The Invid prince takes off to do just that despite Sera's protests. The princess is miserable. "Maybe he's right. I don't know if I have the determination to carry out this task. I still don't understand what prevents me from destroying the human rebel.... It's more

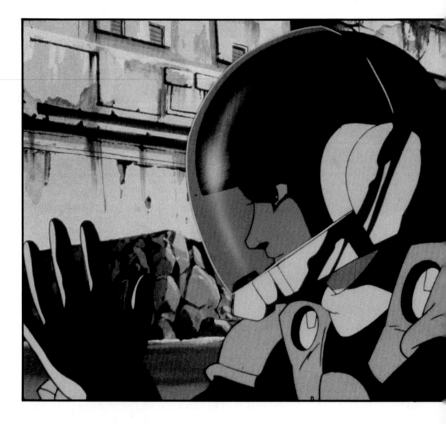

important than ever that I speak with Ariel. I must try to find her."

Corg wastes no time. He assembles his shock troopers and begins a murderous assault on the civilian population. His orders are simple: "Spare no one!"

Alien mecha fill the sky. The inhabitants of the occupied city panic and try to escape as the Invid fire on them. Scott, Lunk, Rook, and Marlene observe the riot. Lancer and Simon watch the old theater go up in flames but manage to move the performers into the safety of the subway tunnels. When Scott and the others catch up with Lancer, Rand, and Annie, the lieutenant shares an idea with the singer: "The people need something to inspire them to fight back against the Invid. The best way I know to do that is to put on a show. Can you do that?"

Lancer agrees and, with Simon's performers as backups, brings comfort out of chaos to the frightened survivors while the resistance fighters wage their own battle against Corg's troops.

While this is going on, Sera finds Marlene. "I don't believe what I'm hearing," Marlene

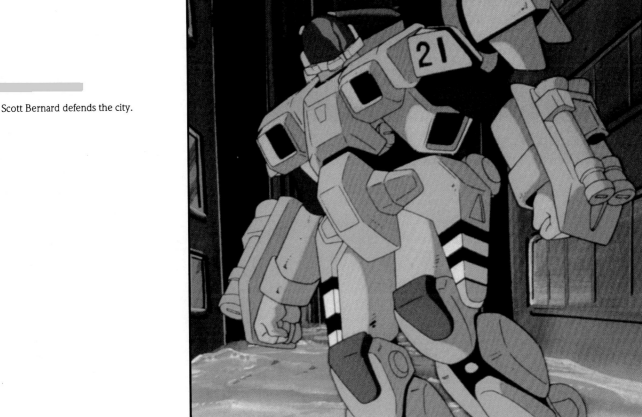

Scott Bernard defends the city.

says. "I am not an Invid!"

Sera is puzzled by her sister's reaction. "You were placed among the people of Earth to learn their plans and report back to our hive. As of this date, the Regis is still waiting for your first report. Do you expect me to believe that you have forgotten who you are and why you're here?"

"No—you're lying. You must be."

Sera takes off as the battle comes uncomfortably close, promising to return. Marlene is left to wonder over this new mystery. She despairs that she could be one of the evil Invid.

The freedom fighters develop a new strategy. Instead of fighting individual shock troopers, they turn their attack on the giant hive itself. They storm the tower with incredible force. When the Invid realize what is happening, they return to the unguarded hive. The aliens are wiped out in the subsequent explosion. Corg rages. He has been vanquished by a handful of renegade humans again.

Afterward, when the Robotech rebels regroup and check their coordinates, they find they are but a few hours away from Reflex Point. The end of their journey is approaching fast.

As the resistance unit nears its destination, they hear an incredible crash. Scarlet sears the horizon as a series of explosions rips the air.

Scott and crew arrive at the scene of a nightmare. One of the ships from the Expeditionary Force has crashed into the planet's surface, driven to ground by Invid assault squadrons. The destruction is so complete, the lieutenant knows there can be no survivors. Still, they check the area and hope for the best. A lone woman appears amid the wreckage holding a video camera. She introduces herself as Sue Graham, a member of the 36th Squadron Intelligence Department, Jupiter Section. As a video journalist, her mission is to keep records for Admiral Hunter's archives. As she interviews the freedom fighters, she warns them that the Invid are circling back.

Sue is right. The aliens arrive as predicted. Since there are too many to fight, the rebels overturn their mecha and hide in the ruins. Sue Graham continues to film the approaching aliens despite the danger of discovery.

"We have to get this on film so Admiral Hunter can view it," Sue explains. "Maybe it will give us a clue as to how these aliens operate."

"So, Admiral Hunter will be here soon," Scott says. "The fleet will be able to take care of the Invid."

"Yes. They're making final preparations for the bombardment of Reflex Point. The third attack unit is in preliminary maneuvers at a base on the far side of the moon. The main Robotech force, however, is coming back with a fleet made up of the new Veritech fighters. The ships have been code named Shadow Fighters."

Rand is fascinated. "Why Shadow Fighters? What are they?"

Sue demonstrates with one of her films. "You can see from this graphic representation that the protoculture generator has been designed with a fourth-dimensional configu-ration, making the Shadow Fighter invisible to the Invid. It's that simple."

The conversation stops as another Invid patrol approaches. Sue speculates the aliens must be looking for the Syncro Cannon, another new weapon that crashed with the fleet. She has hidden it in a nearby cave, out of alien view. They try to salvage the cannon, but it is impossible. Rand destroys it to keep the valuable mecha out of enemy hands.

She films more footage on the Invid. She is especially interested in Corg. Until now, the team believed Corg was a human fighting for the aliens, but when the Invid prince is wounded, they see that he has green blood. They realize Corg is an alien in human form. As shrapnel flies about them, Sue Graham is fatally wounded and Marlene is hit. The freedom fighters are stunned into silence. Marlene has the same color blood as the Invid. Marlene is an alien, too. Devastated, the woman runs, sobbing, from the crash site. Scott and the others can only stare after her.

Scott and Rand can't believe the destruction.

Lunk protects Annie.

DARK FINALE

Episode 84

Lancer joins the Robotech Assault Force.

On the outskirts of Reflex Point, Rand is unhappy at being left behind.

The freedom fighters rendezvous at Reflex Point in time to join Admiral Hunter's assault force. There has been a major rift in the team. Scott, Lancer, and Lunk are official military personnel. Rook, Rand, and Annie are not. As the soldiers mobilize for battle, the "civilians" are not happy to be left behind.

But orders have never stood in their way before, and Scott's directives don't stop Rook and Rand now. Disregarding the probable dangers, the two form their own strategy to attack Reflex Point. After all, they haven't come this far to be left out of the grand finale. As they soar into the sky, Lunk discovers stowaway Annie hidden in the back of his jeep. The terrain is too dangerous to drop her off. He has no choice but to take the girl along.

Marlene finally accepts her Invid identity of Ariel and becomes one with her tribal memory. Her heritage has become clear at last, but when she enters the Great Hive to meet with the Regis, Ariel speaks for the humans. Sera and Corg listen, too. "They are only fighting to regain the land that is rightfully theirs. The land we're taking away from them. Have we forgotten our past? Have we forgotten that our own planet was stolen from us? What gives us the right to inflict the same evil on these people?"

"We have gone too far to worry about that now," Sera tells her. Still, the Invid princess is distressed, and, as she launches into battle, Ariel's words stay with her. Later, when she finds Lancer in trouble, Sera can't stop herself from saving his life.

Scott, Lunk, and Annie rally to Lancer's side. Rook and Rand join them. Suddenly, Ariel appears to them as if transformed. The team hardly recognizes her. She seems to be a different person.

"I am neither human or completely Invid," Ariel tells them. "I am a new form of life that is a blending of the two. You must believe that the Invid never planned to destroy humanity. We are only trying to find a place where we can live in peace and security."

Scott and the others don't know what to make of this concept, but they follow Ariel into the central core of the Great Hive. There they meet the Invid Queen Regis for the first time.

The alien's voice seems to come from everywhere. "Behold—I am the Invid. I am the soul and the spirit. I have guided my people across the measureless cosmos from a world that was lost to a world that was found. I have led my people in flight from the dark tide of shadow that engulfed our forefathers, that threatens to engulf us even now. I am the power and the light. I am the embodiment of the life force, the creator-protector. In the terminology of your people, I am . . . the Mother. Ariel, it is true. You are a traitor. Was it you who led these children of the shadow to the Hive?"

"Yes," Ariel admits. "But you must see now that they are not children of the shadow, that they have a life force that is almost as strong as our own. If they oppose us, it's because we are trying to do the same thing to them that was done to us so many years ago. Perhaps if we could begin again, we might be able to find a way for our two peoples to share this planet in peace."

"I'm sorry," Scott says. "You know that's not possible. Not at this point."

"You'd rather have the death and destruction continue?"

Lunk becomes angry. "Hey, lemme tell ya something maybe you've forgotten. Your people invaded us, remember?"

Ariel sighs. There is no way she can forget. None of her people can deny truth, any more than they can neglect the instincts of their ancestral history. "Lunk, you traveled with me. You took care of me. I even think you liked me a little bit. I am no different a person now than I was then. The fact that I could travel among you as a friend means that we are not so different—your people and mine."

"Ariel, look at these 'friends' of yours," the Regis says. "Notice how they stare at you in fear and confusion, emotional states which in their species inevitably lead to hatred and

Marlene accepts her Invid identity of Ariel.

Rook and Lancer battle Invid invaders.

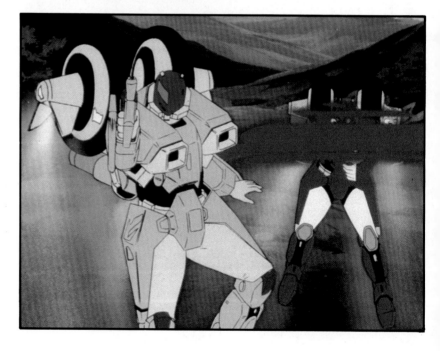

The freedom fighters come face to face with the Invid Regis.

violence. Your contact with them has blinded you to their true nature, my child. It is the genetic instinct of their species to destroy what they cannot understand.

Rand has had enough. "Wait a minute, dragon lady! How do you know what we're thinking? So Marlene's an Invid . . . okay, that was kind of a surprise. But we don't hate her for it. We know she's risked a lot to help us."

Sera speaks up as well. "Forgive me, Regis, but I've begun to doubt whether we are any better than they are. You say this species is guilty of murdering and making slaves of their enemies, but how is that any different from what we are doing on this planet?"

"Have you all gone mad?" Corg demands. "This pathetic species cannot be allowed to stand in the way of our future! Sera, your contact with the rebels has made you weak and spineless."

"And has made a monster out of you, Corg, consumed by vengeance and evil passions. You are the child of shadow. Not the humans."

Lancer stands with Sera. "Fool! If you keep fighting, there won't be a future for any of us."

Corg won't be denied the execution of his vendetta. He runs from the Hive for his battle armor with Scott Bernard close behind. The others follow and watch as the two take to the air for combat. The sky has darkened. The sun is blocked by the tremendous battle fleet that has arrived to rout the invaders and reclaim the planet.

"Oh, wow!" Annie cries. "I didn't think there were that many ships in the whole universe."

Lancer shakes his head wearily. "Well, that does it. Any hope of a peaceful settlement has just gone down the drain. . . . Heaven have mercy on us all."

In the depths of the Hive, the Invid Mother already begins to mourn: "No—they have come from beyond the stars! The dark tides of shadow have come to engulf us again. . . ."

SYMPHONY OF LIGHT
Episode 85

Scott races to battle Prince Corg.

Corg and Scott engage in a brutal aerial dogfight. The intensity of their conflict is reflected in the battle between the Earth and alien forces. The shock troopers are no match for the new Shadow Fighters. The Invid cannot fight what they cannot see and are being destroyed despite their best efforts. As Admiral Hunter's fleet blasts the Invid battalions, Scott finishes Corg with his teammates' help.

The Regis feels the death of her children. The aliens have a choice—stay and be slaughtered, or leave the planet forever. For the Invid Mother, there can only be one decision: "Whether one race or the other emerges victorious is of little meaning. Such hatred can only breed more hatred. Oh, my children...if we stay, this conflict will rage from generation to generation. Hear me! When we sensed the first indications of the protoculture resources on this world, we thought that, at last, we had found the home for which we searched. We called together all our people scattered through the galaxies to begin life anew on this planet. We rebuilt a world that had nearly been destroyed by evil, and we constructed the Genesis Pits in order to pursue the path of enlightened evolution...but it was not enough. The Earth is reviving and will eventually regain its proper balance in accordance with the laws of nature. However, the humans have been too strongly influenced by the malignant shadow of the Robotech Masters and are only intent upon the destruction of their race. We, the Invid, will continue our evolutionary development elsewhere. We shall consume all the protoculture and rise to a higher plane. Come with me! Discard this world and follow the spirit of light as he beckons us onward!"

The Invid leave. With nothing to fight, Hunter's fleet ceases its attack. Lancer and Sera guard the Great Hive and the Regis as she beckons her children to the stars. Sera chooses to remain on Earth. Lancer seems

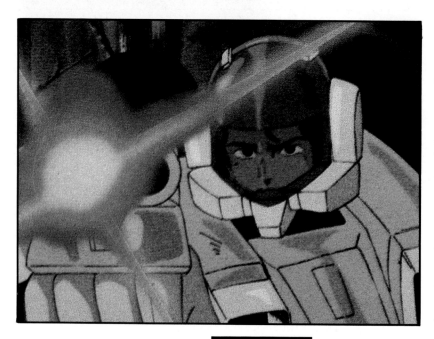

Scott's fatal shot

content to have her stay with him.

The humans celebrate their victory. Lancer gives his last performance as Yellow Dancer, revealing his true identity to the public at last. Scott Bernard accepts a final military mission. With the threat of war behind him, he can enjoy space duty and look forward to his return as well. Rand and Rook decide they have a more permanent partnership in store for their future. Annie and Lunk form their own family.

Lancer dedicates his last song to the

Lancer prepares for his final concert as Yellow Dancer.

commander of the freedom fighters, Scott Bernard. "He's leaving the Earth behind and with it, the most precious of possessions—his friends—the people who love him most. But when he comes back, we'll be here to welcome him home with open arms."

Scott Bernard has more than friends to come home to. Ariel promises to wait for him on their new home—Earth. As the lieutenant bids goodbye to the planet, he abandons old memories as well. The pain of the past is forgotten in the future's bright promise.

Battle rages over the city.

A new beginning.

CHAPTER 2

THE MACROSS SAGA

Characters & Mecha

RICK HUNTER

Rank: Lieutenant
Age: 19

As an amateur pilot and close friend of Lieutenant Commander Roy Fokker, Rick Hunter makes his first appearance in the Macross Saga by "buzzing" the audience at the historic launch of the SDF-1 in his private, flying-circus aircraft. "Big brother" Fokker is not amused by the antics of his young friend, but all fun and games are put aside when the launch is disrupted by the appearance of the alien Zentraedi Armada intent on reclaiming the SDF-1 as their own. In a matter of minutes this playful young man must grow up.

Throughout the series, Rick struggles with his feelings in regard to his role as a soldier and, eventually, as a leader. He does not approve of violence, and his reluctant commission into the Robotech air force is tainted by his unspoken fear of the giant alien invaders. Rick's feelings are also torn between two women: Lynn Minmei, a young Chinese girl he rescues, and Lisa Hayes, his commanding officer. After his best friend's death, Rick's sense of responsibility and purpose strengthens. Eventually, Rick becomes one of the major figures in the intergalactic war which will determine the fate of Earth. Rick is a continuing character throughout the odyssey of **ROBOTECH.** In the New Generation segment, Scott Bernard refers to him as Admiral Rick Hunter. Rick's compassion, skill, dedication, and sense of responsibility make him a leader his people look up to with trust and respect.

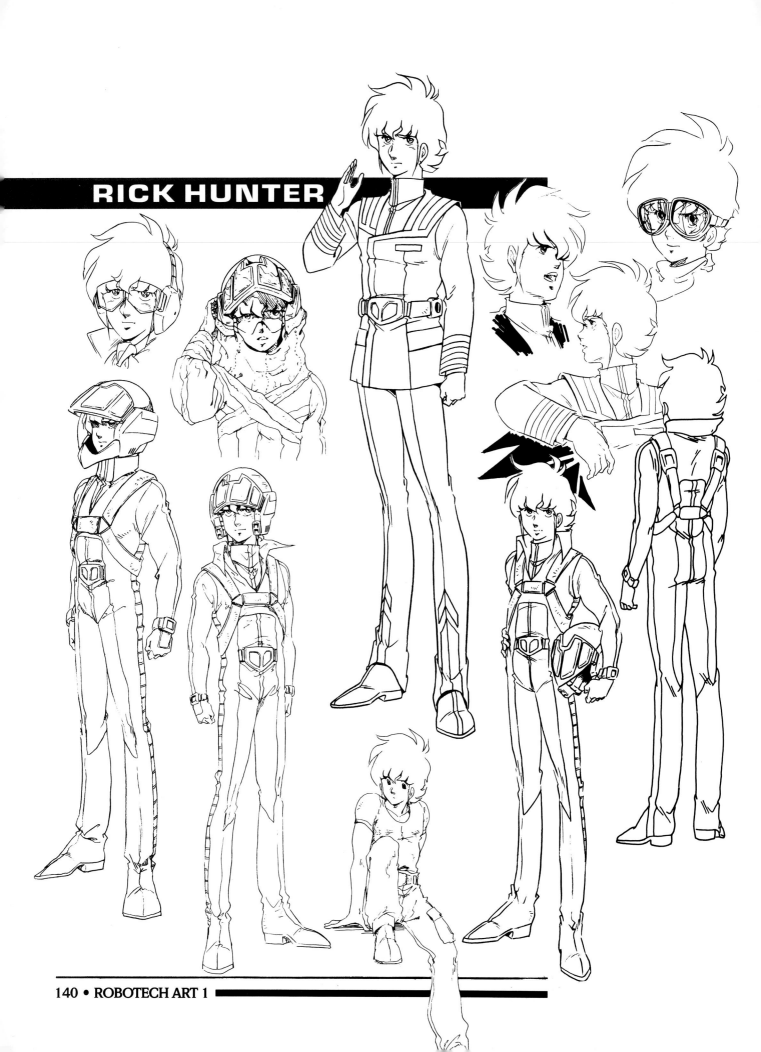

RICK HUNTER

LYNN MINMEI

Rank: Non-military Status
Age: 15

At the beginning of the Macross Saga, it would seem that Lynn Minmei is a 15-year-old girl going on the age of 5. Hers is a butterfly personality at best, although she is always a scene-stealer. Lynn Minmei is one of the brightest stars of the **ROBOTECH** story. Talented, charismatic, and beautiful, the young Chinese girl becomes the darling of the SDF-1. Out of the 70,000 residents of Macross City living onboard the SDF-1, Minmei competes in a beauty contest and becomes "Miss Macross," a morale-lifting symbol for civilians and soldiers alike. But this seems only a game for the girl. A natural flirt, Minmei accepts her role as spiritual cheerleader with enthusiasm, but little real responsibility. Unfortunately, her innocence and lack of maturity prevent her from recognizing the seriousness of Rick Hunter's interest.

Still, it is Lynn Minmei's singing that inspires many of the Zentraedi to defect, and ultimately turns the tide for the humans in this initial encounter. Minmei grows to accept her responsibility as a leader in the reconstruction of Earth after its destruction during the Robotech Wars.

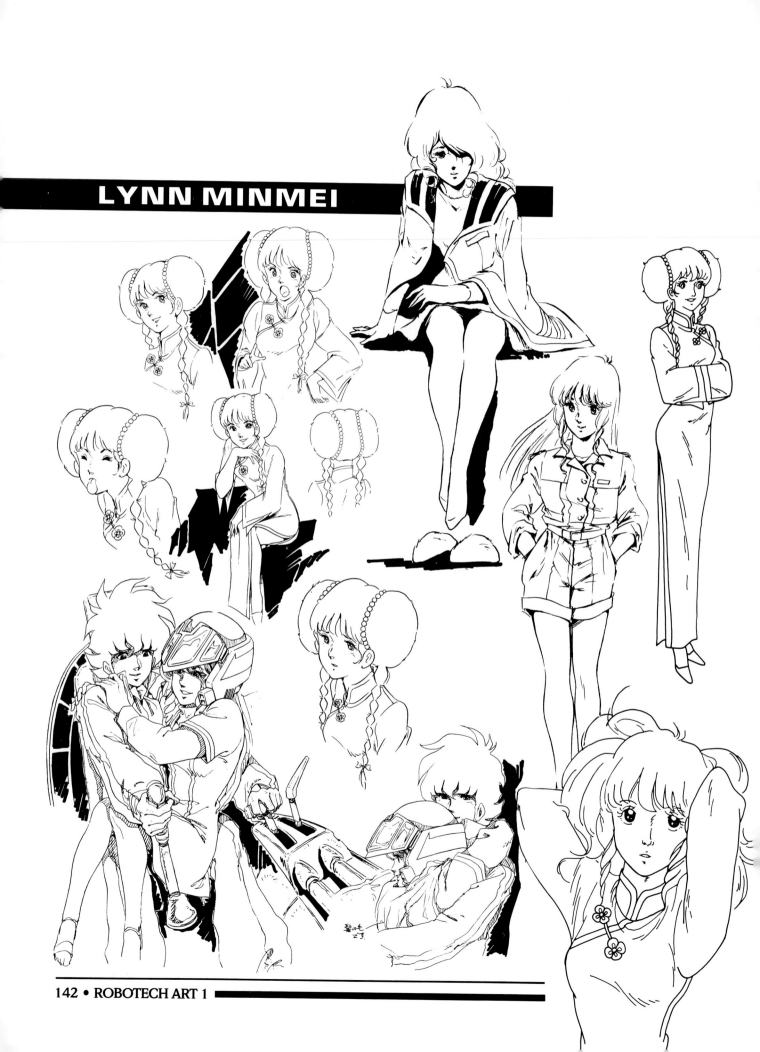

LYNN MINMEI

LISA HAYES

Rank: Lieutenant Commander
Age: 24

As the daughter of Admiral Hayes, Lisa could have chosen any position in the United Earth Defense Forces. But when her fiancee, Karl Riber, decides to request duty on Mars Base Sara in order to avoid involvement in the global civil war, Lisa chooses the Space Corps hoping to eventually join her intended at the Martian Colony. The arrival of the SDF-1 changes her plans. Lisa is assigned as First Officer on board the ship and is in charge of all operations, including defense controller. It is a position she handles with authority and intelligence. Because she devotes all her energy to her work, she gains a reputation as a "cold fish," especially with new recruit Rick Hunter. However, her hardline career woman attitude is only a mask for the gentle, loving woman she really is.

After the Zentraedi attack and the subsequent Space Fold maneuver, Lisa learns that Karl Riber, along with the rest of the personnel on Mars Base Sara, has been killed by the aliens. As a result of this loss, Lisa becomes even more involved in her work. But there are new complications. Lisa falls in love with Rick Hunter, and, although she is an able advocate of the SDF-1 and its mission, she cannot find a voice to express her feelings to Rick. It is a rocky romance with missed opportunities and endless problems for Rick as well as Lisa.

ROY FOKKER

Rank: Lieutenant Commander
Age: 30

Roy Fokker is the devil-may-care commander of the famed "Skull Squadron" and combat veteran of the civil war that has ravaged Earth. With the arrival of the SDF-1, Fokker enlists in the United Earth's Government's Robotech Defense Force. He appears to be the classic swashbuckling hero, but Fokker is able to transcend this mold and be as compassionate and human as any of his crew. It was during his stint as a famed air circus pilot, before his involvement in the military, that Roy met and befriended young Rick Hunter. Then, while he was training on the Veritech Fighter, Roy met and fell in love with Claudia Grant. His death in battle comes as a shock to all who knew and cared for this generous, affectionate man. Still, Roy Fokker's dynamic presence continues to be felt throughout the series. He becomes the inspiration for Rick Hunter's increased devotion to duty.

CLAUDIA GRANT

Rank: Bridge Officer
Age: 28

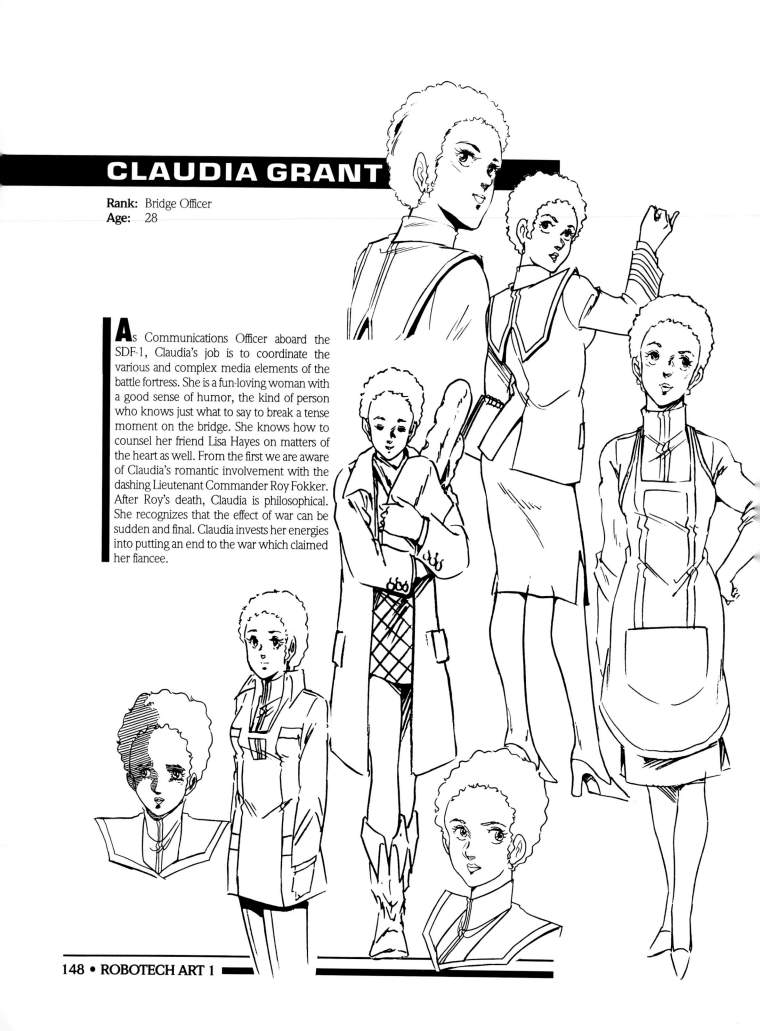

As Communications Officer aboard the SDF-1, Claudia's job is to coordinate the various and complex media elements of the battle fortress. She is a fun-loving woman with a good sense of humor, the kind of person who knows just what to say to break a tense moment on the bridge. She knows how to counsel her friend Lisa Hayes on matters of the heart as well. From the first we are aware of Claudia's romantic involvement with the dashing Lieutenant Commander Roy Fokker. After Roy's death, Claudia is philosophical. She recognizes that the effect of war can be sudden and final. Claudia invests her energies into putting an end to the war which claimed her fiancee.

CAPTAIN GLOVAL

Rank: Captain
Age: 52

Captain Gloval is a perfect example of what a person can accomplish in the face of overwhelming odds. He enters the Macross Saga as a war-weary veteran placed in command of the SDF-1. Not only must he put the mysterious battle fortress through her paces, he has the added responsibility of breaking in a crew of raw recruits. The initial shakedown cruise of the SDF-1 turns out to be rougher than expected when Gloval must defend Earth against invading aliens...aliens who have been bred for countless generations to be perfect fighting machines.

With the possibility of total annihilation all too imminent, Captain Gloval fights back with a vengeance. He plots strategy for strategy against the Zentraedi, always keeping one step ahead. His courage, skill, and determination become the essence of the Robotech Defense Force.

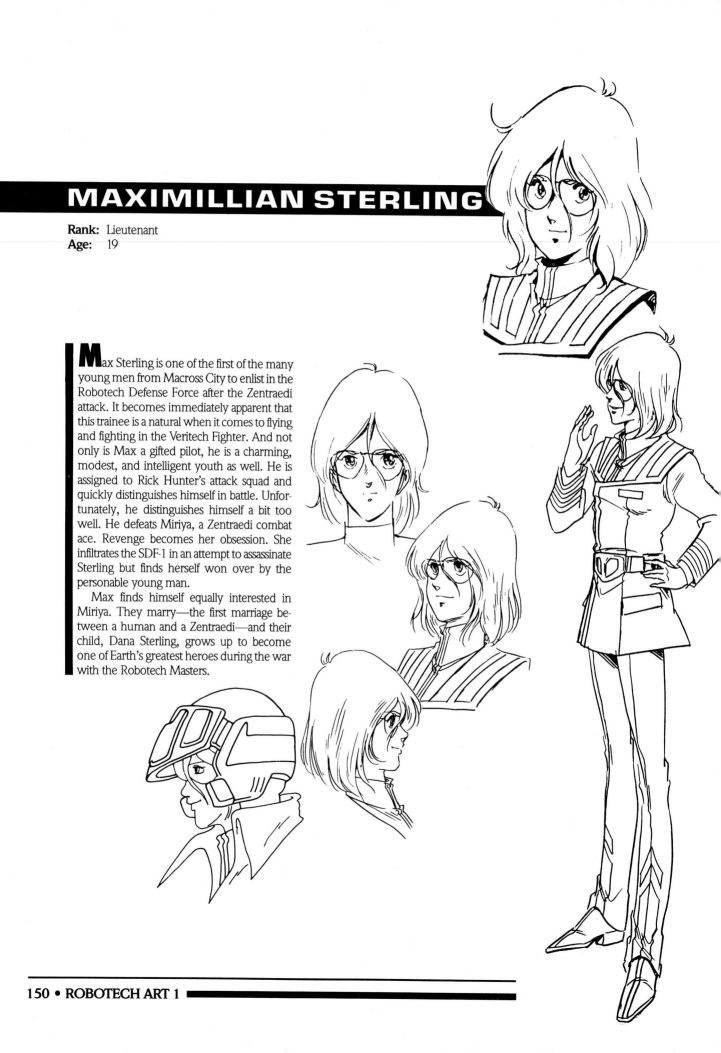

MAXIMILLIAN STERLING

Rank: Lieutenant
Age: 19

Max Sterling is one of the first of the many young men from Macross City to enlist in the Robotech Defense Force after the Zentraedi attack. It becomes immediately apparent that this trainee is a natural when it comes to flying and fighting in the Veritech Fighter. And not only is Max a gifted pilot, he is a charming, modest, and intelligent youth as well. He is assigned to Rick Hunter's attack squad and quickly distinguishes himself in battle. Unfortunately, he distinguishes himself a bit too well. He defeats Miriya, a Zentraedi combat ace. Revenge becomes her obsession. She infiltrates the SDF-1 in an attempt to assassinate Sterling but finds herself won over by the personable young man.

Max finds himself equally interested in Miriya. They marry—the first marriage between a human and a Zentraedi—and their child, Dana Sterling, grows up to become one of Earth's greatest heroes during the war with the Robotech Masters.

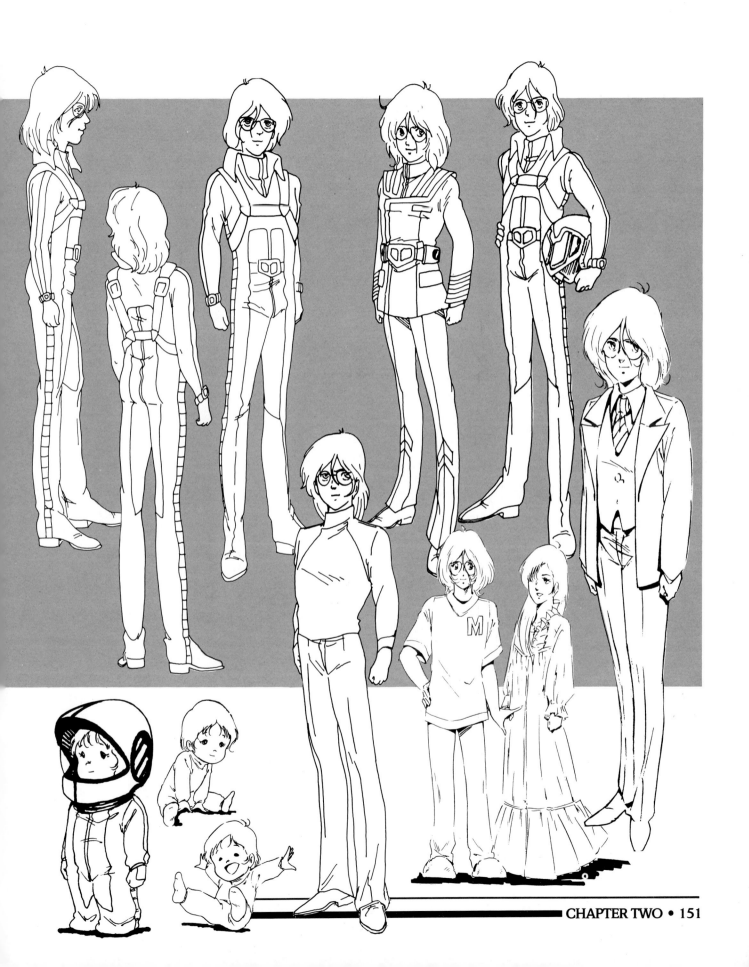

BEN DIXON

Rank: Second Lieutenant
Age: 20

Ben is a lighthearted combat pilot whose braggadocio generally outweighs his skill and natural fighting abilities. Courageous and determined, he is well liked by his comrades. Assigned to a position directly under Rick Hunter, it comes as quite a blow when Ben is killed in the line of duty.

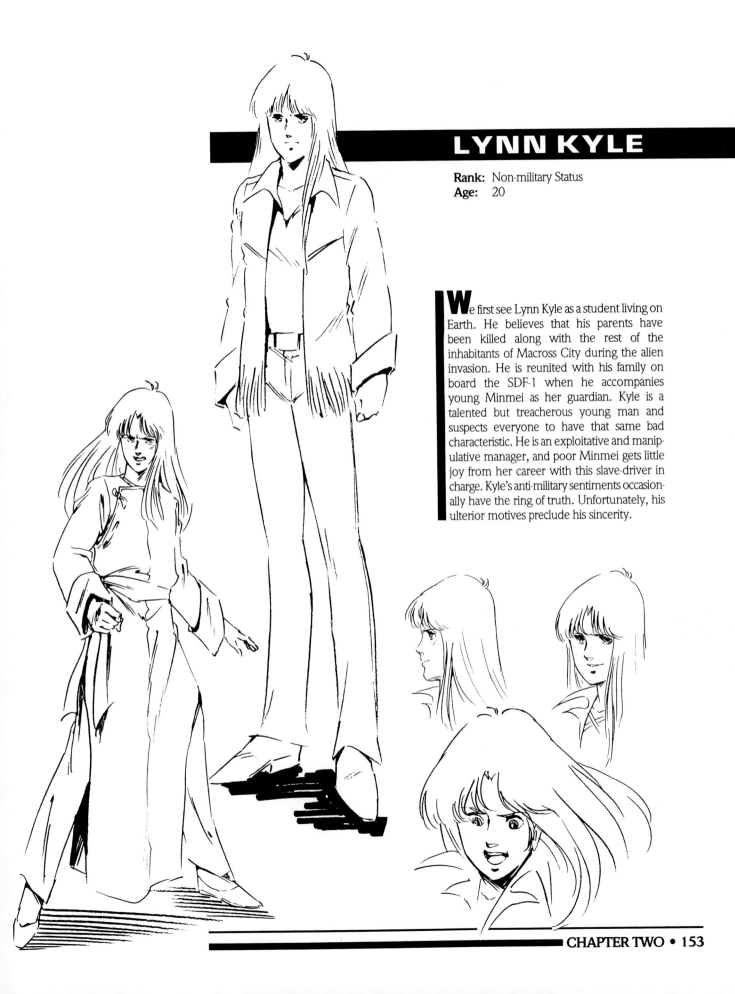

LYNN KYLE

Rank: Non-military Status
Age: 20

We first see Lynn Kyle as a student living on Earth. He believes that his parents have been killed along with the rest of the inhabitants of Macross City during the alien invasion. He is reunited with his family on board the SDF-1 when he accompanies young Minmei as her guardian. Kyle is a talented but treacherous young man and suspects everyone to have that same bad characteristic. He is an exploitative and manipulative manager, and poor Minmei gets little joy from her career with this slave-driver in charge. Kyle's anti-military sentiments occasionally have the ring of truth. Unfortunately, his ulterior motives preclude his sincerity.

KIM YOUNG

Rank: Enlisted Operative
Age: 23

Kim is Claudia Grant's communications assistant. Her assignment to the bridge crew is indicative of her abilities, although in her spare time she is more concerned with having a good time and flirting with the pilots. She is aided in this pursuit by her best friends and bridge mates, Sammie Porter and Vanessa Leeds.

SAMMIE PORTER

Rank: Enlisted Operative
Age: 20

Sammie is the youngest of the bridge crew on the SDF-1. Her naivete and obvious sense of wonder in **ROBOTECH's** world of scientific marvels lay the groundwork for a strong, heroic character. When the time comes for Sammie to take charge of defending the SDF-1, she accepts the position without hesitation.

VANESSA LEEDS

Rank: Enlisted Operative
Age: 23

As part of the terrible trio of Porter, Young, and Leeds, Vanessa feels it's her mission to fill her off-duty time with as much fun and excitement as possible. She is the computer operator assigned to the bridge of the SDF-1 and although she loves her work and shipmates, she becomes quite homesick for Earth after years of isolation on the space fortress.

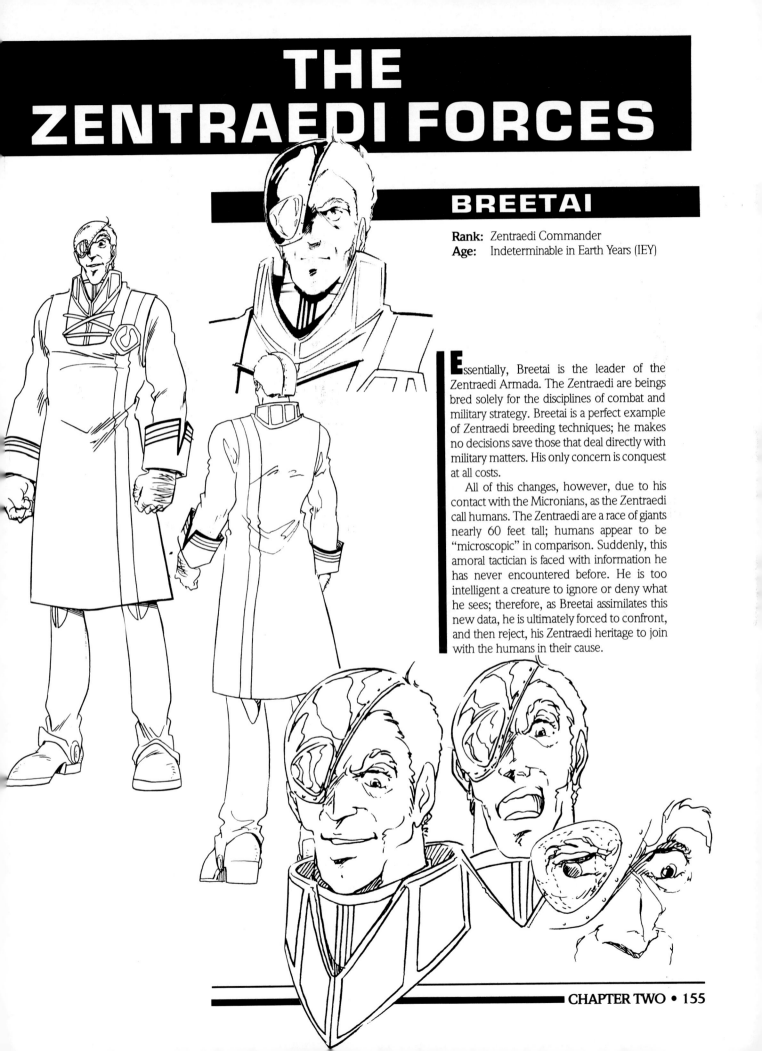

THE ZENTRAEDI FORCES

BREETAI

Rank: Zentraedi Commander
Age: Indeterminable in Earth Years (IEY)

Essentially, Breetai is the leader of the Zentraedi Armada. The Zentraedi are beings bred solely for the disciplines of combat and military strategy. Breetai is a perfect example of Zentraedi breeding techniques; he makes no decisions save those that deal directly with military matters. His only concern is conquest at all costs.

All of this changes, however, due to his contact with the Micronians, as the Zentraedi call humans. The Zentraedi are a race of giants nearly 60 feet tall; humans appear to be "microscopic" in comparison. Suddenly, this amoral tactician is faced with information he has never encountered before. He is too intelligent a creature to ignore or deny what he sees; therefore, as Breetai assimilates this new data, he is ultimately forced to confront, and then reject, his Zentraedi heritage to join with the humans in their cause.

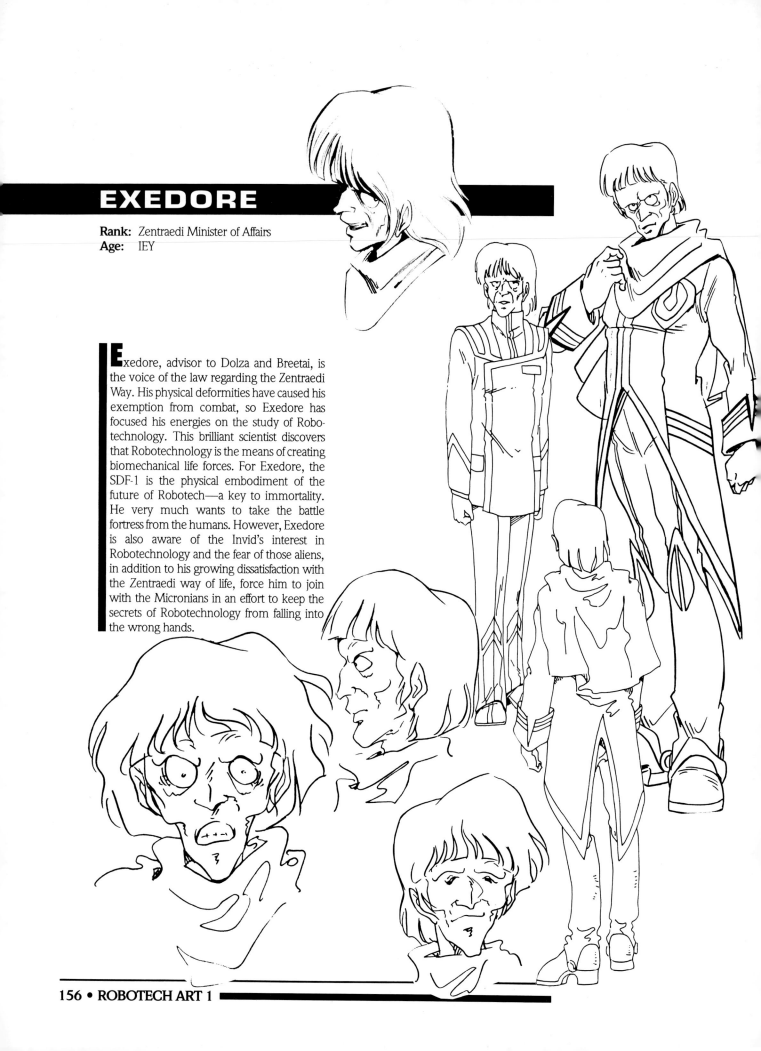

EXEDORE

Rank: Zentraedi Minister of Affairs
Age: IEY

Exedore, advisor to Dolza and Breetai, is the voice of the law regarding the Zentraedi Way. His physical deformities have caused his exemption from combat, so Exedore has focused his energies on the study of Robotechnology. This brilliant scientist discovers that Robotechnology is the means of creating biomechanical life forces. For Exedore, the SDF-1 is the physical embodiment of the future of Robotech—a key to immortality. He very much wants to take the battle fortress from the humans. However, Exedore is also aware of the Invid's interest in Robotechnology and the fear of those aliens, in addition to his growing dissatisfaction with the Zentraedi way of life, force him to join with the Micronians in an effort to keep the secrets of Robotechnology from falling into the wrong hands.

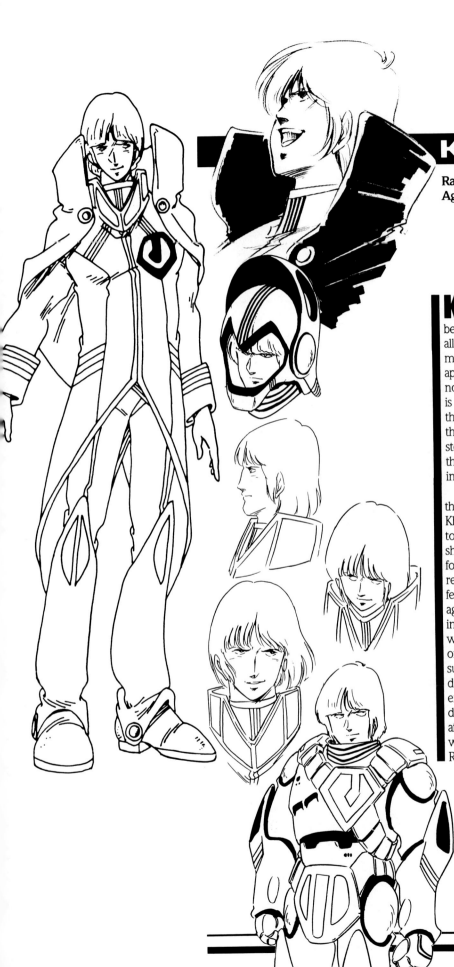

KHYRON

Rank: Zentraedi Warlord
Age: IEY

Khyron has a nickname—the Back Stabber—and he does his best to live up to it! Of all the Zentraedis, Khyron probably exhibits more human characteristics when he first appears than his fellow aliens. Unfortunately, none of these attributes is good or noble. He is a glory-hungry opportunist who delights in the slaughter of his victims. The end justifies the means—that's Khyron's motto. He will stop at nothing to achieve his own ends, from the annihilation of entire planets up to and including the sacrifice of his own men.

While Breetai and Exedore seek to capture the SDF-1 and the knowledge it holds, Khyron, bored with the lengthy war, schemes to destroy the fortress. He is not reluctant to show his contempt for his superior officers or for the Zentraedi lifestyle. He shares a hidden relationship with Azonia, a high-ranking female Zentraedi Commander. This goes against the Zentraedi culture, which forbids interpersonal relationships between men and women. With the exception of Azonia, most of the Zentraedi regard Khyron with fear and suspicion. He is so unlike his fellows, they don't seem to know what to do with him—except to try and stay out of his way. Khyron deserts his post during battle hoping to return after the fighting is over to defeat the weakened victor and capture the secrets of Robotechnology for himself.

MIRIYA

Rank: Captain, Zentraedi Air Force
Age: IEY

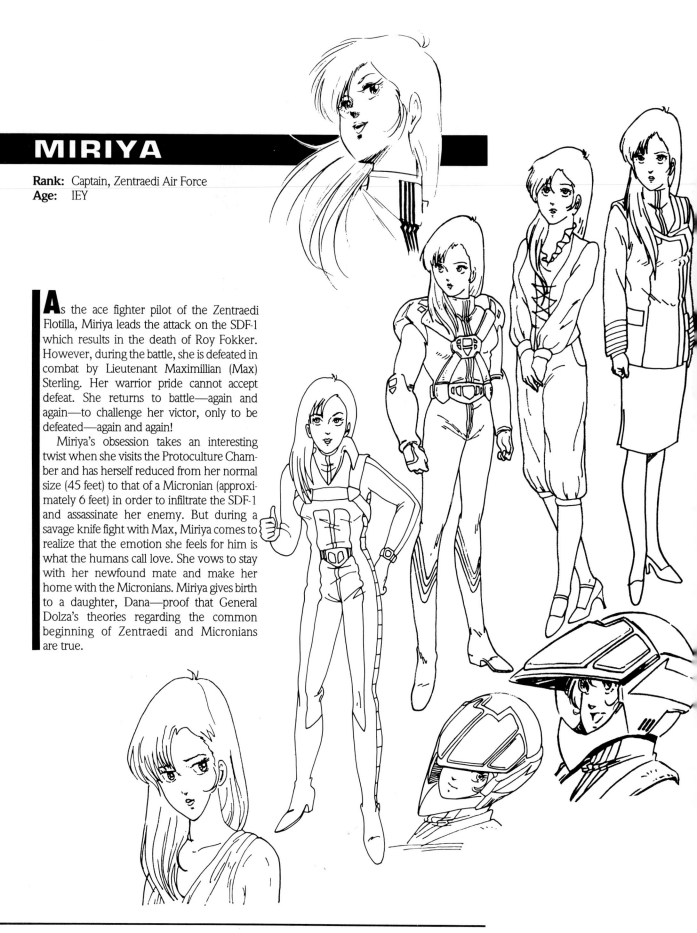

As the ace fighter pilot of the Zentraedi Flotilla, Miriya leads the attack on the SDF-1 which results in the death of Roy Fokker. However, during the battle, she is defeated in combat by Lieutenant Maximillian (Max) Sterling. Her warrior pride cannot accept defeat. She returns to battle—again and again—to challenge her victor, only to be defeated—again and again!

Miriya's obsession takes an interesting twist when she visits the Protoculture Chamber and has herself reduced from her normal size (45 feet) to that of a Micronian (approximately 6 feet) in order to infiltrate the SDF-1 and assassinate her enemy. But during a savage knife fight with Max, Miriya comes to realize that the emotion she feels for him is what the humans call love. She vows to stay with her newfound mate and make her home with the Micronians. Miriya gives birth to a daughter, Dana—proof that General Dolza's theories regarding the common beginning of Zentraedi and Micronians are true.

DOLZA

Rank: General
Age: IEY

Dolza is the supreme commander of the Zentraedi Armada. His interest in Robotechnology and the SDF-1 stems from the Zentraedi's inability to repair any of the equipment in their vast armada. This was one of the safeguards built into the system by the Robotech Masters when the Zentraedi were created. While Dolza is unaware of the details of the system, he is intelligent enough to guess at these secrets with amazing accuracy. Dolza forbids his soldiers to come into contact with the Micronians in any way other than assigned military missions. He reasons that there is more of a connection between the Zentraedi and the Micronians than either side is aware of. Eventually, he discovers that his theories are true.

AZONIA

Rank: Zentraedi Warlord
Age: IEY

Azonia is the commander of the female pilots. She is a skilled, respected, and powerful warrior. It would seem that her unusual relationship with Khyron is as confusing to her as it would be to her fellow Zentraedi—if it were openly known. In her way, Azonia is as arrogant as her lover. . .a trait too common among the Zentraedi Warlords during the various battles for the SDF-1.

BRON, RICO, and KONDA

Rank: Intelligence Operatives
Age: IEY

Bron, Rico, and Konda are Zentraedi spies sent to infiltrate the SDF-1 to gather information which would be of value in plotting the defeat of the Micronians. As spies, they try to blend into their surroundings, to become an unnoticeable part of the Micronian culture. They succeed too well. Not only are they seduced by the Micronian way of life, they fall in love with the SDF-1 bridge crew trio—Kim Young, Sammie Porter, and Vanessa Leeds—as well. They become typical of the Zentraedi deserter. Impressed with what they perceive to be an ideal lifestyle—and Lynn Minmei's singing—they flock in droves to the SDF-1 and, ultimately, Earth for sanctuary. Bron, Rico, and Konda are three of the first Zentraedi to be incorporated into the refugee population of Macross City.

SDF-1—ATTACK MODE

In the attack mode as seen here, the SDF-1 is a powerful weapon system. Its main guns are capable of destroying thousands of targets in a single energy blast. There is also a pin-point barrier system which is in effect when the ship is in the Attack Mode. A modification of this Barrier System itself becomes a weapon as the crew of the SDF-1 learns more about this mysterious vessel.

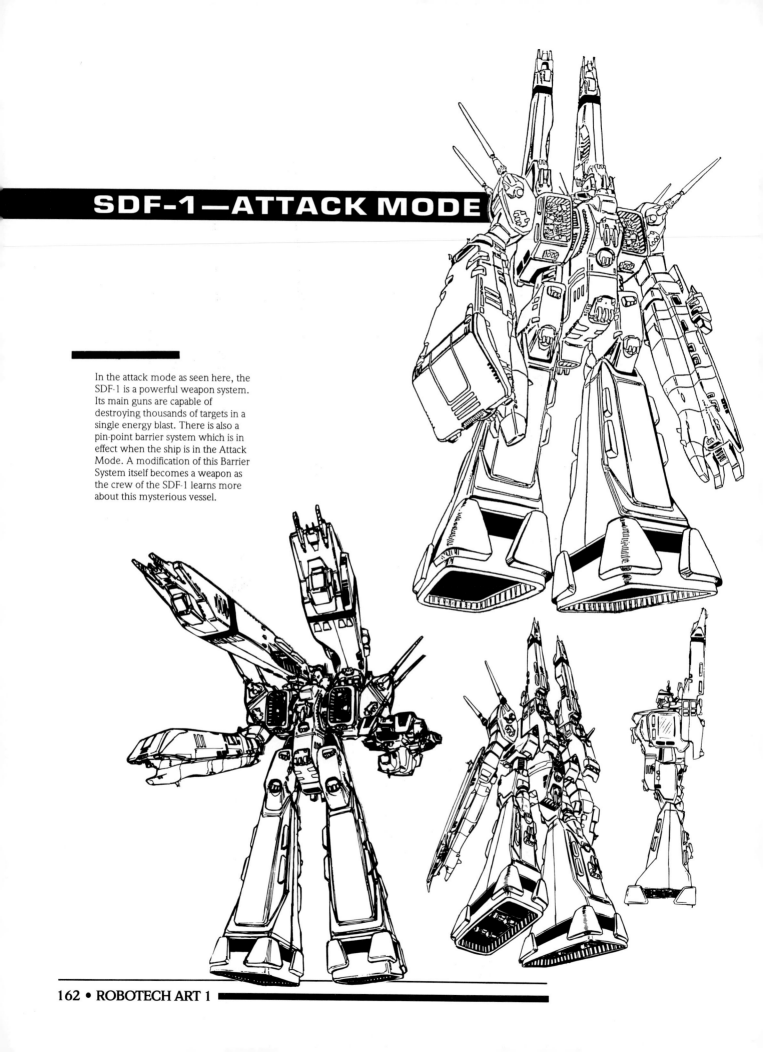

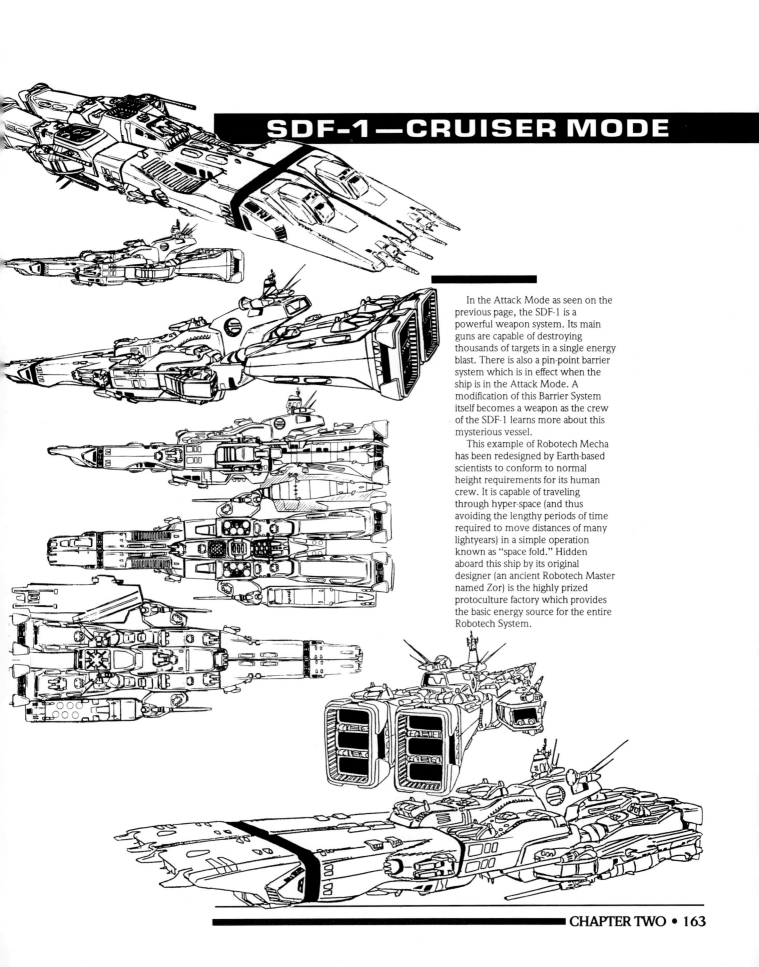

SDF-1—CRUISER MODE

In the Attack Mode as seen on the previous page, the SDF-1 is a powerful weapon system. Its main guns are capable of destroying thousands of targets in a single energy blast. There is also a pin-point barrier system which is in effect when the ship is in the Attack Mode. A modification of this Barrier System itself becomes a weapon as the crew of the SDF-1 learns more about this mysterious vessel.

This example of Robotech Mecha has been redesigned by Earth-based scientists to conform to normal height requirements for its human crew. It is capable of traveling through hyper-space (and thus avoiding the lengthy periods of time required to move distances of many lightyears) in a simple operation known as "space fold." Hidden aboard this ship by its original designer (an ancient Robotech Master named Zor) is the highly prized protoculture factory which provides the basic energy source for the entire Robotech System.

SDF-1 INTERIORS

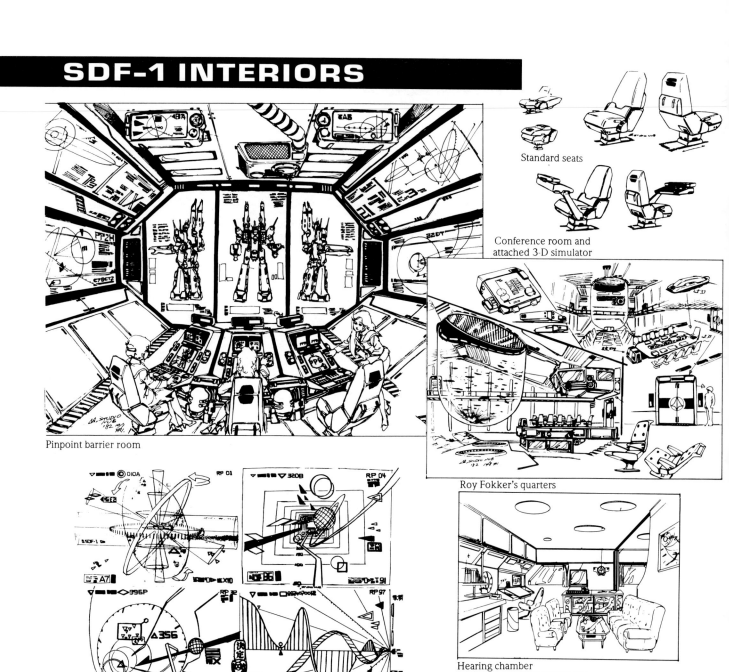

Pinpoint barrier room

Standard seats

Conference room and attached 3-D simulator

Roy Fokker's quarters

Hearing chamber

Standard examples of 3-D projector readings

Deca-missile launcher

Captain Gloval's private room

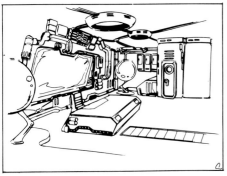

Captain Gloval's quarters

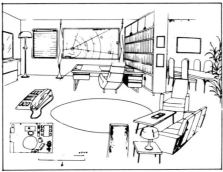

Investigation room

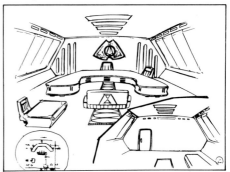

Panoramic view of the barrier systems

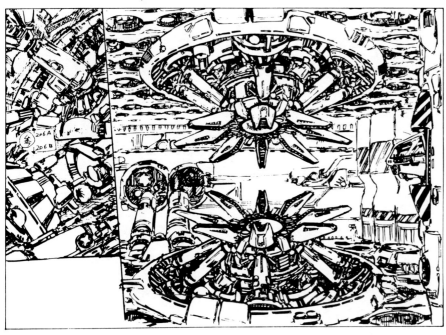

Bridge in transition

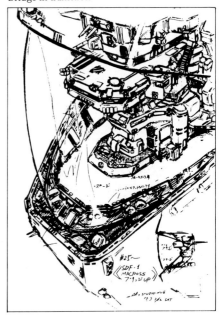

Mechanical passageway

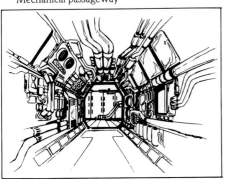

Shipboard corridor

Waiting room

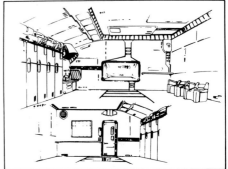

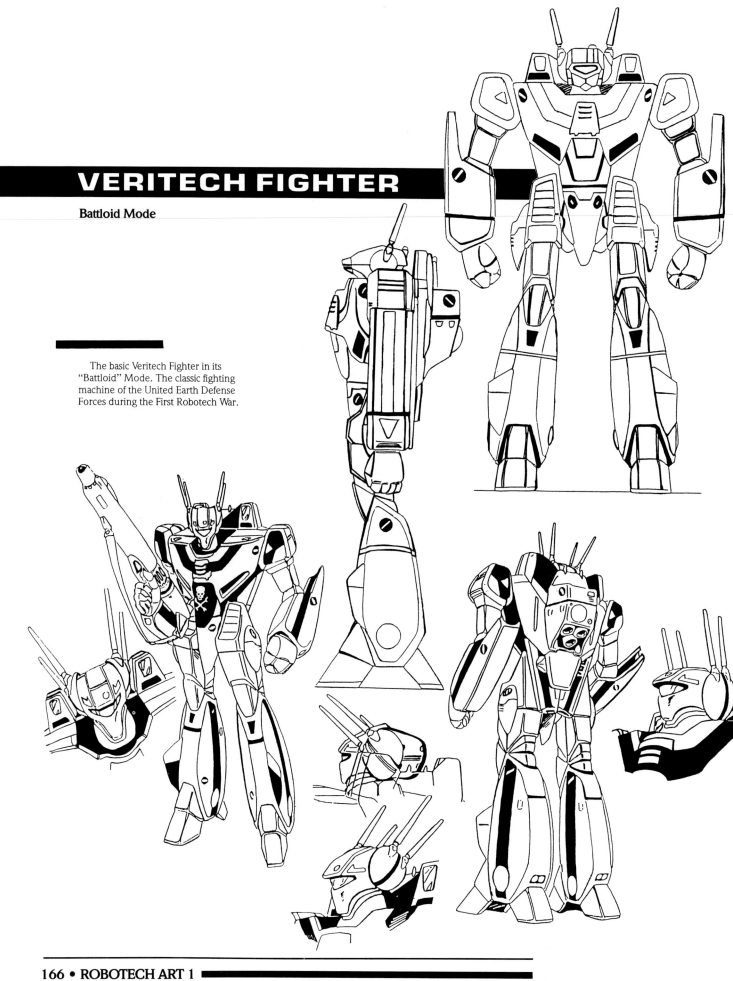

VERITECH FIGHTER

Battloid Mode

The basic Veritech Fighter in its "Battloid" Mode. The classic fighting machine of the United Earth Defense Forces during the First Robotech War.

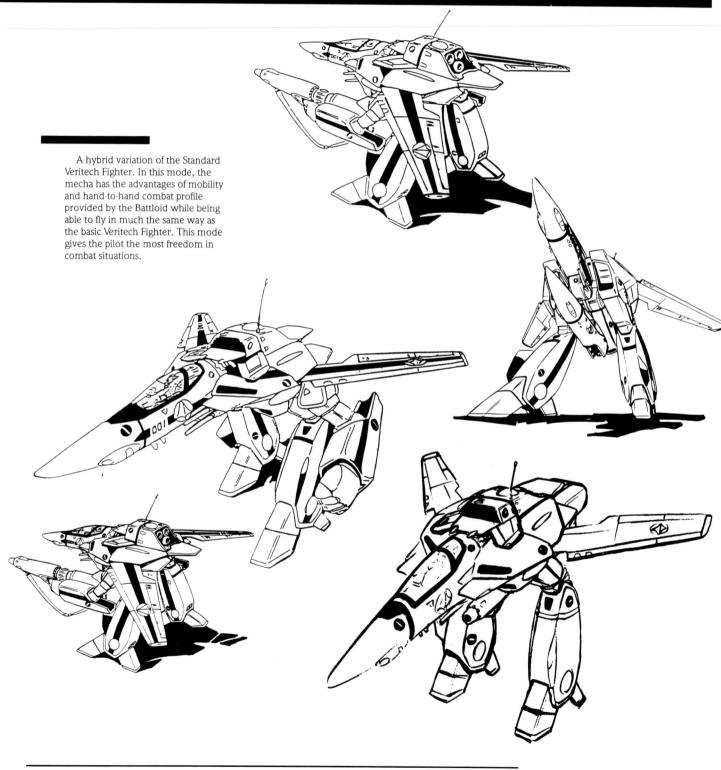

A hybrid variation of the Standard Veritech Fighter. In this mode, the mecha has the advantages of mobility and hand-to-hand combat profile provided by the Battloid while being able to fly in much the same way as the basic Veritech Fighter. This mode gives the pilot the most freedom in combat situations.

ZENTRAEDI FLAG SHIP

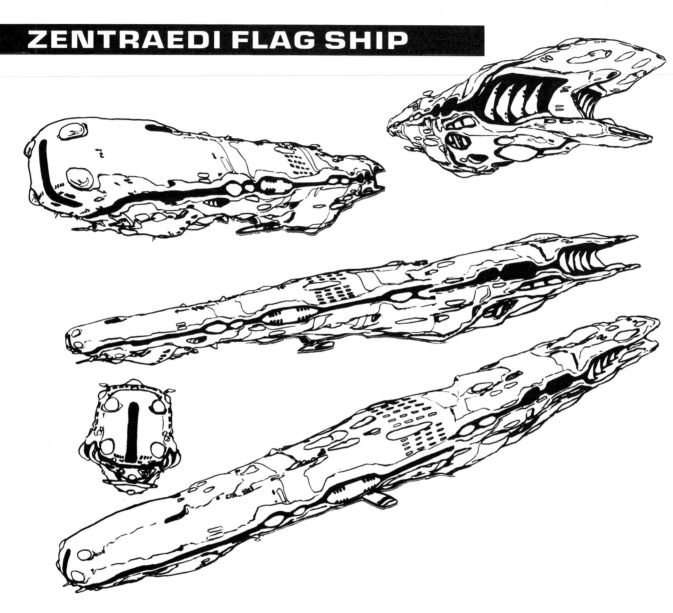

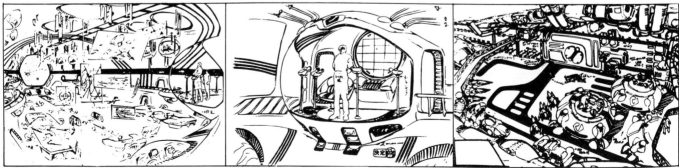

Bridge   Commander's room   Mid-size hangar

TACTICAL BATTLE POD

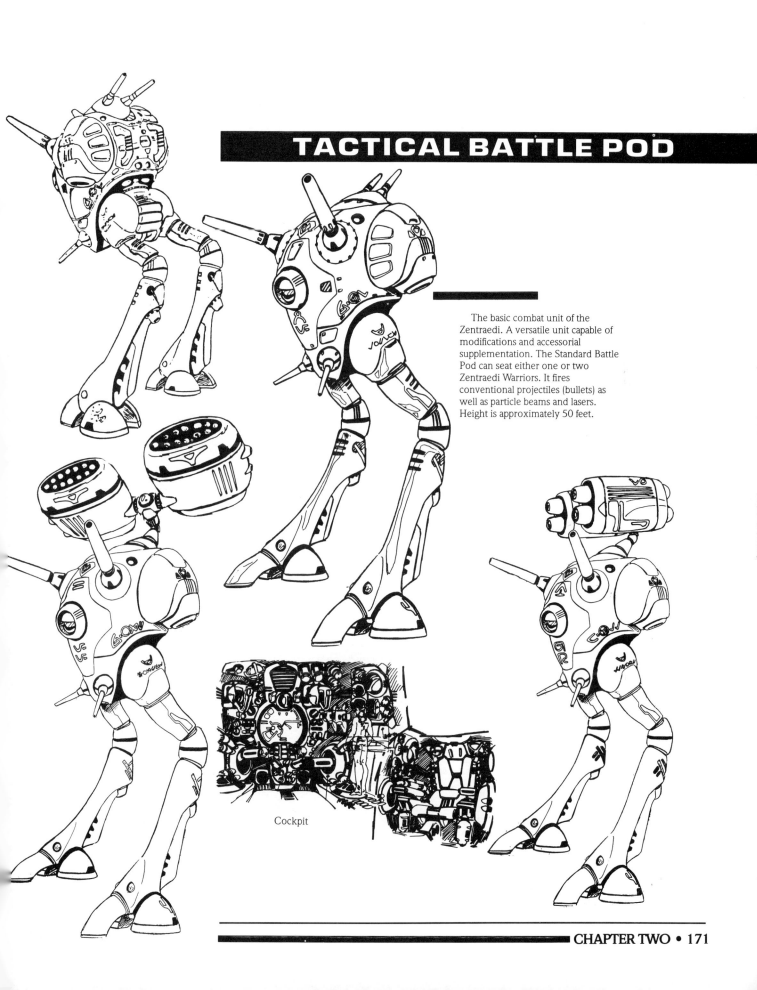

The basic combat unit of the Zentraedi. A versatile unit capable of modifications and accessorial supplementation. The Standard Battle Pod can seat either one or two Zentraedi Warriors. It fires conventional projectiles (bullets) as well as particle beams and lasers. Height is approximately 50 feet.

Cockpit

OFFICER'S BATTLE POD

Standard Issue of Combat Armour for use by the elite Officer Class of the Zentraedi Army. It is able to function in deep space as a highly maneuverable weapon system as well as act as an effective combat unit on terrain found on planets such as Earth. An impressive array of weapon systems is made available to the pilots of these mecha systems.

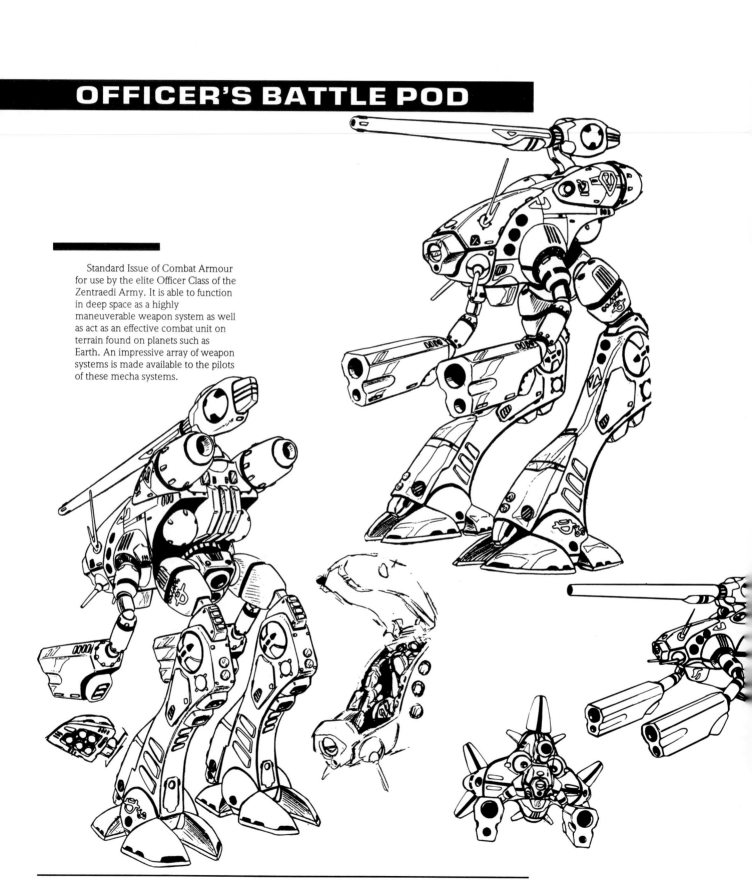

CHAPTER 3 THE ROBOTECH MASTERS
Characters & Mecha

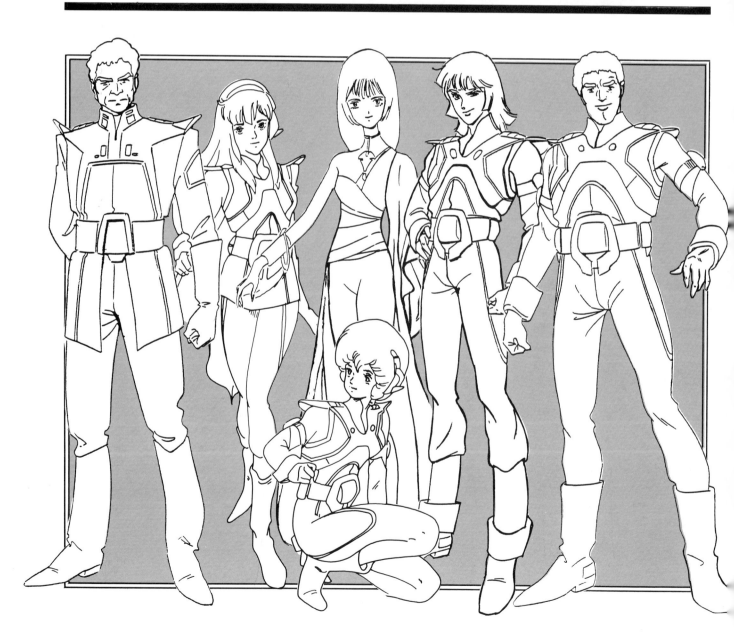

DANA STERLING

Rank: Lieutenant
Age: 18

The daughter of Max and Miriya Sterling, Dana is not only the first child born from a union between two races, she is the first child to be born from the womb of a clone. Dana is among the first graduates of the Robotech Military Academy founded in the aftermath of the First Robotech War. Dana is very feminine. Her child-like curiosity combined with her natural intelligence, compassion, and curiosity seem odd combinations to make a successful soldier, but somehow, it works. Crossbreeding gives her the added dimension of precognition concerning the Robotech Masters and their schemes. She also shares an unusual psychic bond with the renegade clone, Zor Prime. Dana is the catalyst for much of the action that takes place during the Second Robotech War.

DANA STERLING

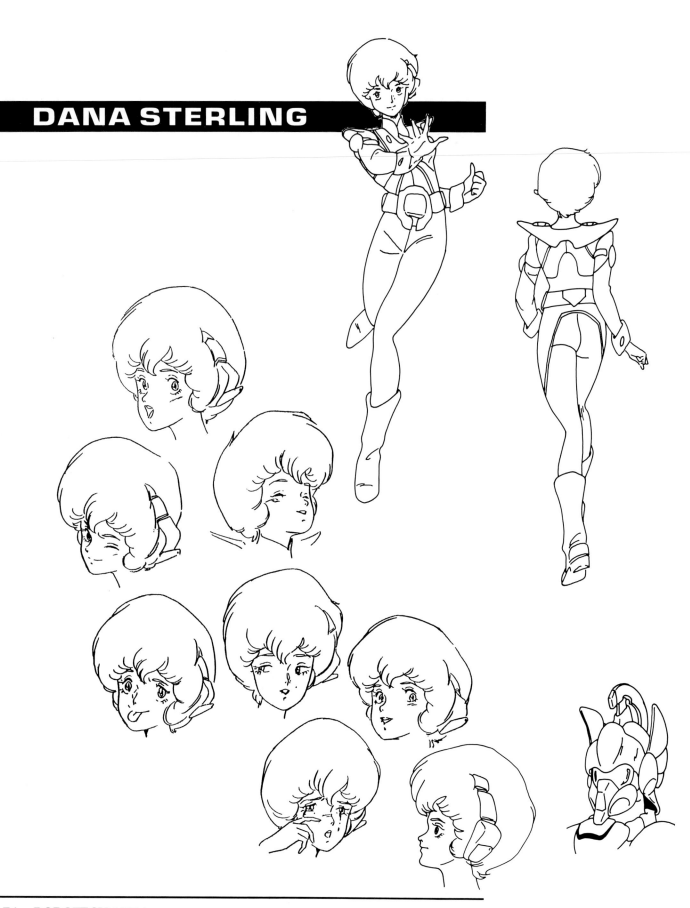

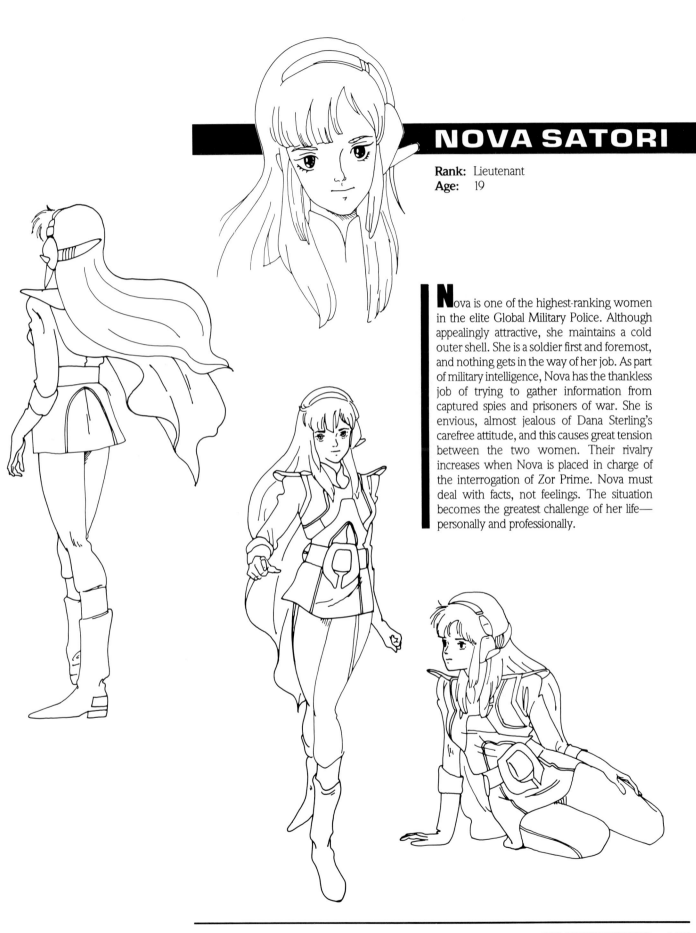

NOVA SATORI

Rank: Lieutenant
Age: 19

Nova is one of the highest-ranking women in the elite Global Military Police. Although appealingly attractive, she maintains a cold outer shell. She is a soldier first and foremost, and nothing gets in the way of her job. As part of military intelligence, Nova has the thankless job of trying to gather information from captured spies and prisoners of war. She is envious, almost jealous of Dana Sterling's carefree attitude, and this causes great tension between the two women. Their rivalry increases when Nova is placed in charge of the interrogation of Zor Prime. Nova must deal with facts, not feelings. The situation becomes the greatest challenge of her life—personally and professionally.

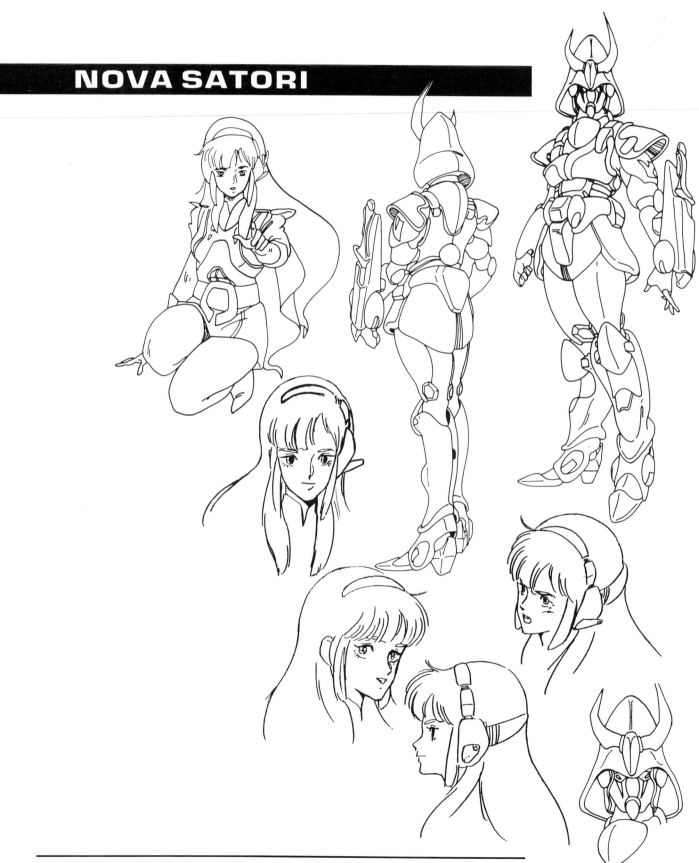

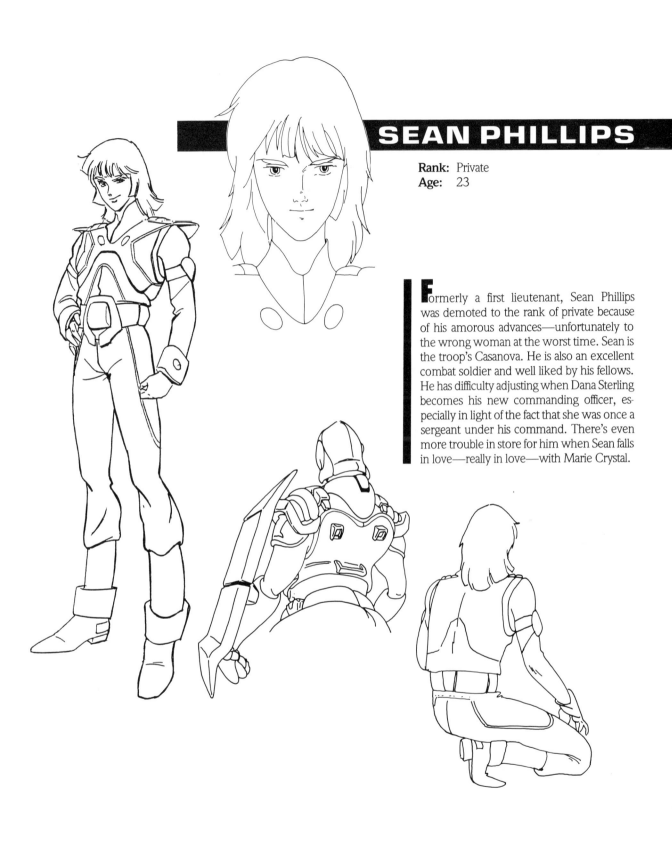

SEAN PHILLIPS

Rank: Private
Age: 23

Formerly a first lieutenant, Sean Phillips was demoted to the rank of private because of his amorous advances—unfortunately to the wrong woman at the worst time. Sean is the troop's Casanova. He is also an excellent combat soldier and well liked by his fellows. He has difficulty adjusting when Dana Sterling becomes his new commanding officer, especially in light of the fact that she was once a sergeant under his command. There's even more trouble in store for him when Sean falls in love—really in love—with Marie Crystal.

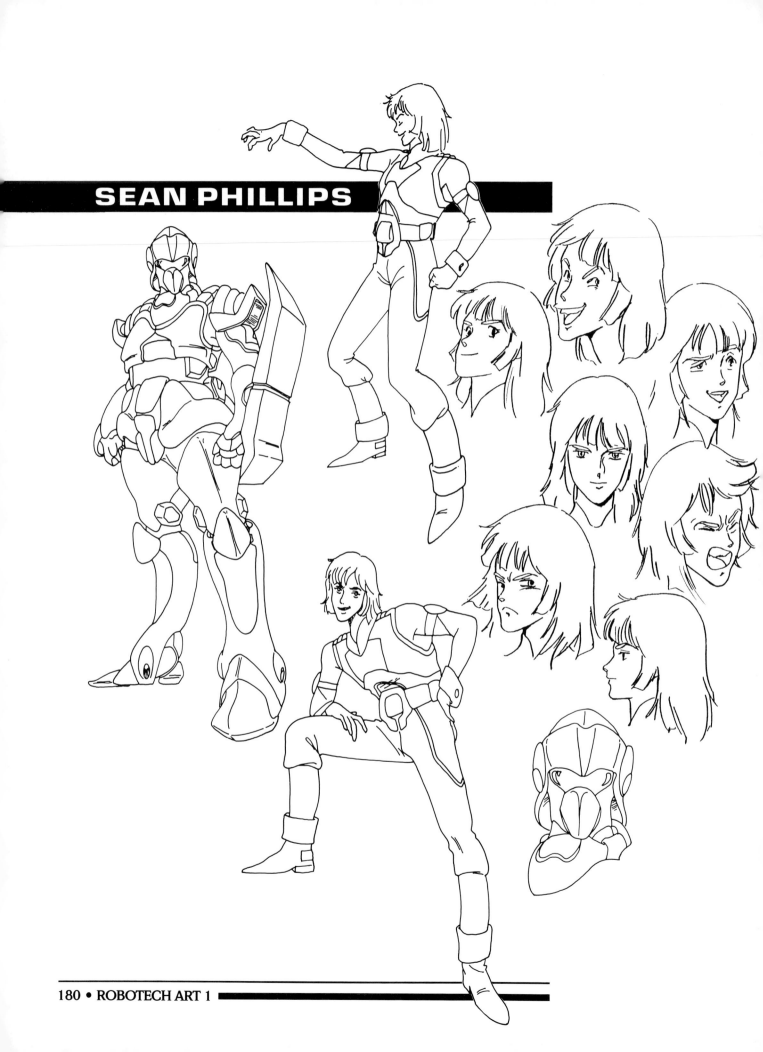

SEAN PHILLIPS

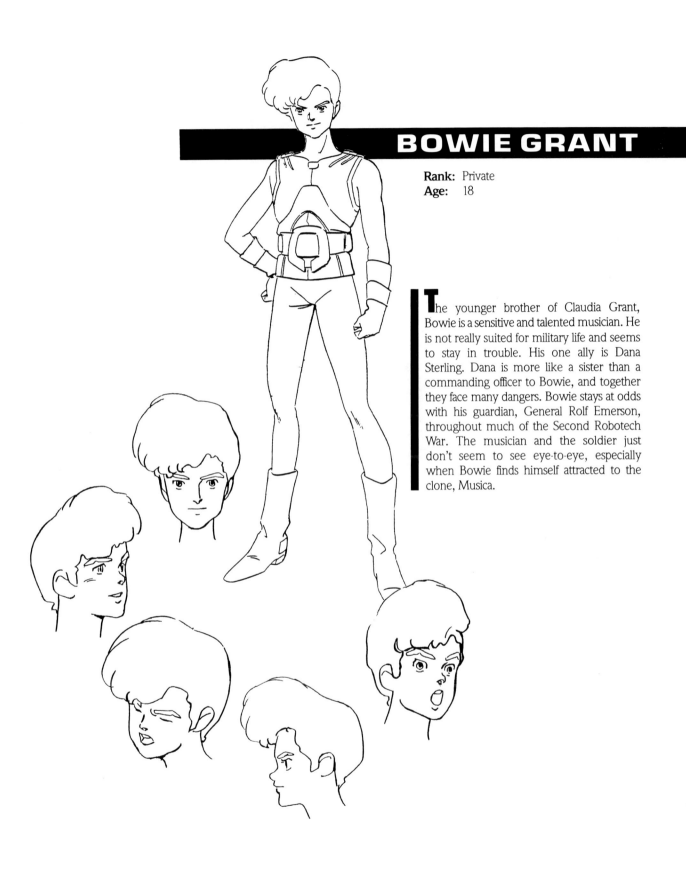

BOWIE GRANT

Rank: Private
Age: 18

The younger brother of Claudia Grant, Bowie is a sensitive and talented musician. He is not really suited for military life and seems to stay in trouble. His one ally is Dana Sterling. Dana is more like a sister than a commanding officer to Bowie, and together they face many dangers. Bowie stays at odds with his guardian, General Rolf Emerson, throughout much of the Second Robotech War. The musician and the soldier just don't seem to see eye-to-eye, especially when Bowie finds himself attracted to the clone, Musica.

MARIE CRYSTAL

Rank: Lieutenant
Age: 20

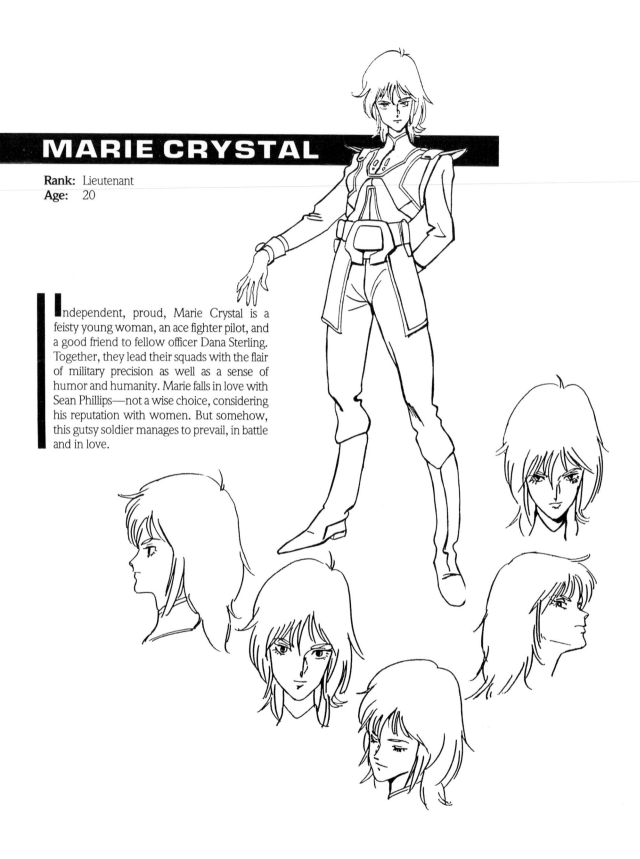

Independent, proud, Marie Crystal is a feisty young woman, an ace fighter pilot, and a good friend to fellow officer Dana Sterling. Together, they lead their squads with the flair of military precision as well as a sense of humor and humanity. Marie falls in love with Sean Phillips—not a wise choice, considering his reputation with women. But somehow, this gutsy soldier manages to prevail, in battle and in love.

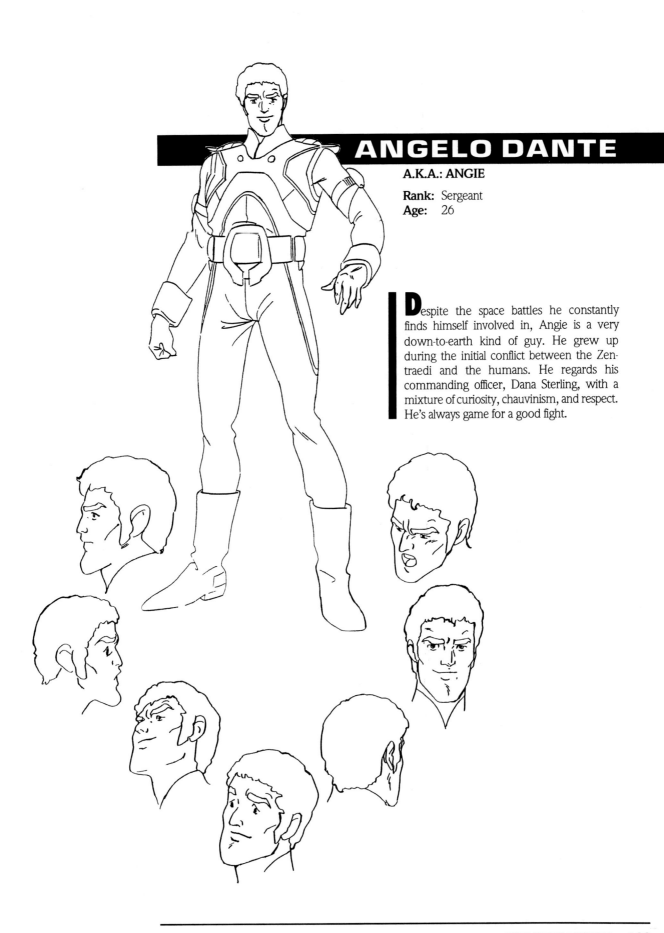

ANGELO DANTE

A.K.A.: ANGIE

Rank: Sergeant
Age: 26

Despite the space battles he constantly finds himself involved in, Angie is a very down-to-earth kind of guy. He grew up during the initial conflict between the Zentraedi and the humans. He regards his commanding officer, Dana Sterling, with a mixture of curiosity, chauvinism, and respect. He's always game for a good fight.

LOUIE NICHOLS

Rank: Corporal
Age: 20

Louie lives in a world of his own creation. A lanky hybrid of punk and nerd, the young genius excels in mechanical dexterity and lives only for the study of Robotechnology. He is constantly tinkering with various "mecha." As a result, he becomes quite an inventor. It would seem that if Louie can think of a machine he needs to solve a certain problem, all he has to do is sit down long enough to fiddle with enough circuits, chips, and metals, and—*Voila!* His only dissatisfaction comes about when his machinery is put to use in ways he did not intend.

ROLF EMERSON

Rank: General
Age: 46

Rolf Emerson is an example of the military's finest. Respected by his troops and fellow officers for his skill and humanity, he plays out his hand in the Second Robotech War with a singular sense of purpose. He is Bowie Grant's guardian. While he feels responsible for the young man and takes his commitment seriously, it's obvious that he feels genuine affection for Bowie as well. He is constantly at odds with Supreme Commander Leonard, and despite his own rank, Emerson finds himself and his men in the unhappy position of playing sacrificial pawns in Leonard's futile attempt to destroy the Robotech Masters.

LEONARD

Rank: Supreme Commander, Earth Forces
Age: 56

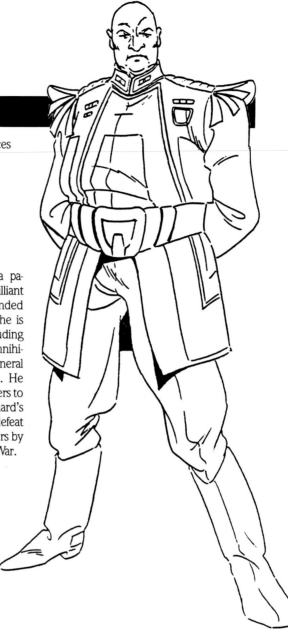

Supreme Commander Leonard is a pathetic bigot. A skilled soldier and brilliant tactician, the man is nevertheless so blinded by his fear of the invading aliens that he is willing to sacrifice everything—including Earth and her people—in an effort to annihilate the Robotech Masters. Unlike General Emerson, he is unwilling to negotiate. He would prefer the murder of alien prisoners to their interrogation. In the end, it is Leonard's unreasoning fear that brings about the defeat of the humans and the Robotech Masters by the Invid during the Second Robotech War.

THE ROBOTECH MASTERS

Rank: Masters of Robotechnology
Age: IEY

The Robotech Masters are the ones who first send the Zentraedi Forces after the SDF-1 and the protoculture factory hidden on board the ship. After the end of the First Robotech War, the Robotech Masters make a fifteen-year journey to Earth. They are desperate to obtain the protoculture factory.

During the journey, the Robotech Masters use up most of the precious protoculture matrix in order to allow their mecha and clone workers to function properly. These aliens are enveloped with a keen sense of urgency. They must have the protoculture for their race to continue along the path they have devised! Not only that, they have discovered an Invid sensor nebula scouting the fourth quadrant of the galaxy in the vicinity of Earth. Now it becomes a race against the biological clock to get the protoculture before it has a chance to mutate into the Invid Flower of Life. The Robotech Masters know that if they cannot recover the protoculture, or if it is found in its mutated condition, their only alternative to preserve the balance of the universe (as they see it) is to destroy the matrix and the host planet—Earth!

The Robotech Masters are ageless and arrogant. They have devised a lifestyle where the lesser peoples—clones—wait on their betters, the Robotech Masters. These aliens originally created the Zentraedi Warriors and the clones to serve the Robotech Masters. This class structure has continued for countless generations and has evolved into a lifeless, stagnant situation. The Robotech Masters cannot conceive of their creations as individual units, only as property. As a matter of course, in order to preserve a sense of dependency, they have devised a triad lifestyle wherein the clone slaves live and mate in groups of three. Independent thought and/or action outside the triad is severely punished.

Why did the Robotech Masters devise such a class structure? The original Masters were obviously brilliant to have been able to develop and nurture the sciences their descendants live by. Unfortunately, during the time of the Second Robotech War, the society has closed in on itself. It has already reached the height of its grandeur and seems to be waiting to die.

ZOR PRIME

Rank: Bioroid Pilot
Age: Undetermined

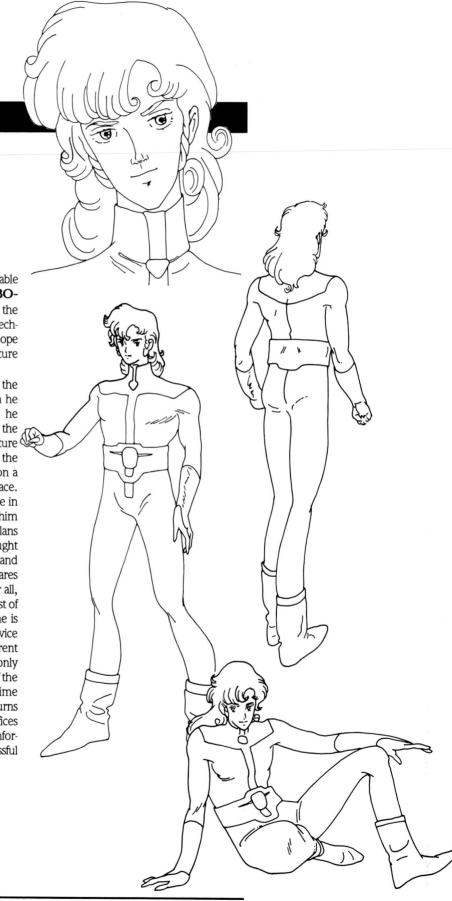

Zor Prime is one of the most memorable and tragic heroes in the story of **ROBO-TECH.** The handsome youth is actually the first clone of Zor, the father of Robotechnology. He is the Robotech Masters' last hope to regain the secrets of the protoculture factory and Robotechnology.

The original Zor did not agree with the philosophy of his fellow scientists. When he developed the science of Robotech, he safeguarded the material by hiding all of the data along with the only existing protoculture seed factory in the reflex furnaces of the SDF-1. Then he sent the battle fortress on a one-way trip into the nether regions of space. The Robotech Masters activate Zor Prime in an effort to regain Zor's secrets and to use him as a spy against the humans. Their plans backfire. The clone shares the same thought patterns as the original Zor. Old images and memories return in a series of nightmares that are a source of untold torment. After all, Zor Prime is literally thrown into the midst of the humans. His military captors think he is one of the humans shanghaied into service for the invading aliens and an apparent amnesia victim. This cruel treatment is only another example of the callous attitude of the Robotech Masters. Eventually Zor Prime discovers who and what he is. He turns against the Robotech Masters and sacrifices himself to destroy the galactic tyrants. Unfortunately, his noble act results in the successful Invid invasion of Earth.

MUSICA

Rank: Clone, Non-military Status
Age: Undetermined

Musica, with her sisters Musell and Musie, are responsible for keeping the worker-clones content. Musica plays the cosmic harp, an instrument as lovely and resonant as its musician. Musica is happy in her position until she meets the human (and fellow musician), Bowie Grant. Her immediate and impossible attraction to the young man changes her life. To the alarm of her sisters and friends, she begins to question the ways of the Robotech Masters. Unable to condone the life-style imposed on her and her people, the gentle Musica eventually becomes one of the leading figures in the rebellion against the Robotech Masters.

KARNO

Rank: Lieutenant
Age: Undetermined

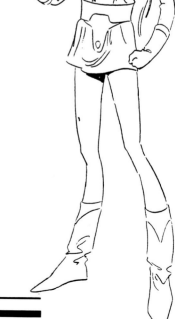

Karno is an example of the Robotech Masters' breeding and conditioning. The Robotech Masters intend him to be Musica's mate. The lovely musician rejects him because of her love for the Micronian, Bowie Grant. Karno is more upset over her independent thought, her rebellion against the "Robotech Way," than her personal commitment to another man. He cannot accept any changes in "the way." As a result, he seeks retreat in the military, hoping to destroy the Micronian menace before it corrupts any more of the Robotech people.

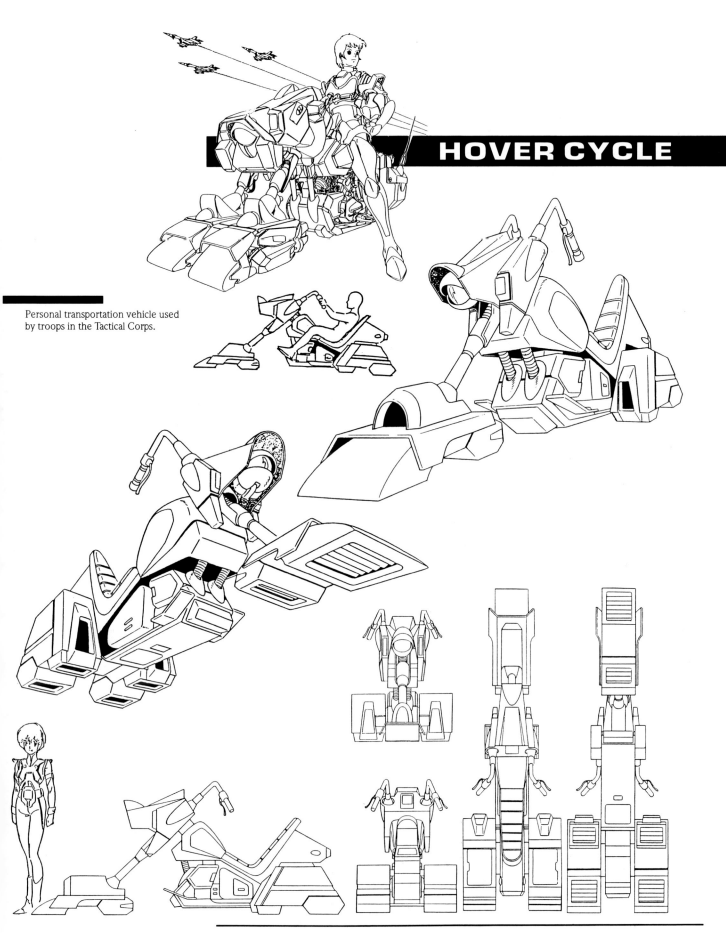

HOVER CYCLE

Personal transportation vehicle used by troops in the Tactical Corps.

VERITECH HOVER TANK

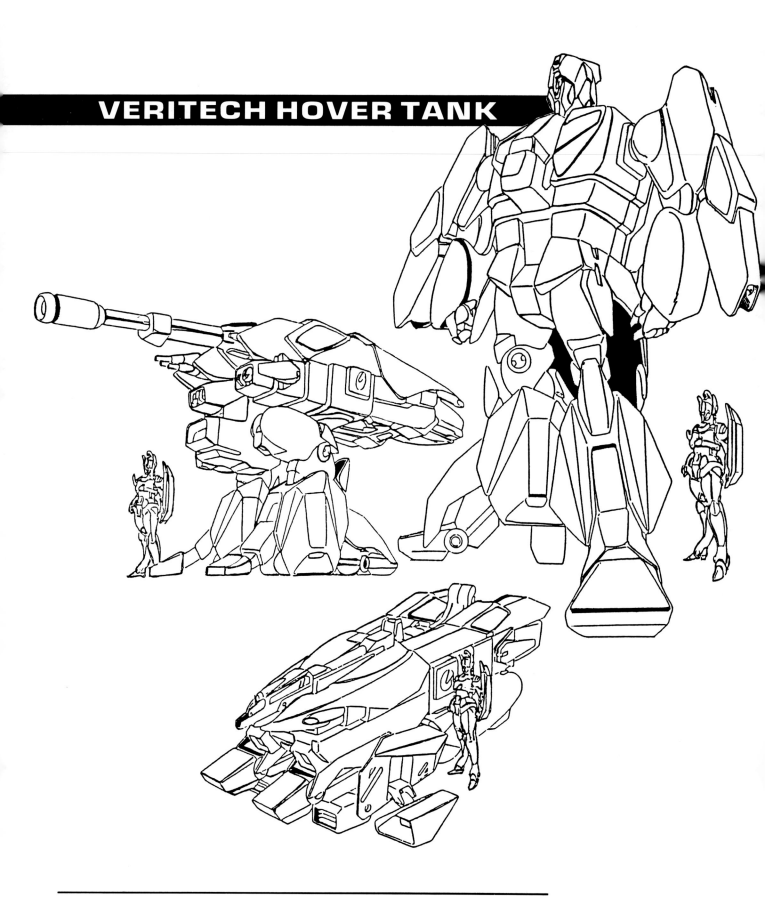

VERITECH COPTER

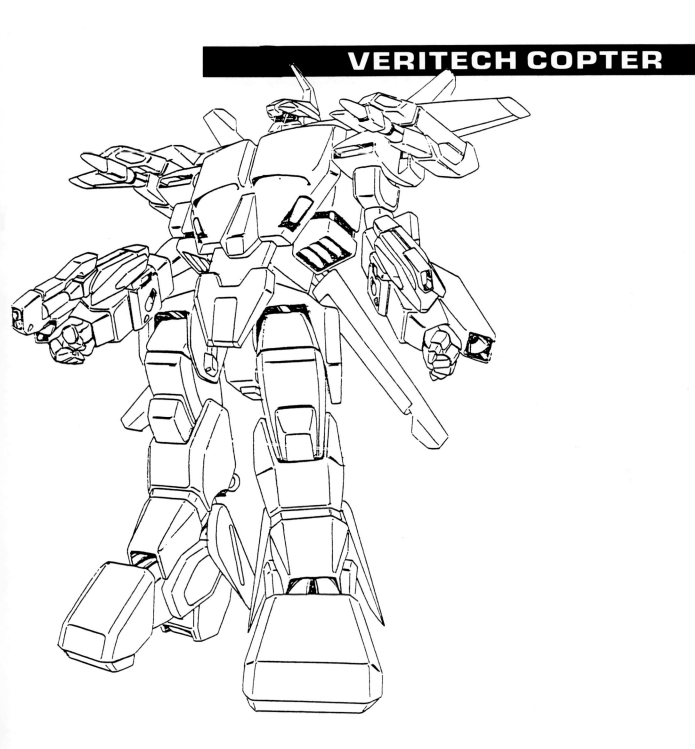

STANDARD COMBAT BIOROID

A unique symbiotic coupling of an enlarged android and a first-stage clone pilot. Controlled telepathically by Clonemasters who direct up to 200 Bioroids at a time, they are the most common element of the Robotech Masters' personal army following the fall of their Zentraedi warriors.

The clone pilot sits in a control unit which translates simple monitor responses of the unthinking clone into articulated movement in corresponding areas of the larger Bioroid. In instances when the Bioroid is piloted by second- and even third-stage clones who show marked signs of increased intelligence, the response time of the Bioroid increases in direct relationship to the mental level exhibited by the clone pilot.

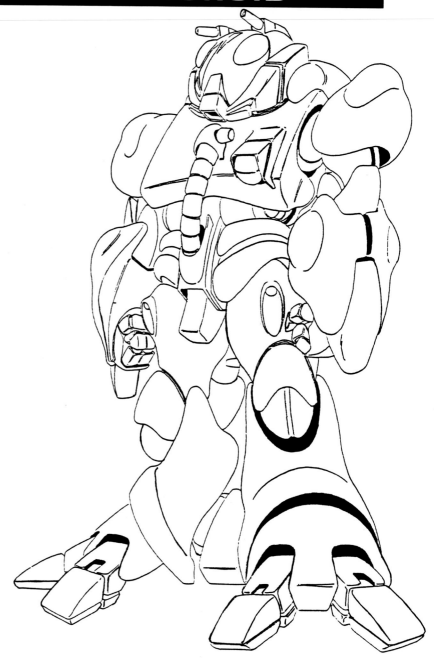

BIOROID HOVER CRAFT

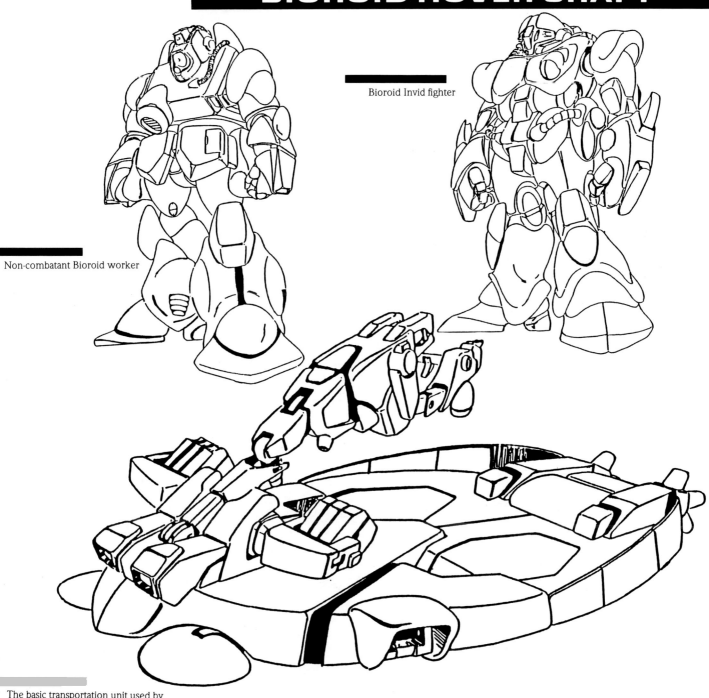

Bioroid Invid fighter

Non-combatant Bioroid worker

The basic transportation unit used by the Bioroid to travel through the vast maze-like confines of the Robotech Masters' massive floating planetoids. They can be used in both combat and non-combat situations.

TACTICAL AIR FORCE

The basic Air Force Division of the United Earth Government. This is the division which trains combat pilots and all technical support teams for conventional (non-space-related) missions.

CIVIL DEFENSE UNIT

This division is used as basic civilian policing force. They are assigned to protect the local cities and encampments and provide a high profile for the United Earth Government.

CIVIL DEFENSE FLYING CORPS

A self-explanatory concept. This squad works in conjunction with the Civil Defense Unit to police the non-military outposts and cities which have sprung up after the First Robotech War.

COSMIC UNITS

These are the troops of the United Earth Government who guard the various off-world military outposts and orbiting space stations which provide security and research for the Robotech Research Group. They can function as pilots in case of emergency.

GROUND-BASED MILITARY POLICE

A highly secretive organization which reports directly to the supreme commander of the United Earth Government's Army of the Southern Cross. This secret police group monitors internal affairs and functions as the headquarters for intelligence gathering. The most elite division of the Government's military profile, the GMP often acts on its own without the approval or knowledge of their superiors.

ALPHA TACTICAL ARMORED CORPS

The elite unit of the tactical corps assigned the task of piloting the remarkable Veritech Hover Tank—a transformable heavy armoured personnel combat vehicle. The Alpha Corps is able to work with most of the various divisions of the United Earth Government's other tactical groups. Only the best soldiers are inducted into the Alpha Corps.

TACTICAL CORPS

The basic infantry unit of the United Earth Government. This division is the equivalent of the contemporary United States Marine Corps. They are able to go into a variety of terrains and environments with a simple change of uniform.

TACTICAL ARMORED SPACE CORPS

The equivalent of the Alpha Squad in regard to their elite status in the United Earth Government's Air Force. The pilots of the Armoured Space Corps are assigned to the Veritech AJACS—a transformable attack 'copter capable of prolonged flight in outer space. They also pilot a version of the Veritech Drone Bomber—in the "Logan" Mode—which is a powerful offensive weapon system.

JUNGLE SQUAD

Variation on standard tactical corps. Difference is in ordnance of weaponry and combat armour.

RE-CON ESCORT PATROL

These are the members of the tactical corps responsible for all communications-related missions. They function as intelligence gatherers and provide tactical support for Groundbased Military Police.

MOUNTAIN OFFENSE SQUAD

A specialized branch of the tactical corps. This Squad is assigned the task of patrolling the many mountain ranges on the planet. A groundbased unit.

SEA SQUAD

Basically, the Navy Division of the Army of the Southern Cross. These troops work as either re-con or offensive units. Their action is confined to deep-water research in the development of protoculture.

HUMID CLIMATE OFFENSIVE SQUAD

Basically, the "Green Beret" of the tactical corps. These troops are assigned to marshy environments. They are masters at camouflage and infiltration.

DESERT SQUAD

The United Earth Government version of the "French Foreign Legion." Stationed at remote desert outposts, these troops man heavy artillery. They are savage fighters who relish the opportunity to engage in hand-to-hand combat.

COLD-WEATHER OFFENSIVE SQUAD

Another variation of the basic tactical corps. Assigned to the polar regions, these troops are assigned to protect the Robotech Research Scientists who are active in the region. They are also trained for first-strike capability.

BATTLE ARMOR

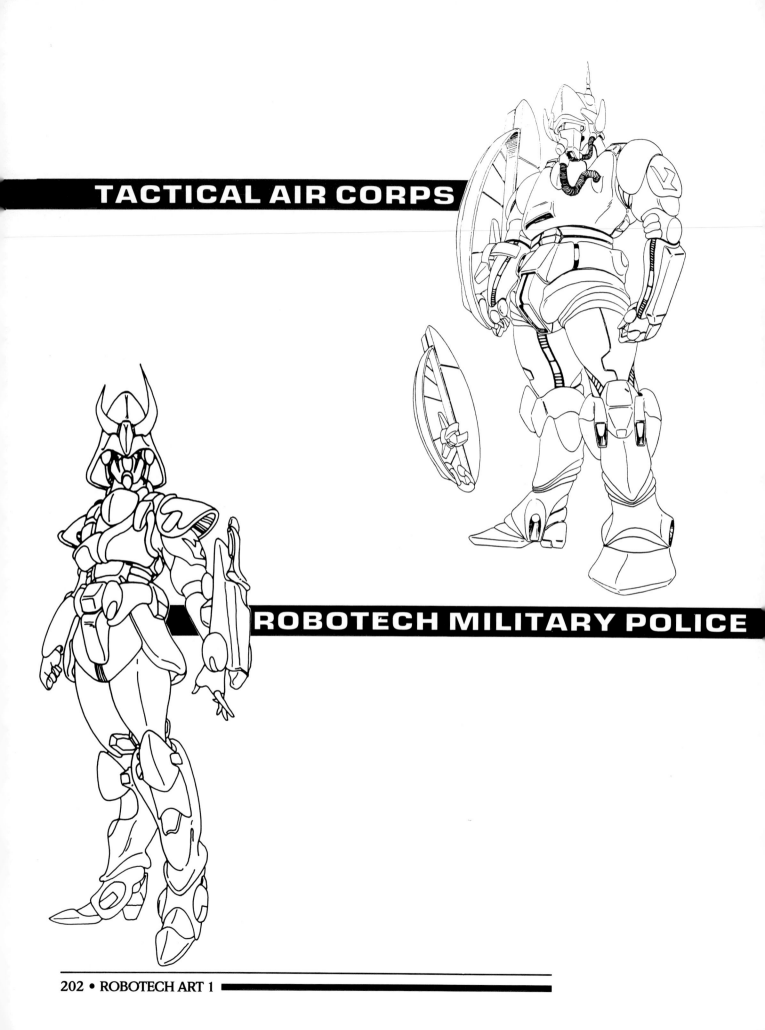

TACTICAL AIR CORPS

ROBOTECH MILITARY POLICE

CHAPTER 4 THE NEW GENERATION
Characters & Mecha

SCOTT BERNARD

Rank: Lieutenant
Age: 20

Born in outer space during the United Earth Government's Expeditionary Mission, Scott Bernard is one of the new generation of Robotech Defenders. He is a pilot in the Mars Division, one of the advanced interstellar battalions trying to reclaim Earth from the Invid. He returns to his ancestral planet as one of the only survivors from this advance Robotech detachment. Scott's fiancee, Marlene, was killed in the initial battle. When he recovers from the shock of his disastrous landing, Scott sets about to fulfill his mission to reach Reflex Point and join Admiral Rick Hunter's new army at all costs. A natural but sometimes reluctant leader, Scott accumulates other Earth rebels on the way to Reflex Point and forms a resistance force that battles the Invid invaders as they make their way to the ultimate battleground. A moody and driven young man, Scott must relearn the value of friendship from his new acquaintances as he moves toward his final goal.

Armored cyclone rider—Scott Bernard's model

Armored cyclones

LANCER

A.K.A.: YELLOW DANCER

Rank: Non-military status, Resistance Fighter, Entertainer

Age: 22

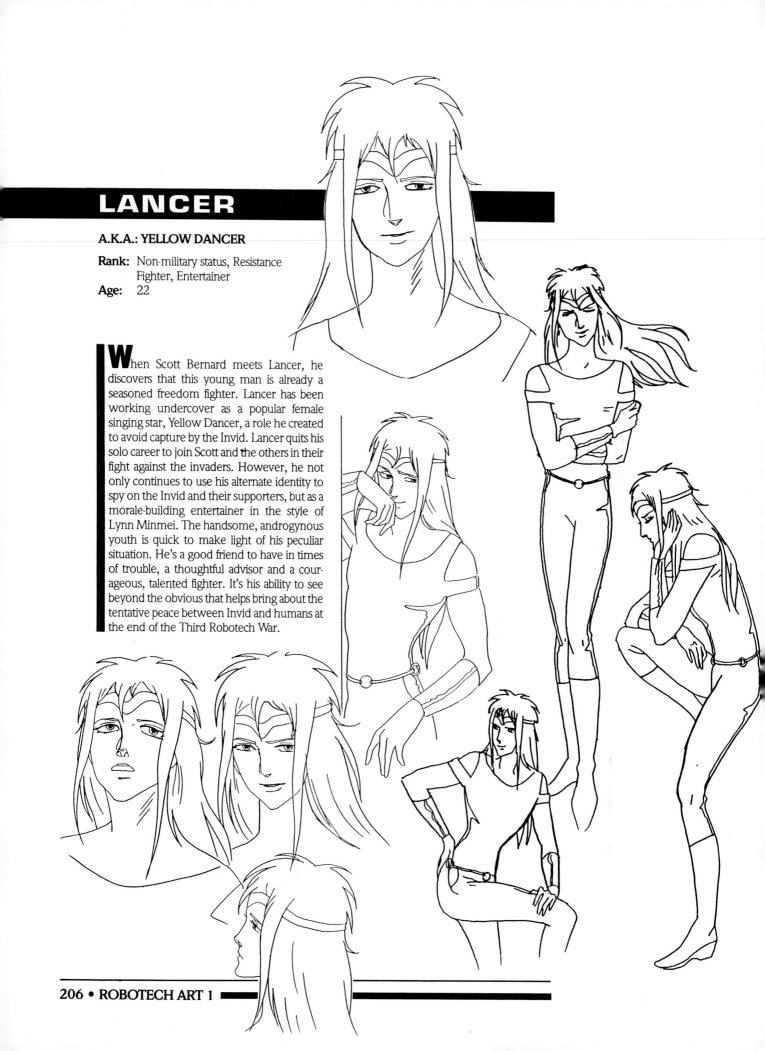

When Scott Bernard meets Lancer, he discovers that this young man is already a seasoned freedom fighter. Lancer has been working undercover as a popular female singing star, Yellow Dancer, a role he created to avoid capture by the Invid. Lancer quits his solo career to join Scott and the others in their fight against the invaders. However, he not only continues to use his alternate identity to spy on the Invid and their supporters, but as a morale-building entertainer in the style of Lynn Minmei. The handsome, androgynous youth is quick to make light of his peculiar situation. He's a good friend to have in times of trouble, a thoughtful advisor and a courageous, talented fighter. It's his ability to see beyond the obvious that helps bring about the tentative peace between Invid and humans at the end of the Third Robotech War.

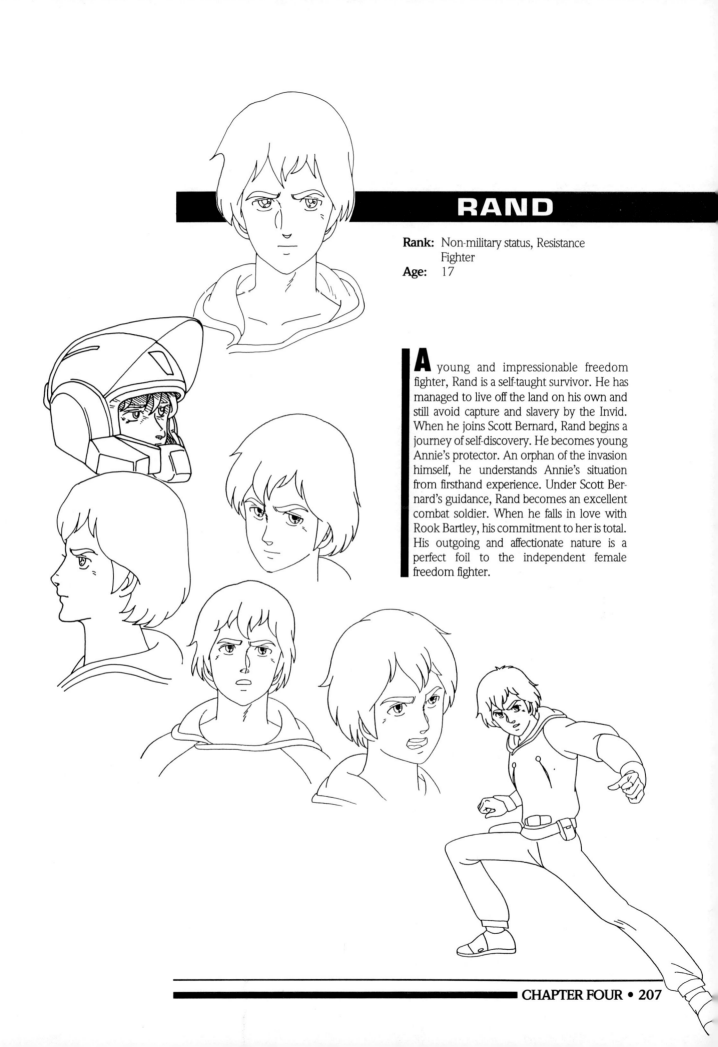

RAND

Rank: Non-military status, Resistance Fighter
Age: 17

A young and impressionable freedom fighter, Rand is a self-taught survivor. He has managed to live off the land on his own and still avoid capture and slavery by the Invid. When he joins Scott Bernard, Rand begins a journey of self-discovery. He becomes young Annie's protector. An orphan of the invasion himself, he understands Annie's situation from firsthand experience. Under Scott Bernard's guidance, Rand becomes an excellent combat soldier. When he falls in love with Rook Bartley, his commitment to her is total. His outgoing and affectionate nature is a perfect foil to the independent female freedom fighter.

RAND

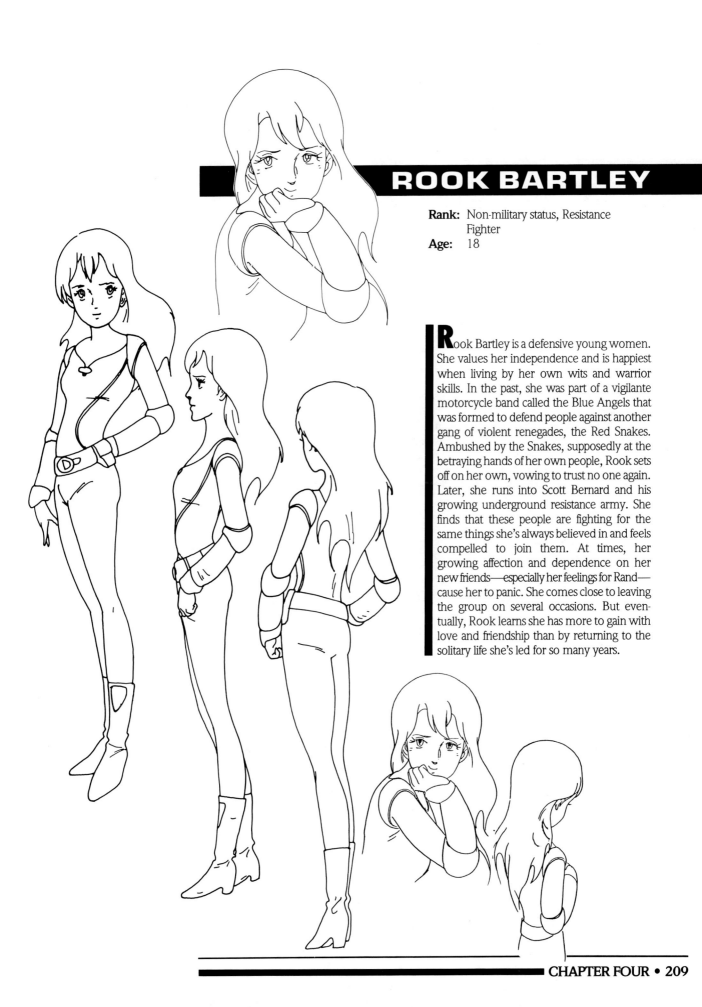

ROOK BARTLEY

Rank: Non-military status, Resistance Fighter

Age: 18

Rook Bartley is a defensive young women. She values her independence and is happiest when living by her own wits and warrior skills. In the past, she was part of a vigilante motorcycle band called the Blue Angels that was formed to defend people against another gang of violent renegades, the Red Snakes. Ambushed by the Snakes, supposedly at the betraying hands of her own people, Rook sets off on her own, vowing to trust no one again. Later, she runs into Scott Bernard and his growing underground resistance army. She finds that these people are fighting for the same things she's always believed in and feels compelled to join them. At times, her growing affection and dependence on her new friends—especially her feelings for Rand—cause her to panic. She comes close to leaving the group on several occasions. But eventually, Rook learns she has more to gain with love and friendship than by returning to the solitary life she's led for so many years.

ANNIE

A.K.A.: MINT

Rank: Non-military status
Age: 13

Spunky little Annie has the distinction of being the youngest in the family of resistance fighters that revolves around Scott and his mission to get to Reflex Point. Annie has lost her parents to the invasion, but it's apparent she has never known a happy home life. She sets about adopting a new family with a vengeance. Annie is an outrageous flirt, and frequently her enthusiasm gets her into more trouble than she can handle.

LUNK

Rank: Non-military status, Resistance
Fighter

Age: 25

In size alone, Lunk seems to be the resident brute of the underground army. However, his size is at war with his instincts, and he wages a personal battle against what he perceives to be his feelings of cowardice and inadequacy. His is a loving personality whose compassion for others is balanced by strength and courage. Lunk has a good sense of humor, a talent he frequently calls on—especially when he must take care of Annie.

THE
INVID
REGIS

Rank: Invid Queen Mother
Age: IEY

The Invid live by the word—and whim—of their Queen. As a representative of her race, Regis seems to exhibit the same arrogance and curiosity of Earth's previous invaders, the Robotech Masters. Like the Robotech Masters, the Invid have left their home to search for the protoculture substance they need to survive. They feel they can't afford to show the conquered humans any consideration; the Invid enslave what they don't destroy. They are unable to put down all of Earth's rebels. Scott Bernard's band of freedom fighters seem especially resistant to the Invid force. The Invid Queen Mother is a cool and calculating being, intelligent and ruthless. In her quest for knowledge, she has devised the Genesis Pits where she subjects Invid larvae to radical genetic reprogramming, turning them into various life forms such as dinosaurs, dragons, and humanoids in an effort to gain as much knowledge of the Earth, its inhabitants, and its history as possible.

Despite her alien nature, Regis feels responsible for her people in the same way Admiral Rick Hunter feels responsible for Earth and its people. When faced with the thought that the humans would annihilate the planet rather than subject themselves to life under Invid rule, Regis leads her people back into space. They consume the remnants of the protoculture and "rise to a higher plane."

MARLENE

A.K.A.: ARIEL

Rank: Non-military status, Invid Simulagent
Age: IEY

Marlene is one of the Invid larvae developed into a humanoid simulagent. She is placed within Scott Bernard's group of freedom fighters to act as a spy. The resistance force finds her at the scene of a recent Invid attack. They believe this beautiful young woman is an amnesia victim, still in shock and unable to talk due to the horrible traumas she's endured. Scott, Lancer, Rook, Rand, and the others adopt her into their family. Scott names the girl "Marlene" after his dead fiancee. Later, they discover that she is an Invid agent and her name is Ariel.

But Marlene *has* experienced trauma—although at the hands of her own people. She has been "dropped" in the humans' hands with little care or consideration. She has no idea that she is an Invid. She grows to trust and care for her companions. She also falls in love with Scott Bernard.

SERA

Rank: Invid Shock Trooper
Age: IEY

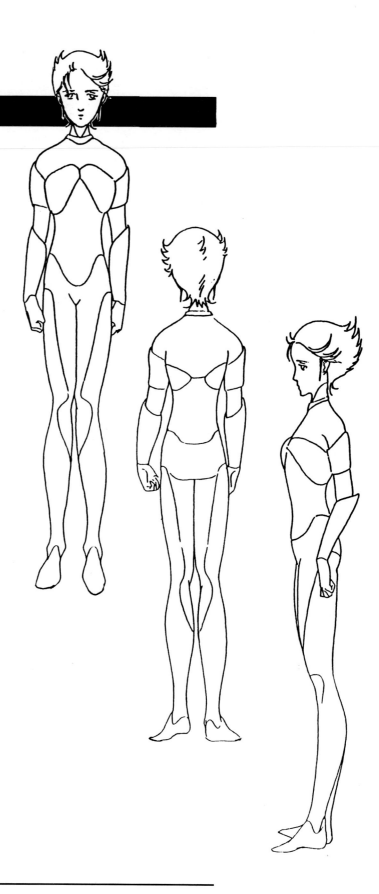

Sera is one of the Invid Mother's young queens. Like Ariel, she is an Invid larvae humanoid. Unfortunately, as a human-like creature, she is prey to emotions that the Invid have managed to avoid. Like Musica and Bowie Grant, Max and Miriya Sterling, Sera knows her mate when she meets him. Sera rejects her Invid training for Lancer. Sera maintains her sense of duty and tries to protect the Queen Mother as the Regis leaves the planet. Her love recognizes the justice of her duty and helps her. It is this effective team-up between alien cultures that helps bring about the end of the Third Robotech War.

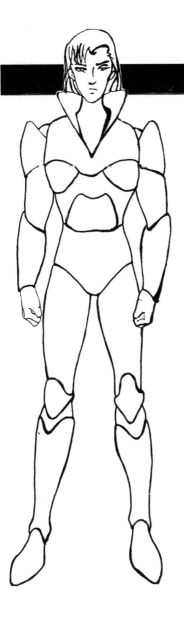

CORG

Rank: Invid Shock Trooper
Age: IEY

Like Sera, Corg is another Invid larvae that has taken on human shape to live on Earth. His instincts are warlike and aggressive. He is unable to feel either compassion or a sense of identity with the humans. In the end, his narrow-minded pursuit of conquest costs him his life.

INVID™ SHOCK TROOPER

The most deadly element of the Invid arsenal. This powerful weapon system gives one Invid soldier the power of a small army. Reserved for officers and evolved Invids.

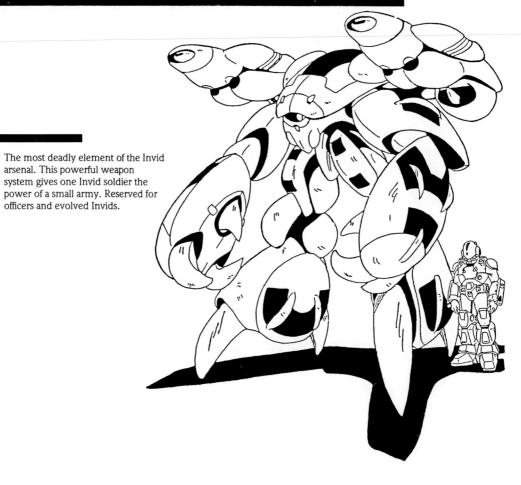

INVID™ SCOUT SHIP

The most common Invid unit, this is the all-purpose Invid combat and transportation system. It is equipped with a sensor device which detects protoculture emanations. It is a hunter which constantly patrols the wastelands on the outskirts of the Invid Zones of Control.

ALPHA FIGHTER™

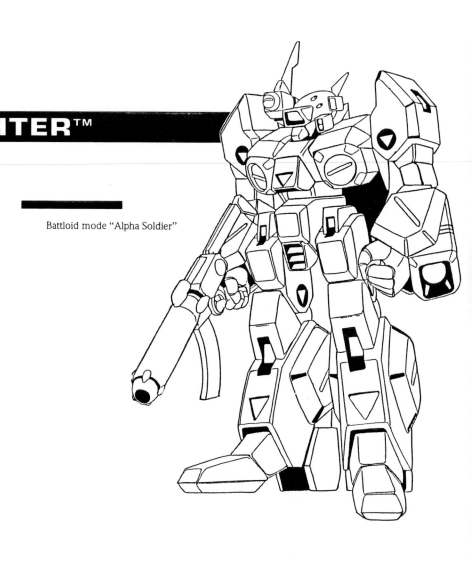

Battloid mode "Alpha Soldier"

CYCLONE

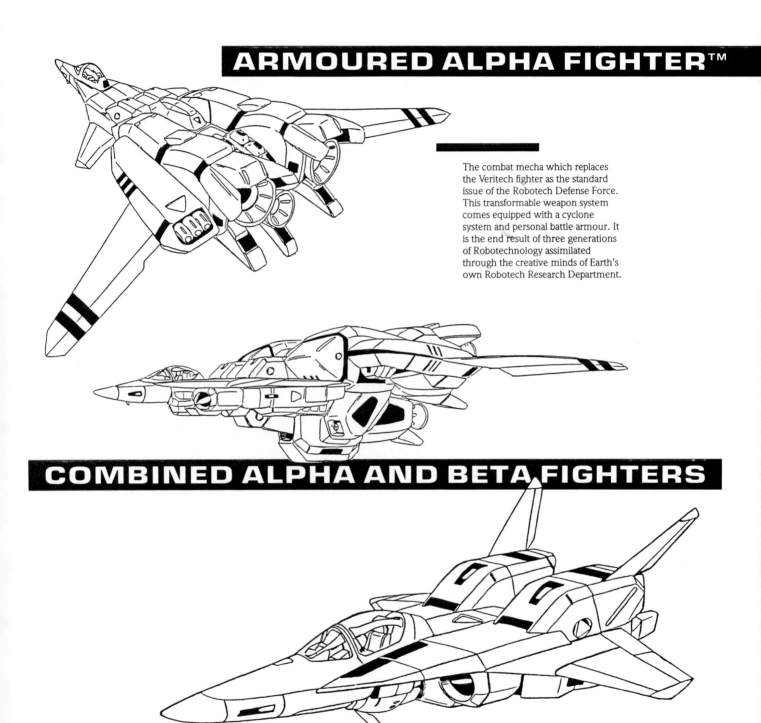

ARMOURED ALPHA FIGHTER™

The combat mecha which replaces the Veritech fighter as the standard issue of the Robotech Defense Force. This transformable weapon system comes equipped with a cyclone system and personal battle armour. It is the end result of three generations of Robotechnology assimilated through the creative minds of Earth's own Robotech Research Department.

COMBINED ALPHA AND BETA FIGHTERS

CHAPTER 5

Lieutenant Rick Hunter—The Macross Saga.

Adorable two-dimensional characters whose eyes fill seven-eighths of their faces...handsome young heroes who have mastered the mystic art of seeing through their low-hanging forelocks...rows of giant robots defending Earth from moronic monsters while alien villains rant on as they come up with yet another plan to take over the world, the galaxy, the universe....

For many people, these are the images that the words "Japanese Animation" bring to mind. They are conjured up by memories of half-remembered television cartoon series or wincing glimpses of recent animated fiascoes. Of the dozens of Japanese animated series and movies imported to the United States in the last two decades, only a scant handful have survived with their original footage, storyline, and integrity left intact. The rest have been rerouted by editors and scripters to appeal to young children, or rather to what these people feel young children will accept. Unfortunately, their concept of rewriting falls into the hack 'n' slash area; series are "written down" to the child's level using simplistic story lines and even simpler characterization. Very little energy is wasted on continuity or complexity. So, Japanese animation, or *anime* (the Japanese word for the genre, pronounced **ah**-*nee-may*) has been saddled with the uniquely American stigma that "cartoons are just for kids." As a result, instead of earning respect for their sweeping, epic-scale stories, their tragic heroes and heroines, their delightful sense of style and farce, anime has only drawn ridicule for catering to youngsters.

But in March of 1985, a show called **ROBOTECH** appeared in this less-than-promising video environment. A high-powered hybrid of Japanese science fiction anime serials *Macross, Southern Cross,* and

The Invid battle **ROBOTECH's** New Generation for the most precious prize of all—Earth!

(*Popeye* and *Betty Boop*), Walter Lantz (*Woody Woodpecker*), MGM (*Tom and Jerry*), and Warner Brothers (*Bugs Bunny, The Road Runner*) joined those of Disney in aiming for all ages...and at times, their satirical wit and saucy storylines went to the opposite extreme, reaching far over children's heads for pure adult entertainment.

With the advent of American television, cartoons were shown in early evening hours and could be enjoyed by the whole family. Shows like Jay Ward's *Rocky And His Friends* in the late 1950s and Hanna-Barbera Studios' offerings of the 60s (*The Flintstones, Top Cat,* and *Jonny Quest*) were especially popular. Adults could appreciate the double entendre lines and sophisticated humor while their children delighted in the animated visuals and clever characters. But soon after that, cartoons were exiled to Saturday mornings and all the elements that appealed to adults stayed in bed with the older crowd. Violence of the "see your favorite superhero punch out the villain and save the world" variety became the new bill of fare. These shows prompted campaigns by protective parental pressure groups to clean up children's television. They wanted TV cartoons to contain wholesome elements. Unfortunately, this only seemed to translate into more unnecessary violence as the characters evolved—or rather devolved—into mindless clichés of good and evil, still trashing each other with no other purpose in mind. The marriage between those adults and those whose business it is to turn out the shows as fast as possible, with as much hype as possible "cost-effectively" has been less than satisfactory. Is it any wonder that many Americans feel they have outgrown animation by the time they reach their teens?

Programs like **ROBOTECH** show us that

Mospeada, **ROBOTECH** wanted to make an impact in the audience age barrier. And it succeeded!

That age barrier—the aggravatingly American view that cartoons are only suitable for children—actually hasn't been with us long. In fact, American animation first came into its own as entertainment for all ages. Walt Disney set lofty standards for the field starting as far back as the 1920s with animated shorts that progressed to feature films like *Snow White and the Seven Dwarfs, Fantasia, Pinocchio,* and others. Throughout the 1930s and 40s, theatrical shorts such as Max Fleischer's

Breetai and Exedore, two of the upper echelon Zentraedi. Their lives change dramatically when they come in contact with the Micronians in The Macross Saga.

Dana Sterling—The Robotech Masters

animated programs don't have to be like that. What storyline could be more violent than the premise of an alien force trying to take over the planet as initiated in the first episode of the series? We actually come into the program seeing that Earth is embroiled in the midst of a global civil war. With the arrival of the mysterious SDF-1, personal battles are put aside as the commanders come to the startling realization that there are outside forces threatening the safety of their world. For the first time in decades, television cartoon characters are allowed to think, to reason. The heroes and heroines, even the villains become three-dimensional characters. In **ROBOTECH,** we can experience Rick Hunter's trauma, passing from childhood to adulthood in less than a day as he comes face to face with the Zentraedi giants. What began as a holiday for Rick turns into a living nightmare with amazing rapidity. The tragic death of Roy Fokker and its effect upon his friends and companions is equally memorable. We see Scott Bernard's all-but-overwhelming grief at the loss of his fiancee, Marlene . . . how he carries her image with him throughout the whole of The New Generation segment of **ROBOTECH,** finally coming to terms with and building a new life on the memory of their relationship. It is a powerful statement that turns him into one of the strongest characters in the **ROBOTECH** series. Even the happy-go-lucky warrior woman, Dana Sterling, initiates her own rite of passage when she realizes that the enemy she's killing

could be her own relatives. It's a staggering fact that only she can come to grips with—and she does!

The people at Harmony Gold—the producers of **ROBOTECH**—have received many letters from parents and teachers commending them for their insight in the creation of the series. "Thank you for showing the children that it's all right to mourn, to grieve at the loss of a friend. Thank you for showing us what it's like to lose someone," one teacher writes in regard to the episode dealing with the death of Roy

The death of Roy Fokker, one of the most moving segments of The Macross Saga.

Starzinger (U.S. Title: *Spaceketeers*) was a tongue-in-cheek space-opera rewrite of the *Monkey King/ Alakazam the Great* legend in which three friendly aliens defend a human princess on her mission to restore galactic peace. (Copyright © 1978 Toei Animation.)

Fokker. On the surface, this may seem to be a logical step in plot development—showing the aftermath of violence, the loss and grief that result from killing, and the no-win nature of war. However, **ROBOTECH** is one of the few animated programs on television today that takes the time to investigate these complex themes. Harmony Gold is giving their audience credit for something other programming specialists have ignored for quite some time. They are assuming their audience can think.

In Japan, Canada, Europe, and other parts of the world, the broadcasting of animated films and series is far ahead of us. Japan, in particular, has taken the lead in creating fine new animated films and series of incredible diversity and ingenuity. Pioneering animators in the 1910s and 20s produced their own short films using both cut-out paper silhouettes and line animation to bring eons-olds Oriental art styles to life. Strangely enough, the Japanese military government took the first big step toward the production of Western-style animation in 1943. Fledgling Nipponese animators were commissioned to create

MANGA

Manga is the word for Japanese comic art albums. Manga are easy to read once you know they are laid out "backward" from American comics. Start at the top of the right-hand page and work to the left, then down the page always scanning from right to left. Confusing? Not really. In good manga, action and attention to characterization make it easy for Western readers to follow the storyline even if they can't read a word of Japanese.

Popular manga series usually evolve into equally popular anime series. Here are two examples:

CATSEYE is an up-to-date *It Takes A Thief* saga, although in this case, it takes three thieves—sisters. In this manga, Hitomi eliminates an eyewitness to one of her recent capers. She eliminates the camera—not the photographer.

SPACE COBRA is full of "muscles, monsters and mammaries" according to Frank Strom of *Animato*. Cobra, a retired thief/con artist on the run from the Space Mafia finds old habits die hard. In this sequence, Cobra is confronted by a sentient sword, a weapon with delusions of grandeur. Somehow, the hero remains unimpressed. Note Cobra's arm in the cell. Yes, it is a bionic wonder weapon.

Catseye copyright © 1983 Tsukasa Hojo, Shueisha Publishing, Tokyo Movie Shinsha and Nippon TV.
Space Cobra copyright © 1982 Buichi Terazawa, Shueisha Publishing, Tokyo Movie Shinsha and Fuji TV, CIC.

propaganda shorts featuring darling little animals waging war for Japan and trashing the Allies with character designs that closely resembled Disney's often-imitated wide-eyed style of that decade. Later, after World War II, the United States occupation of Japan brought a cultural crossover that included comic books and animated theatrical shorts and features of the 1940s. The imports became very popular and the Western style of cartoon art overturned all other forms of animation in Japan. When you watch ROBOTECH, you are really seeing a film whose roots got their start in American animation of years past.

Anime found its feet with the formation of Toei Animation Company in 1951. The first successful studio to produce Western-style animated features, Toei's efforts, like the internationally released *Alakazam the Great,*

became solid hits with the Japanese public; television arrived just in time to showcase all sorts of anime serials.

First and foremost among Japanese TV anime studios was Mushi [Bug] Productions, founded in 1961 by Osamu Tezuka. A fan of the works of Walt Disney and Walt Kelly (the creator of *Pogo*), Tezuka had long been the leader in the far-flung field of *manga* (pronounced **mahn**-*gha* with a soft "a" in both syllables). Manga is the word for Japanese comic-art novels that frequently run into several volumes and many thousands of pages. The cinematic quality of Tezuka's works lent itself perfectly to anime adaptations. Mushi Productions got off to a sparkling start with serialized anime versions of Tezuka's fantastically popular manga creations of the mid-50s, *Mighty Atom* (1963) and *Jungle*

写真をとられずにすんだわ

サンキュー姉さん

瞳…

あ…!!

きゃあああ

あ!!

たしかにソード人は狩猟民族だ

獲物をつきさすことによってその生命エネルギーをすいとっている話だぜ

だが人間は殺さなかった

あんたが王の時はどうだった

あの男はおのれが王になりたいばかりに非道な手段でワシをおとしいれたのだ

あの裏ぎり者ののろわれた野心家バベルのせいだ

王だって!? なんでまた死刑に…

つまり…バベルが王になってから人の生命エネルギーの味をしったというわけか

まさに暴君は民族の道徳までかえてしまったのだ

まあいいさ あんたらの民族の道徳などきいていられないんでね

あんたが王だとしたらこの船について外へでる方法はくわしいだろう? ないのか?

残念ながらおまえひとりでは無理だろうな

あの男が王になってからソード人の誇りも騎士道精神も地におちてしまった

もはやソード人は殺リクと暗竜をくりかえす殺人集団になりさがってしまったのだ

Emperor (1965)—the first color anime series for Japanese TV. (That's right. Many of the first animated films were created in black and white!) Through arrangements with the American television network, NBC (which partially funded the production of *Jungle Emperor*), the two programs were brought to the U.S. in the mid-60s under the titles *Astro Boy* and *Kimba the White Lion*. These two programs not only earned a following in the States that still exists, they also paved the way for more anime imports. As a flurry of other television anime studios formed to take advantage of the booming Japanese TV market, they found an eager American market for their shows, too. The TCJ/Eiken studio had a pair of hot hits on both sides of the ocean with *Eight Man* (1963) and *Iron Man 28* (also 1963, but known in the U.S. as *Gigantor*), a show that would win a color remake 17 years later in Japan. Tokyo Television didn't last long, but it is remembered for *Fight! Marine Kid* (1966) and its sequel, *Sea-Bed Boy Marine* (1969) which

were combined for U.S. airwaves as *Marine Boy*. Mushi Productions followed up its previous successes with the tale of an alien animal trio, *Wonder Three* (1965, U.S. title, *Amazing Three*). And a studio that formed in 1964, Tatsunoko ("Seahorse") Productions, would go on to become familiar to audiences abroad through their series *Mach Go Go Go* (1967, retitled *Speed Racer* in America), *Science Ninja Team Gatchaman* (1972, also known as *Battle of The Planets*), and the three series that make up **ROBO-TECH:** *Super Dimension Fortress Macross* (1982), *Genesis Climber Mospeada* (1983), and *Super Dimension Cavalry Southern Cross* (1984).

In the years that followed, an anime broadcast timetable took shape with upward of a dozen new anime series being produced each year. Variety was a necessity, and the scope of TV anime widened to offer something for everyone. Shows didn't always have mass appeal but were made with various groups of viewers in mind.

Jungle Emperor (U.S. title *Kimba, The White Lion*) first appeared as a manga drawn by the "god of manga," Osamu Tezuka, between 1950 and 1954. After it was animated in 1965 as the series that would become *Kimba*, a second series called *Susume Leo! (Forward, Leo!)* followed in 1966, but it took 17 years for that sequel to reach these shores as *Leo the Lion*. (Copyright © 1965 Osamu Tezuka and Mushi Productions. Copyright © 1950 Osamu Tezuka.)

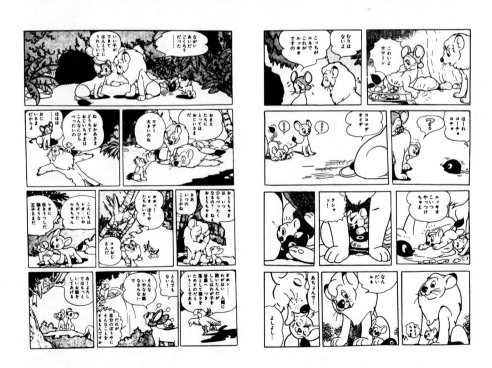

Mach Go-Go-Go (American title, *Speed Racer*). One of the most popular Japanese anime to reach America in the 1960s. (Copyright © 1967 Tatsunoko Productions.)

Iron Man No. 28 (American name, Gigantor). A color remake of the original 1963-1967 black and white series. (Copyright © 1980 Mitsuteru Yokoyama and Tokyo Movie Shinsha.)

Jun (Princess) and Jinpei (Keyop), two of the five-member *Gatchaman* team. A heavily revised version was brought to America in 1977 under the title *Battle of the Planets*. (Copyright © 1972 Tatsunoko Productions.)

Anime music and the actors and actresses who create the voices are popular with Japanese fans. *Genesis Climber Mospeada* produced several albums and singles featuring Yellow—**ROBOTECH's** androgynous rock'n'roller. Lynn Minmei of The Macross Saga was by no means ignored in the anime music hall of fame. *Macross* albums and singles are very popular in Japan.

In the area of science fiction—or sf, as it is called in both English and Japanese—anime adventures had first been aimed for a younger crowd. But as the audience grew up, sf anime became more serious and sophisticated. When sf anime matured in the late 1970s, it triggered a popularity boom for the entire genre. For years it had been just one of many forms of entertainment, but now it began to garner a massive fan following. Today those legions of devotees are catered to by upward of seven different monthly anime magazines, each packed with more than 150 pages—on glossy stock and in color—with first-class freebies enclosed such as posters, mini-books on new series and other printed fun-fare material. Fans can buy singles and albums of their favorite anime theme songs and BGM (**B**ack**g**round **M**usic) soundtracks. They can go to concerts featuring theme song vocalists and the actors and actresses who provide voices for the anime characters. Several chains of anime specialty shops keep up a steady stock of stationery, posters, beach towels, rice bowls, pre-recorded home video cassettes, actual cels. . . well, *anything* that can be decorated with a favorite anime character's likeness can be made available— and *is* made available to the interested fan. In less than ten years, anime and its merchandising has ballooned into an industry bringing in the equivalent of billions of dollars a year.

The turnaround began in 1977 with *Space Cruiser Yamato,* a spectacularly popular theatrical feature culled from a modest 1974 series of the same name. Buoyed a bit by the worldwide success of *Star Wars,* the *Yamato*

feature arrived at exactly the right time to give both sf and anime a boost in the eyes of the Japanese public. A scant two years later, the saga of the star-sailing, reborn World War II battleship's journey to save Earth would be seen on North American television right along with its 1978 sequel, *Space Cruiser Yamato II,* under the title *Star Blazers.*

Hot on the heels of the *Yamato* boom came another milestone of sf anime, 1979's *Mobile Suit Gundam.* Before this aired, giant robots had been portrayed as sort of cast-iron characters—rarely sentient, but embodying nobility, honor, and all the righteous requisites every good defender of justice requires. In *Gundam,* however, robots were established as high-tech battle machines that the heroes—or villains—just happened to use as weaponry or for transportation. They were first cousins of the powered suits in Robert Heinlein's sf novel of off-world war, **Starship Troopers.** Throughout *Gundam's* 43-episode epic of civil war and the unfolding of mankind's budding psychic abilities, technological details were lavished on orbiting space colonies and robotics. Not only did this

contribute to the show's sizable following (which prompted a 1985 sequel series, *Zeta Gundam*), but it also began a trend in anime *meka* (mechanics) that is still being expanded upon.

If *Yamato* sparked sf anime to new heights, *Gundam* whetted the audiences' appetites for the technology of the future that anime could make plausible, if only on the TV and movie screens. Foundations were laid for a new kind of series, something unique in the annals of anime. It would come to be called *Super Dimension Fortress Macross,* the first segment of the story of **ROBOTECH.**

In 1980 anime's popularity continued to swell. The production world was charged with new creative energy. A legion of late-teen anime fans-turned-animators combined with fever-pitch public support to spark that energy with fantastic results.

Shōji Kawamori was part of that tidal wave of young animators, and during 1980 he rode the crest of the wave to fame. Two years earlier, at the age of 18, Kawamori was plucked from his first-year studies at the prestigious Keio University (the Japanese

The crew of the *Space Cruiser Yamato.* This program not only helped trigger Japan's anime boom in the late 70s, but also collected a sizeable North American fan following when the program appeared in the United States as *Star Blazers.* (Copyright © 1983 West Cape Corporation.)

Char Aznable, the charismatic "Red Baron" villain in *Mobile Suite Gundam*. This 1979 television serial from Nippon Sunrise went on to inspire three feature film condensations as well as the sequel series, *Zeta Gundam*. *Gundam* introduced the most technically advanced period of anime with its depiction of realistic battle meka and space colony life. Its success set the stage for the triumph of *Macross*. (Copyright © 1979 Nippon Sunrise.)

Named for the leader of a rough and tumble team of intergalactic mercenaries, the *Crusher Joe* anime began as a series of sf adventure novels written by the head of Studio Nue, Haruka Takachiho and was illustrated by Yoshikazu Yasuhiko. Well known on both sides of the ocean as "Yas," Yasuhiko also helped to bring the quick-draw quartet to the big screen as director of the Nippon Sunrise Studio's *Crusher Joe* feature film in 1983. (Copyright © 1983 Haruka Takachiho Yoshikazu Yasuhiko and Nippon Sunrise.)

equivalent of an Ivy League school) to join Studio Nue, an extremely small and select group of anime meka designers. Put to the task of working on meka for the sf robot serial, *Fighting General Daimos* (1978, seen in North America as *Starbirds*), Kawamori's debut in professional anime was an impressive one. By the time 1980 rolled around, he had become one of the chief members of Studio Nue's five-man band and would help lead the group to glory as one of the main masterminds behind *Macross*.

Unlike young Kawamori, Studio Nue was anything but the "new kid on the block." In fact, Nue's reputation was that of one of the most accomplished meka design studios in Japan. The group was organized by Haruka Takachiho, a man with no small reputation himself—the huge anime hits, *Crusher Joe* (a 1983 feature film), and its 1985 prequel, the TV serial *Dirty Pair,* were adaptations of two different series of sf adventure novels he penned in the 70s. Picture, if you will, the galactic adventures of a brooding young Han Solo and crew as "heroes for hire" in space, and you've got a good idea of how and why *Crusher Joe* was and continues to be so popular.

Studio Nue actually began life under the name SF Central Art and made a quiet start in 1973 drawing up character and meka designs for an anime serial partially inspired by Gerry Anderson's **Supermarination** works, *Zero Tester.* The very next year brought a stroke of luck that would lead to later successes as the group got the call to clean up the rough meka and character design sketches by famed manga-man Reiji Matsumoto for the *Space Cruiser Yamato* series. Matsumoto, long revered as the manga master of meka, could appreciate fine work and no doubt kept an interested eye on Takachiho's team for the next three years as they changed their name to Studio Nue and created superior meka and robot plans for programs like *Brave Raideen* (1975), *Combattler V* (1976), and *Voltes V* (1977). When the Toei Animation Company began the task of turning Matsumoto's creation, Captain Harlock, into a celluloid reality, Matsumoto went straight to Studio Nue for advice in designing Harlock's seemingly sentient spaceship, the *Arcadia*. With these designs appearing in the 1977 *Space Pirate Captain Harlock* series, the 1978

Galaxy Express 999 series, and Matsumoto's own manga versions of the sf serials, as well as a new-style *Arcadia* gracing the screen in the films *Galaxy Express 999* (1979), *Adieu Galaxy Express 999* (1981), and *Arcadia of My Youth* (1982), Studio Nue became a major force in the anime industry. Shows like *Zambot 3* (1977), the aforementioned *Fighting General Daimos,* and *Gordian the Warrior* (1979), added to Nue's meka accomplishments. By 1980, their reputation for fine sf anime work was unsurpassed. The demand for their designs increased.

1980 was a pivotal year for Studio Nue. Contracted to work on the feature film *Technopolice 21C (Century)* by Toho, one of Japan's biggest film producers, Nue began to expand from being just a meka designer to becoming an essential part of anime planning. With the writing skills of founder Takachiho and Kenichi Matsuzaki (a scriptor on the side for *Mobile Suit Gundam* and another robot drama of high repute, 1980's *Space Runaway Ideon*), and the meka designing wizardry of Naomi Katō, Kazutaka Miyatake, and the budding Kawamori, Nue went about creating the entire world of *Technopolice 21C*. A ground-breaking project was next on the agenda, an sf anime series co-produced by Japanese giant Tokyo Movie Shinsha (ani-

Space Pirate Captain Harlock (Toei Animation, 1978-79). The stoic Captain appears in many of Reiji Matsumoto's manga and anime. He is one of the most popular animation heroes in Japan and the United States. (Copyright © 1978 Reiji Matsumoto and Toei Animation.)

The mysterious Maeter of *Galaxy Express 999.* (Copyright © 1978 Reiji Matsumoto and Toei Animation.)

Daigo and his bionic panther, Clint, in *Gordian the Warrior.* (Copyright © 1979 Tatsunoko Productions.)

mators of *Mighty Orbots,* a 1984 series broadcast exclusively in North America) and the French company DIC Films called *Ulysses 31.* The quick-learning Kawamori was given free rein on the job and came through with another conquest for his comrades. By summer, Studio Nue was solidly established as one of the best in the industry.

And then, the chance of anime immortality came knocking at Nue's door. In August of 1980, a group called the Uizu Corporation approached the band with some vague ideas for a new sf show. The opportunity to develop an entire prospective anime series was a new challenge and Nue jumped at the chance to be part of the team. An agreement was reached that Studio Nue would be in charge of planning and design while the Uizu Corporation would handle production.

The Uizu Corporation had their hearts set on creating a robot show and they had certainly come to the right people. Nue had helped pioneer multiple-piece combining robots in their designs for *Combattler V, Voltes V* and *Daimos.* During early planning conferences, Nue and their new employers batted around possible combinations. Thanks to a new *Space Cruiser Yamato* film released that very month, *Be Forever Yamato,* battleships were high on the public's hit parade. Transforming robots were well-liked too, so

The *Yamato*—ready for battle again. (Copyright © 1980 West Cape Corporation.)

why not create a battleship that could change into a robot? Kawamori took the concept a step further and, borrowing from some of his unused meka ideas for *Ulysses 31,* placed an inhabited city of 56,000 people within a 1,200-meter-long space battleship. Thus, the roots of *Macross* were born—but it was originally titled *Battle City Megarōdo!*

Megarōdo was a dual pronunciation play on the English words "mega-road" in reference to a great road made up of a man's life and "mega-load" comparing those 56,000 people to extra baggage onboard the ship.

As the brainstorming continued, a background for the *Megarōdo* began to take shape. With Nostradamus' predictions for the future firmly in mind, the massive battleship became an alien vessel that crashed on Earth in 1999. In the initial story line, the Earth people establish a finders-keepers possession of the ship and rebuild it during a ten-year period. The scriptors had no idea who owned/built the mysterious mammoth. Enemy alien robots were briefly considered and Nue served up some small-scale ten-to-twenty-meter-tall Earth battle robot models that could be piloted to fight the foe hand-to-hand. But the sentient alien robots were eventually dismissed as being too credibility-straining. The villains eventually evolved into

a race of otherworldly humanoid giants which would still be in scale with Earth's battle robots.

At the start of 1981, *Megarōdo* was still a sketchy skeleton of plot fragments and meka projects-in-progress. However, some differences had developed in the way the Uizu Corporation viewed their brainchild. Uizu wanted *Megarōdo* to have an extremely silly slant—to be a grandiose parody that would lampoon the entire genre of giant robot epics and itself as well. Nue wasn't comfortable with that concept. Not only did they prefer "hard" science sf that kept to science fact as closely as possible while preserving anime's sense of wonder, they also had their hard-earned status in the anime world to uphold. Studio Nue could appreciate light comedy and farce as much as anyone, but the parody Uizu was pushing for worried them.

Then the studio was faced with yet another dilemma. For nearly a year before Uizu first contacted them, Nue had been developing a unique new kind of transforming battle suit. Now the plans were finished and although high hopes had been pinned on using it in the project, Nue wasn't sure they wanted to squander their promising design on a show that wouldn't put it to its intended use. Rather than dismiss the idea entirely,

The bridge crew of the SDF-1.

Max and Miriya Sterling, a meeting of alien cultures—and more!

Nue decided to shelve it temporarily and pondered possibilities for its use in another show.

Plans for *Megarōdo* continued. Each new plot-puzzle gave way to circumstances for new developments. Plans for an all-female bridge crew led to a female captain, which in turn led to a plot for a male alien spy to sneak aboard the *Megarōdo* to have an illicit love affair with her. The problem of the two races' size difference was solved further down the line when the inspiration of the Micronian reduction system struck. Suddenly one shrunk-down spy became a crowd of male Micronian-size spies, which prompted the addition of a female spy for variety. Then the parody aspect reared its head again, and the lone female evolved into a genius alien warrior who would eventually meet her match in a genius Earth boy—a show-stopping, scene-stealing youth who just happened *not* to be the hero. It had long been an anime institution that the hero of the feature was the most charismatic of good-guy characters (although usually overshadowed by tragic, honorable villains). This new twist tore down the tradition with great glee and gusto. In the saga of **ROBOTECH,** we know this plot development as the story of Max and Miriya Sterling.

Still, there were many more characters to be developed for the story, and they made their initial appearances in unexpected ways. In February 1981, Shōji Kawamori was skimming the sketchbook of high-school buddy Haruhiko Mikimoto, when some renderings of a Chinese girl caught his eye. Mikimoto, or "HAL," as he signed his work and liked to be called, had specialized in drawing the female form for years, as Kawamori was well aware. In high school the two had collaborated on a 90-page sf manga effort, **The Last Soldier,** along with Fujihiko Hosono, who would later gain fame for his original manga versions of the anime slapstick series **Sasuga No Sarutobi** (1983) and **Gugu Gammo** (1984). Mikimoto went on to assist Hosono on the art for the **Crusher Joe** manga and, at age 21, became an apprentice animator for the Artland studio on the recommendation of Studio Nue's Kazutaka Miyatake. Conveniently, Mikimoto first entered Artland in the same month *Megarōdo* was launched. Since then, Mikimoto had animated scenes for the second *Lupin the Third* series and the *Mighty Atom* remake. He was promoted to creating original character designs for a variety of shows. However, through it all, HAL continued to perfect his powers of illustration. It paid off when his winsome Chinese girl captivated Kawamori. Mikimoto signed on as *Megarōdo's* character designer and the girl who guaranteed his job would soon make him one of the most well-known personalities in anime.

The girl came to be known as Lynn Minmei and her arrival spurred a shake-up in *Megarōdo's* story. Originally cast as a cute Chinese restaurant delivery girl trotting egg rolls up to the *Megarōdo's* bridge, Minmei became increasingly popular with the planning staff as Mikimoto's pen clarified her

The captivating Lynn Minmei.

character. She made the leap from secondary character to co-star in a mere month. As the *Megarōdo* storyline solidified, Minmei emerged as a popular singing star and morale-lifting movie idol cut from the same cloth as Lili Marlene. She was also given a parody purpose—broadcasts of her songs and movies would be intercepted by the aliens who would become so excited by her representative view of human society, they would all have themselves reduced to Micronian size and defect to the *Megarōdo*. Sound familiar, **ROBOTECH** fans?

With Minmei commanding more and more of the spotlight, the *Megarōdo* project reached its first anniversary. However, half of its co-creators weren't there to celebrate. The Uizu Corporation had been dissolved in 1981 leaving Studio Nue with custody of the prenatal series—a somewhat unsettling situation for a meka design studio that had never before soloed on the production of a show. But Nue stoutly picked up the pieces and hoped for the best. At least they could now redirect the series away from its parody slant to an area the studio would be more at ease with. A love triangle involving Minmei and the still undeveloped hero and heroine could be both entertaining, yet make a memorable contrast set against the cosmic-scale war that

The Super Dimension Fortress Macross.

Captain Gloval of the SDF-1.

blazed between the humans and the aliens. Nue took the plunge and when *Megarōdo* changed courses in mid-stream, it shed its title for a new one: *Super Dimension Fortress Macross.*

Mikimoto hit the inks in earnest and began to "audition" prospective characters in quick-sketch cartoons as the Nue staff went to work roughing out a 52 episode storyboard for their series. A premiere date of April 1982 had been targeted, but as Nue reconsidered their deadline and the lack of manpower, the 52 episodes were reduced to 48 and then chopped once more to 39. By December 1981 things were looking a little more hopeful. The 39 half-hour episodes had been completely roughed out, Mikimoto had created a stable of sketch-tested characters, and the promising new battle suits had even been put to good use as the intermediate stage of a new Nue innovation—a fighter plane that could change into a small-scale robot. Still, the situation was rapidly turning out to be more than one studio could handle and, as the year drew to a close, Nue formally asked the Artland studio to help produce *Macross.*

Noboru Ishiguro was the head of Artland. When Nue approached him, his stint as chief animation director of the color *Mighty Atom* series was coming to a close. The *Macross* proposal interested him, all the more so since HAL, still an apprentice in his studio, was freelancing as the character designer. Ishiguro agreed to have Artland animate the series and was rewarded by having the new captain,

Gloval, of the *Macross* be loosely based on him . . . especially in respect to his eye for the ladies! Fun and games aside, there was a tough task ahead and although the major decisions were made to have Ippei Kuri's studio, Anime Friend, as a co-producer, Tatsunoko Productions as a distribution company and Takutoku Toys as a sponsor, the starting airdate had to be postponed until September 1982.

The nine month countdown for the broadcast date passed in a flurry of preparations. Mikimoto took a brief break to work on some secondary character designs for the *Technoboyger* series (shown in North America as *Thunderbirds 2086*) and returned just in time to draw up the final storyboards for *Macross*. The scenarios for the first three *Macross* episodes were completed and September arrived—along with another delay! *Macross* finally reached the air on October 3, 1982 and although its story was trimmed from 39 episodes to 36 soon afterwards, the series was a tremendous success—in *every* respect!

The impact of *Macross* on the genre of anime is immense. It has eclipsed its still recent forerunners, *Yamato* and *Gundam*. Years have passed since the premiere of *Macross* in Japan, but so far nothing has been able to replace it in the public's esteem. In July 1984 the feature film, *Macross: Love—Do You Remember?*, a revised version of the series' saga animated with state-of-the-art techniques, proved that its following is still faithful. Today, in Japan, *Macross'* merchandising, usually nonexistent after a series leaves the air, and continuous mention in anime magazines goes on. Rather than a case of chronic overkill, it's a testimony to the tenacity of *Macross'* popularity and to the changes the series has indelibly stamped on the anime world.

One of the marks *Macross* made was to push the popularity of transforming battle robots to new heights. Several shows tried to cash in on the phase, but only a few found comparable favor with the Japanese public. The most successful to date, Tokyo Movie Shinsha's *Super Dimension Century Orguss* (1983), filled *Macross'* television time slot when that series ended. *Orguss* and *Macross* had a lot in common, too, such as sharing chief animation director Ishiguro, character

designer Mikimoto and meka marvel Kawamori. It was not only a logical outgrowth of the transforming meka introduced in *Macross*, it also mentioned some interesting crossover flings between *Orguss* hero Kei Katsuragi and *Macross* misses Minmei, Sammy and others! After the completion of *Orguss*, the same potent trio of Ishiguro, Mikimoto and Kawamori went on to create the extraordinary feature film, *Megazone 2-3*.

When *Orguss* ended at episode 36, a third "Super Dimension" series, *Super Dimension Cavalry Southern Cross*, followed it onto the air. Like *Orguss*, *Southern Cross* involved direct descendants of the meka in *Macross* but had no ties to either of its predecessors' storylines. With *Southern Cross*, Tatsunoko

Licensing is an important aspect of **ROBOTECH**, too. The efforts of people like Carl Macek, Susan Christison, Gabriela Aranda, Mark Freedman, Caryl Liebmann, and others make the world of **ROBOTECH** accessible to its fans through companies (Comico, Matchbox International, Peter Pan Industries, etc.) licensed to produce **ROBOTECH** material. Pictured here, John Rocknowski, president of marketing, and Frank Agrama, president, CEO Harmony Gold, discuss a potential licensee.

Productions finally got their shot at animating a "Super Dimension" show. *Southern Cross* carried the hallmark of many Tatsunoko shows with some of the studio's characters from the past popping up every so often for the sharp-eyed viewer to spot.

One year before, Tatsunoko had animated another short-lived but popular program, *Genesis Climber Mospeada.* While the "Super Dimension" series were gifted with the choice Sunday afternoon weekly time slot, *Mospeada* had to contend with the near disastrous Sunday morning time period. It didn't have much of a chance to attract a large audience by the time it ended at episode 25. But while they are a small group, *Mospeada's* fans have proven to be a very vocal minority. As a result, an all new continuation of the adventure titled *Genesis Climber Mospeada: Love Live Alive* was released on home videotape in Japan in September 1985. *Mospeada's* meka was the basis of a marketing blitz of transforming toys, but in the case of this program, the characters outshone the meka in the fan's eyes. In fact, most of *Love Live Alive* is a new concert by celluloid singer, Yellow Belmont, also known to **ROBOTECH** fans as Yellow Dancer or Lancer.

Mospeada is a unique case—the only anime series that was a first run television bust but was revived for its insistent fans. Other shows may get similar second chances if the *Mospeada* video is successful. This could be

particularly significant in light of the increasing amount of anime being produced exclusively for the booming home videotape market.

Audience ratings may dictate a television show's fate in America, but in Japan, an anime series faces a double-edged sword. Each show must earn a following or risk having its storyline come to a sure and definite finale. To be considered for animation, a prospective series must be marketable, able to earn its keep through the sale of goods (toys, clothing, records, models, etc.) cranked out by manufacturers who sponsor the show. When *Macross* triggered the 80s avalanche of meka-dependent sf adventure series—and the tons of toys and models that went with it—it also set the stage for **ROBOTECH's** arrival.

For years, North American specialty shops and importers supplied collectors and fans with the quality anime meka goods. Fans looked for this material even though the selection was usually anemic and prices increased anywhere from double to ten times the original cost. In the late 70s, American toy makers made robots affordable and available with their Shogun Warriors toy line licensed from Japanese giant, Bandai/Popii. But although many of the Shogun Warrior anime incarnations were brought to North American television with Jim Terry's 1977 *Force Five* package (which included the robot-less *Starzinger* [1978, retitled *Spaceketeers*], the series *UFO Robot Grendizer* [1975], *Getta Robo G* [1975, aired as *Starvengers*], *Gaiking* [1976], and 1977's *Danguard Ace*), the marketing venture didn't last long.

It was only a matter of time until Japan's increasing craze crossed the ocean and sure enough, in early 1984, the first of the meka-mania began its invasion of the North American toy stores. With warehouses full of unsold goods for anime series long off the air, Japanese manufacturers were glad to sell their stock to the shrewd U.S. companies that approached them. By Christmas 1984 the imported meka models and toys were selling better than the popular Cabbage Patch Kids. Few people realized that the converting robots had been originally featured in animated shows and companies obscured that fact by assigning personalities to the meka. Anime had evolved from that scenario years ago. The Japanese put their energies into creating plausible human and alien characters

UFO Robot Grandizer (Toei Animation, 1975-77). This serial made headlines when it appeared on French TV as Goldorak, winning a 100% share in its time slot for several months. (Copyright © 1975 Go Nagai, Dynamic Productions, and Toei Animation.)

who used the meka for what it was—machinery—rather than anthropomorphising the material. Fortunately, Revell Incorporated, a company that had invested in hundreds of thousands of meka models, chose to forego foistering personas on properties. They treated the battle weapons as they had been designed to be and christened their line Robotech Defenders. Many of the models just happened to be from *Mospeada* and the Super Dimension duo of anime series.

The metamorphosis of *Macross, Southern Cross* and *Mospeada* into an American program named **ROBOTECH** was nothing short of inspired ingenuity brought about partly by design and partly by chance. While many people had a hand in the actual happenings, the key figures who guided **ROBOTECH** through its distinctive development were two men, Ahmed Agrama and Carl Macek.

Born in Cairo, Egypt in 1955, Ahmed Agrama got an early start in the film industry. His family founded Graffitti Italiano in Rome and Agrama got plenty of experience as a teenager absorbing the fine points of choosing promising American films for his parents' company to translate and distribute. Equipped with this considerable know-how, Agrama traveled to Los Angeles in the 1970s to study theatrical arts at USC. Frank and Oli Agrama

followed to spearhead the organization of Agrama Films. In 1980 Jehan (Gigi) Agrama joined the business, too.

Traditionally, films are translated from one language to another by subcontracting a score of smaller firms to each handle one special aspect of the job. The Agramas wanted to create a company that could perform the whole process under one roof. In April of 1979, Intersound Incorporated became a reality. The studio was outfitted with the best in sound and film technologies. It took two years for Intersound to satisfy the standards of its creator, but during that time, it kept busy dubbing the television properties of Agrama Films (including several anime programs) for the European, African, Latin American, and Middle Eastern markets.

In 1982 Agrama Films was ready to make its mark in the lucrative but fiercely competitive American television market, and formed Harmony Gold U.S.A. With a sizable stable of international programming to choose from, Harmony Gold got its start by preparing English-language pilot episodes of the parent company's anime acquisitions. They also transferred feature-length anime adaptations of *The Call of the Wild, Frankenstein*, a telefeature based on Marvel Comics' *Tomb of Dracula*, and others into English. As they were finishing this first round of projects in

Susan Christison (vice-president, international licensing), Gigi Agrama (chief operating officer), and Frank Agrama (chief executive officer) of Harmony Gold, U.S.A.

Tomb of Dracula (Toei Animation, 1980). A two-hour animated movie based on the Marvel comic book. (Copyright © Marvel Productions)

Visual Medium and was the curator of the Archive of Popular Culture at California State University at Fullerton for several years before moving on to the West Coast editorship of *Mediascene* magazine and the now defunct publishing company, Atlas Comics. Utilizing his kaleidoscope of abilities and talents, Macek did freelance research and publicity for several films including animated features like Ivan Reitman and Leonard Mogel's *Heavy Metal*. He wrote the text for the art book, **The Art of Heavy Metal: Animation for the Eighties,** and worked as a marketing and promotional coordinator for Canada's Nelvana Animation studio. Finally, unhappy with the film industry's emphasis on monetary returns over and above creativity, he left the industry in 1982 to open the Carl F. Macek Gallery, specializing in original cels, pencil art, and posters from animation shorts and features the world over.

The Gallery's stock of cels included a few pieces from Tatsunoko Productions and Macek found that the Japanese cels sold extremely well. By speaking with his customers and area animation fans, he began to learn about the wide and wondrous world of Japanese anime and its growing stockpile of sf adventure serials. He absorbed the anime topics being discussed by fans, heard the horror stories of how Tatsunoko's *Science Ninja Team Gatchaman* had been butchered into *Battle of the Planets* and listened to the fans' expressions of hope that someday more anime series could have English versions that would remain faithful to the original stories and concepts of their creators. Macek got the opportunity to witness firsthand what American audiences were missing when anime was "kiddified" for the children's market when friends lent him anime videotapes sent by their Japanese pen pals.

When a representative from Harmony Gold visited the Gallery in April 1984, it was the perfect chance for Macek to discuss the anime dilemma with people in a position to do something about it. Harmony Gold was impressed with his insight. Macek advised Harmony Gold to aim for a young adult audience—the teenagers who kept the film industry's box office booming. Macek's arguments were so convincing that Harmony Gold decided to try his suggestions. He was hired as production executive and given the

early 1984, word came of a nearby animation art gallery exhibiting some of the original celluloid paintings (called "cels") used to create some of their properties. The cels could certainly come in handy for publicity, so Harmony Gold contacted the gallery's owner, Carl Macek.

Carl Macek is a man of myriad talents. He was born in Pittsburgh in 1951. Macek is the only person in the United States to earn a college degree in *Theory of Criticism in the*

go-ahead to produce a show that would appeal to their new target.

Macek examined Harmony Gold's hefty collection of anime programs and emerged with *Super Dimension Fortress Macross*. Its track record in Japan was remarkable, but just as important, Macek knew the series was extremely popular with stateside anime fans as well. Remembering the plight of those fans and considering the integrity of his proposed new audience, Macek set out to create an English-language version of *Macross* as close to the original as possible. In June 1984 work began on a mega-pilot episode in English—the first three episodes of the series, end-on-end as a 70-minute feature. Not only would Harmony Gold have a pilot episode guaranteed to knock the socks off TV programmers jaded by slopped-and-chopped-together English-dubbed anime pilots, but this high-quality introduction to *Macross* would make an excellent initial entry into the North American home videotape market for the young company.

Macek also believed that movies and television programs should be kept in the public's view through the medium of publishing, and what better way to show off the visual aspects of an exciting new animated series than in a comic book format? With work on the *Macross* pilot on the move, Harmony Gold tested the waters for any interested comic book publishers. Comico, the Comic Company, seized the opportunity to put the **ROBOTECH** saga into print. Comico became the first independent comics publisher to license a major anime property. By the end of June 1984, *Macross* was operating in full forward stride with production of the videotape pilot and the comic book series well underway.

Later that summer, fate altered the future of *Macross* when Harmony Gold discovered that Revell, Incorporated owned the rights to the toy models made for the show. Revell's *Robotech* line had already appeared on store shelves across America. Consequently, Harmony Gold would be unable to sell *Macross* models to merchandise their show. Revell had the models but not the *Macross* name, and so would lose the instant recognition of anyone who would see the program. What a dilemma! The completion of the *Macross* pilot feature made timing that much more

Leonard Araujo records dialogue at Intersound Incorporated as Carl Macek looks on.

crucial and so, in September 1984 while the *Macross* videotape drew raves at its premiere at the World Science Fiction Convention in Los Angeles, Harmony Gold sent a representative to Revell to propose that the two companies work together. A co-licensing agreement was reached, but even though the *Macross* videotape was now racking up sales across North America, the show's future was still uncertain.

In American syndication, a show has to have at least 65 episodes to even rate consideration for purchase by a television station. With one segment run each weekday, a 65-episode program fills thirteen weeks—a good quarter of a year—while a shorter series has less appeal for the station since it will run out of episodes sooner. Since *Macross* was comprised of only 36 episodes, Harmony Gold couldn't expect it to reach the air through syndication. On the other hand, the *Macross* pilot videotape was a success.

Dana Sterling and crew, originally of *Super Dimension Cavalry Southern Cross* sign on board as The Robotech Masters segment of **ROBOTECH**.

They are followed by Rand, Annie, and Scott Bernard, part of **ROBOTECH**: The New Generation.

The company was doing some serious thinking about releasing the entire series exclusively on videotape.

But Revell had other ideas. The wide exposure of a television series was sure to sell more models than an exclusive and comparatively reclusive release of the series on home videotape. The model manufacturers pushed for the switch to TV syndication.

To produce the standard 65 episodes necessary for a syndicated television series, Carl combed the collection once more and came up with two additional Tatsunoko titles: *Super Dimension Cavalry Southern Cross* and *Genesis Climber Mospeada*. The design and formats of these two programs were compatible with the *Macross* material. A new vision formed in Macek's fertile imagination. He knew it would be possible to create a space odyssey of epic proportions that would entertain the public he wanted to reach. Combined with the existing *Macross* programs, the series totaled 84 episodes, 85 when a special transitional piece was added. Revell lent an enthusiastic hand to the new project and supplied the anime trilogy with the name they had spent months creating— **ROBOTECH!**

At first glance, it seemed impossible that the meka and plot predilections of these three individual programs would link believably. But somehow, Carl Macek created a monu-

Zor Prime, one of **ROBOTECH's** tragic heroes.

mental epic that encompassed the visuals in a way that did not insult the integrity of the storylines or his proposed audience. The path to **ROBOTECH** became ironically reminiscent of the "mega-road" concept from the *Macross* planning stages. Subsequently, **ROBOTECH** became a generation-spanning saga of an alien culture's encounters with the people of Earth.

In undertaking such a vast compilation, there were bound to be some changes from the original stories, but they were handled with care and consideration. Protoculture, initially the alien Zentraedi's term for the human's display of emotions that their own race had abandoned long ago, became an elusive goal in **ROBOTECH**—a mysterious energy powering the SDF-1 that prompted the Robotech Masters to send the Zentraedi in search of it. Originally, the Robotech Masters were the elders of the alien race, Zor. A brainwashed human being who was used against his own people by the Zor was

transformed into the tragic hero, Zor Prime in **ROBOTECH**. Of the three programs that make up the series, *Mospeada* underwent the least amount of change. In fact, the Invid got their start as planet-possessing aliens. Annie, Scott, Rook, Rand, Lancer and Lunk are very much the same appealing characters they were in the Japanese version.

ROBOTECH never made pretensions of being a direct translation of its original anime components. It didn't need to. Now, for the first time in decades, watching a cartoon series in America is acceptable for the whole family. **ROBOTECH** has paved the way for more anime to be brought to these shores and to your living room.

ROBOTECH represents an unprecedented phenomenon—Oriental anime and Western ideals successfully combined to create a universe of wonder. To some, it may be "just another cartoon," but to so many more, it is storytelling at its finest—a story that Harmony Gold plans to expand in the

Max Sterling, Ben Dixon, Rick Hunter, and Lisa Hayes—part of the continuing saga of **ROBOTECH**.

months ahead. Within **ROBOTECH**'s celluloid universe exist people we meet and come to care about. We share their battles, thrill to their victories, and suffer at their defeats. We ache when friends are lost forever. We miss them when they travel to new worlds without us. There is more than simple gut-level entertainment in this series. **ROBOTECH** gives its audience something to think about. And maybe, through our visual participation in this amazing voyage, the child in all of us may come away a little wiser and a little happier for the experience.

Harmony Gold

presents

Robotech®

**A Harmony Gold USA, Inc. Production
in association with
Tatsunoko Prod. Co., Ltd.**

**Associate
Producer**
Jehan
Agrama

Story Editor
Carl Macek

Script Editor
Steve Kramer

Executive Producer
Ahmed
Agrama

Producer
Carl Macek

**Supervising
Director**
Robert
Barron

Series Staff Writers
Gregory Snegoff
Robert Barron
Greg Finley
Steve Kramer
Mike Reynolds
Ardwight Chamberlain
Tao Will

Dialogue Directors
Robert Barron
David Estuardo
Greg Snegoff
Steve Kramer
Debbie Alba
Jim Wager

**Featuring the
Voices of**
Greg Snow — Khyron, Scott Bernard
Reba West — Lynn Minmei
Jonathen Alexander — Breetai
Drew Thomas — Angelo Dante
Deena Morris — Sammie
Thomas Wyner — Jonathan Wolf
Brittany Harlow — Claudia Grant
Don Warner — Roy Fokker
Axel Roberts — Rico
Tony Oliver — Rick Hunter
A. Gregory — Robotech Masters
Penny Sweet — Nova Satori, Miriya
Aline Leslie — Lisa Hayes

and
Guy Garrett — Captain Gloval
Jimmy Flinders — Lancer, Max Sterling
Anthony Wayne — Rand
Eddie Frierson — Lynn Kyle
Leonard Pike — Exedore
Sandra Snow — Vanessa
Shirley Roberts — Marie Crystal
Wendee Swan — Kim
Larry Abraham — Bowie Grant
Jeffrey Platt — Rolf Emerson
Mary Cobb — Annie
Celena Banas — Regis
Chelsea Victoria — Musica

Post-Production
Intersound, Inc.
Hollywood, USA
Production Manager
Kent Harrison Hayes

Chief Engineer
Bryan Rusenko

Recording Engineers
Eduardo Torres
Debbie Pinthus

Orchestral Music Producer
Ulpio Minucci

Theme by
Ulpio Minucci

Videotape Engineer
Guillermo Coelho

Final Re-Recording
Joel Valentine

Music Editor
John Mortarotti

**Original Animation
Produced By**
Tatsunoko
Production Co., Ltd.

Producer
Kenji Yoshida

Director
Ippei Kuri

Original Music Composed By
Ulpio Minucci, Arlon Ober, Michael Bradley,
Steve Wittmack, and Alberto Ruben Esteves

Orchestrations By
Arlon Ober

Executive Music Producer
Thomas A. White

© 1985 Harmony Gold
Music, Inc.

NAME CHANGES

American	Japanese	American	Japanese
Robotech: The Macross Saga	**Super Dimension Fortress Macross**	**The Robotech Masters**	**Super Dimension Cavalry Southern Cross**
Rick Hunter	Hikaru Ichijō	Dana Sterling	Jeanne Francaix
Lisa Hayes	Misa Hayase	Nova Satori	Lana Isavia
Lynn Minmei	Lynn Minmay	Marie Crystal	Marie Angel
Roy Fokker	Roy Fokker	Sean Phillips	Charles de Touard
Claudia Grant	Claudia LaSalle	Bowie Grant	Bowie Emerson
Henry J. Gloval	Bruno J. Grobal	Louie Nichols	Louis Ducasse
Vanessa	Vanessa	Angelo Dante	Andrzej Slawski
Kim	Kim	Rolf Emerson	Rolf Emerson
Sammie	Shammie	Alan Fredericks	Alan Davis
Maximilian Sterling	Maximilian Jiinas	Commander Leonard	Claude Leon
Ben Dixon	Hayao Kakizaki	The Robotech Masters	The Zor
Jason	Yo-chan	The Robotech Elders	Zor Lords—Supreme Commanders of the Vanguard (Zosma, Zosmo, and Zosmu)
Lynn Kyle	Lynn Kaifun		
Miriya (Sterling)	Miria Fariina (Jiinas)		
Dana Sterling	Komiria Maria Jiinas		
The Zentraedi	The Zentraedi	The Robotech Masters	Zor Lords—Supreme Commanders of the Fleet (Desu, Dera, and Demi)
Breetai	Britai Kridanik		
Exedore	Exedore Formo		
Khyron	Kamjin Kravshera		
Dolza	Bodolza	Zor Prime	Seifrietti Weisse
Konda	Konda	Musica	Musika
Rico	Rori		
Bron	Walera	**Robotech: The New Generation**	**Genesis Climber Mospeada**
Azonia	Lap Lamiz		
Grell	Oigur		
SDF-1	Macross SDF-1	Scott Bernard	Steik Bernard
VF-1 Veritech fighter	VF-1 Valkyrie aircraft	Marlene	Marlene
		Rand	Rei
Veritech in Guardian configuration	Valkyrie in Gerwalk (**G**round **E**ffective **R**einforcement of **W**inged **A**rmament with **L**ocomotive **K**nee-joint)	Annie	Mint Rubble
		Rook Bartley	Fuke Eroze
		Yellow Dancer (Lancer)	Yellow Belmont
		"Lunk" (Jim Cooper)	Jim Austin
Veritech in Battloid configuration	Valkyrie in Battroid configuration	The Invid	The Invid
		Ariel/Marlene (Invid simulagent)	Aisha
		Sera	Sorji
		Corg	Batra
		Regis	Refles

GLOSSARY

Android:

A robot created in human form.

Bioroid:

A robotic power-augmented suit piloted by clones.

Clone:

A biogenetically grown creature. A clone can be as simple as a "lump of protoplasm" controlled telepathically by a Robotech Clone Master, or a highly sophisticated creature such as the Zentraedi Warlords. The clones are generated from cells of previously existing creatures. In time, clones can develop unique personalities.

Cosmic Harp:

A musical instrument which creates sounds which tend to soothe and control the functions of lower-level clones. It works much in the same way as biofeedback. The harp is tuned in such a way as to be played by only one person for an entire lifetime.

The Flower of Life:

The mature form of the plant which forms the basis of protoculture in the seedling stage.

Genesis Pits:

In essence, a huge protoculture chamber designed by the Invid to simulate various geologic eras and conditions. Rudimentary lifeforms are introduced into these environments for purposes of experimentation and development.

Hive:

A massive structure which serves as a nest for the Invid and also as a supply and storage area for the allocation of the foodstuff processed through the Invid Flower of Life. The major Invid hive on Earth is known as Reflex Point.

Hologram:

An image created by the use of laser. Basically, a three-dimensional phantom which simulates a real object.

Hyperspace:

A dimension between the standard dimensions of time and space. It is a zone which can be used to travel great distances without feeling the effects of the passage of time. If the concept of distance is conceptualized on a linear basis, hyperspace is the medium which surrounds and defines the present. Navigation in hyperspace is not always accurate. This is one of the main hazards in utilizing this concept as a means of traveling long distances.

Protoculture:

An energy source derived from diverting the organic energy in cell division of a specific plant known as the Invid Flower of Life. By containing the gestating seed in a matrix which does not allow the plant to develop, the Invid Flower of Life's desire to reproduce is so strong that the energy derived from this submission of cell division is enough to power the massive Robotech mecha invented by Zor and subsequent Earth scientists.

Protoculture Chamber:

A device which houses protoculture matrix and which, when properly employed, can generate new life forms or structurally alter existing life forms.

Robotechnology:

A science, developed initially by an alien scientist named Zor, which utilized the energy from the cell division occurring in specific plants to introduce a sense of bio-energy in machinery. This bio-mechanical system forms the basis of all the transformable mecha seen in the Robotech universe. The bio-force that is perceived through Robotechnology gives machines an empathetic life.

Sensor Nebula:

A large gaseous cloud utilized by the Invid to discover locations possessing large supplies of protoculture and, potentially, the Invid Flower of Life.

Space Fold:

The method by which vehicles travel through hyperspace. Again, considering the linear nature of time and space, by actually folding the fabric of hyperspace, a vehicle can travel from one point in the universe to another. The actual mechanisms for accomplishing a space fold are rather destructive and are not recommended for everyday travel requirements.

Telepathic Communication:

The ability to communicate to individuals on a purely mental level. Used primarily by the more advanced Robotech Masters and the Invid.

Triumvirate:

A system by which clones function in groups of three. Refers back to the Flower of Life and the three blossoms which are grown from each stem. The triumvirate is the basis of the Robotech Masters' society.

Veritech Mecha:

A generic term used to describe machines which have the ability to transform into various modes. The transformations are based on function, rather than deception. A Veritech fighter does not look like a camera which turns into a robot. Rather the mecha is functional, on a per job function. The name Veritech when used in conjunction with various mecha indicates that the item is transformable (i.e., Veritech Fighter; Veritech Hover Tank).

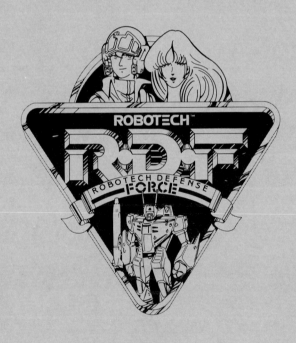

Number THREE   Spring 1980 $2.50

Fanfare

A SURVEY OF
**TV ANIMATION
IN JAPAN**
Galaxy Express 999,
Captain Harlock,
Giant Robots
and more!

**ELDER GOES
COMMERCIAL**
(Occasionally)

**KENNETH
ANGER'S
MAGIC
WORLD**

**WHEN
WRIGHT
WAS
WRONG**

THE PHILOSOPHY OF
MAN-THING

CLOSEUP ON
BEAUTY PAGEANTS
Mrs. America to Miss Bikini

**IN BOTH EARS AND
OUT THE OTHER**

THE K-TEL SELL

And
1984

AFTERWORDS

If you've been reading this book from cover to cover, then you're familiar with **ROBOTECH** from its inception in Japan to its success in the United States as a syndicated series. You know the story, the characters, and the intricate machinery. There's not much more to add except to tell you how this book came into being.

Today, nearly everyone is familiar with animation in one form or another through television cartoons, commercials, and MTV videos. It's easy to forget that it's still a relatively new art form. My first memorable encounter with animation came at the age of five when I saw Walt Disney's *Fantasia* for the first time. Believe you me, it *was* an experience that became a major influence for years to come. Bells rang, doors opened—I don't think I had ever been aware that that much color and sound actually existed prior to *Fantasia*. It was thrilling! However, my second major animation influence was more subtle. It arrived on a small screen, black and white television. There wasn't any color and the sound was pretty tinny, but the story. . . .

I was still in grade school and the story thrilled me from top to toe. It was Osamu Tezuka's *Astro Boy*. As I remember it, *Astro Boy* was as much a story about super-heroic deeds as the story of a charming little creature trying to become part of a society that could not see beyond his metal exterior to the warm-hearted being he was. At the time, *Astro Boy* had the misfortune of being broadcast during our family dinner hour. I can remember several "discussions" concerning dinnertime protocol. As it turned out, I might have missed a meal or two but that was preferable to missing an episode of *Astro Boy*.

Unfortunately, good animation with interesting characters, plots, and quality art became increasingly rare as time went on. It was easy to grow out of this genre as programs like *Astro Boy, Rocky and His Friends,* and the early Disney animated features were shown less and less often. It wasn't until much later, when I was visiting a local comics specialty store, that my interest in animated films and series revived. The issue of the spring 1980 *Fanfare* caught my eye. On the cover was an intriguing, obviously animated character—Captain Harlock. The cover promised an update on "TV animation in Japan—*Galaxy Express 999, Captain Harlock,* Giant Robots and more!" While the prospect of giant robots alone was not especially appealing, Captain Harlock (shades of Errol Flynn!) was. I counted my pennies, made the purchase, read the article (by Fred Patten, one of the contributors to **Robotech Art 1,** by the way), and rejoiced—sort of. Apparently, quality animation was alive and well—in Japan. My chances of pursuing this material seemed rare at best. The odds were something like impossible and none.

Eventually, I met Fred Patten at one of the World Science Fiction conventions. He was kind enough to describe—in detail—the intricate plot line behind the Harlock series and introduce me to new stories and characters from Eastern animated movies like *Phoenix 2772, Andromeda Stories, Harmageddon,* and the original *Gatchaman. Gatchaman* is the original title for the syndicated series, *Battle of the Planets,* a show I was already familiar with. However, when I compared the original against the Americanized or, frankly, kiddified version of what we were seeing in the States, I was appalled. Fred and I found we not only shared a common interest in animation, but a hope that some smart Hollywood type would discover this marvelous material and bring it to the States—intact—to share with people who loved animation as much as we did. We knew the audience potential would be staggering.

The thought was reinforced as I traveled the convention circuit across the country and met more Japanimation fans. At first, there were only small rooms in the hotels where videotapes were shown to a handful of people. Most of the tapes were in Japanese, and someone familiar with the story would provide a running translation of the plot. As interest grew, conventions began to schedule series and movies in the main programming rooms. During this time, I discovered material that went beyond the usual science fiction formats. There were superb movies like *Cagliostro's Castle* about a modern, comic cat burglar—Lupin III—a descendant of a long line of thieves. There was an equally bizarre film and series titled *Patalliro*. Imagine the cast of the *Rocky Horror Picture Show* meeting James Bond meeting the Road Runner, and you begin to get the picture. It is outrageous. Production standards were excellent. Sophisticated and entertaining, the Japanese programs were head and shoulders above anything produced in the United States in more than a decade.

Developing **ROBOTECH** out of three independent series was a major undertaking—creatively and financially. There were several difficulties and limitations inherent in such a task, but integrity and imagination saved the day. For the first time in years, good animation, characters, and stories are gracing the television screen. I can't help but wonder if new dinner confrontations are enacted across the country. I wonder who's winning—green beans or **ROBOTECH?**

Robotech Art I became as unique a project as the series itself. When Japanimation fans discovered that Donning/Starblaze was preparing a quality animation art book based on three favorite series, they got in touch with us by phone and mail. I was constantly impressed by their knowledge, enthusiasm, and willingness to share. Many of them offered to provide information, tapes, and even original art from private collections in order to produce the book you're looking at now. You can't know how helpful this assistance turned out to be. Because of the tremendous output of animated series in Japan, studios do not retain cels and artwork for long periods of time. By the time a series is sold and broadcast in North America, art that would have gone into a book of this sort is no longer available from the original source. While new art can be created, it's not always appropriate. Besides, fans of the series want to see the *original* art from the show.

What to do?

Kathryn Lebherz and Allen Row introduced me to a network of enthusiastic and helpful people. More than fans, these people had put long hours of serious study into animated films and series. James Long donated art and expertise into locating hard-to-find material. Colleen Winters was patience personified in explaining the connection between *manga* (comics) and animated series and how to read them. Ardith Carlton, who began studying Japanese in 1976, was the author of several articles on Japanimation and was the co-author and translator of the underground classic, *Space Fanzine Yamato*. She translated information on the original **ROBOTECH** creators and stayed on as co-author of **Robotech Art I**. There were many more people who helped in a variety of ways, too many to list here. At any rate, what began as a book for fans of the series actually saw publication through their efforts. It's only fitting that we acknowledge and thank them for their help.

All that's left for you readers is to sit back and enjoy our efforts. We had fun putting it together for you. We hope you'll have fun with it, too.

Kay Reynolds
Norfolk, Virginia